it's like that

it's like that

cheryl robinson

 NEW AMERICAN LIBRARY

New American Library
Published by New American Library, a division of
Penguin Group (USA) Inc., 375 Hudson Street,
New York, New York 10014, USA
Penguin Group (Canada), 90 Eglinton Avenue East, Suite 700, Toronto,
Ontario M4P 2Y3, Canada (a division of Pearson Penguin Canada Inc.)
Penguin Books Ltd., 80 Strand, London WC2R 0RL, England
Penguin Ireland, 25 St. Stephen's Green, Dublin 2,
Ireland (a division of Penguin Books Ltd.)
Penguin Group (Australia), 250 Camberwell Road, Camberwell, Victoria 3124,
Australia (a division of Pearson Australia Group Pty. Ltd.)
Penguin Books India Pvt. Ltd., 11 Community Centre, Panchsheel Park,
New Delhi - 110 017, India
Penguin Group (NZ), cnr Airborne and Rosedale Roads, Albany,
Auckland 1310, New Zealand (a division of Pearson New Zealand Ltd.)
Penguin Books (South Africa) (Pty.) Ltd., 24 Sturdee Avenue,
Rosebank, Johannesburg 2196, South Africa

Penguin Books Ltd., Registered Offices:
80 Strand, London WC2R 0RL, England

First published by New American Library,
a division of Penguin Group (USA) Inc.

First Printing, January 2006
10 9 8 7 6 5 4 3 2 1

NEW AMERICAN LIBRARY and logo are trademarks of Penguin Group (USA) Inc.

LIBRARY OF CONGRESS CATALOGING-IN-PUBLICATION DATA:
Robinson, Cheryl.
    It's like that / Cheryl Robinson.
        p.   cm.
    ISBN 0-451-21746-2 (trade pbk.)
    1. African American fire fighters—Fiction.   2. HIV-positive persons—Fiction.   3. Detroit (Mich.)—
Fiction.   4. Single mothers—Fiction.   5. Secrecy—Fiction.   I. Title.
    PS3618.O323I87 2006
    813'.6—dc22   2005022950

Set in Granjon
Designed by Ginger Legato

Printed in the United States of America

PUBLISHER'S NOTE
This is a work of fiction. Names, characters, places, and incidents either are the product of the author's
imagination or are used fictitiously, and any resemblance to actual persons, living or dead, business
establishments, events, or locales is entirely coincidental.
    The publisher does not have any control over and does not assume any responsibility for author or
third-party Web sites or their content.

*To everyone who picks up my book and decides to purchase it,
for allowing me to walk one step closer to my dream
of writing full-time.
Thank you and God bless.*

ACKNOWLEDGMENTS

Happy New Year! And, oh, how happy I am for a new one. Last year was one of those years that I can truly say I'm glad is over. I wasn't able to do all I had planned to in many areas of my life, including promoting my first book, *If It Ain't One Thing;* nonetheless, I did my best to spread the word and I have many to thank for their assistance.

First, to God, for keeping me sane during my many ups and downs and for always being there for me. I had faith that everything would work out and it has. I am grateful for the lessons I have learned along the way.

To my family in the Los Angeles and Oklahoma areas, most of whom I have never met. I made a promise that I would come out to California and see you over the summer of 2005; unfortunately I was unable to. I am making it my priority to come to California in 2006. To my aunts Naomi, Loreene, Louise, and Margaret and my uncles John and Enos. Even though I don't know you, I feel that I don't have to know you to love you, and I can honestly say that I love you because I grew up hearing about you through my mother, who loved each of you very much. To all of my cousins of which there are too many to name. I have spoken to some of you over the phone, and even though it may be too late to develop the type of relationship I longed to have with my cousins back in middle school and high school, I am hopeful that we can one day at least meet face-to-face.

Everything happens for a reason. Meeting Anonymous, an ex-con who was the subject of a novel I self-published in 2003, entitled *When I Get Free,* inspired by true events, led me to Earl Cox of Earl Cox and Associates, a literary consulting firm, who put my book in the hands of literary agent Marc Gerald, who then sold the rights for *If It Ain't One Thing* to New American Library within months. I'd like to thank each of those gentlemen for helping me realize my publishing dream. I'd also like to thank New American Library, particularly my publisher, Kara Welsh, and my editors, Kara Cesare and Rose Hilliard.

Due to space limitations, please forgive me for only mentioning your name or organization and not specifically what you've done. To my parents, Ben and Velma Robinson; my sister, Janice Robinson; my nephews, Sterling Robinson and Brandon Robinson; Delta Sigma Theta Dallas alumnae chapter; Cydney Rax; Emma Rodgers of Black Images Book Bazaar; Avid-Readers.com; Marlive Harris of the GRITS Literary Services; Earlena Butler; Motown Review book club; Rawsistaz; The Mahogany Book Club; Idrissa Uqdah, Circle of Sisters, Kalamazoo, Michigan; Valissa Armstrong; Gregory Chastang; Joy Farrington; Nubian Sistas book club; Women Together.com; Books ThatClick.com; People Who Love Good Books; AALBC.com; Shunda Leigh of *Booking Matters Magazine*; Shaft Washington; Kenyea Dudley; Dee Adams; Pia Wilson-Body; Regina Smith; Eric and Stacy Luecker; Electa Rome Parks; Sisters United book club; Carbette Wade; Dewhana Jones; Agatha Clark; Cynthia Taylor; Desiree Harris; Sistah Circle book club, Dallas.

We don't see things as they are,
we see them as we are.

—Anaïs Nin

1   Porter

Alexander Zonjic was standing on the stage of the Fox theater underneath a V98.7 FUND THE MUSIC banner. I was nervous. This would be my first time performing on sax in front of such an enormous crowd who paid to see Al Jarreau, George Benson, and The Rippingtons—not my band.

"Detroit, I want you to help welcome to the stage an incredible band from your hometown. Put your hands together for Time Out," Alexander Zonjic said.

The other band members went onstage before me and took their positions on instrument. Each musician had three minutes to perform solo as a way to introduce themselves. This was our time to show off, and because we all had really big egos, our objective for the night was to garner the most applause. The person who did was then allowed to come on last for the next performance and was given five minutes to showcase, which was the reason I was the last to walk on-stage. The one with the least applause from the last performance had to introduce me, but we decided just to have Michael Marks, our sit-in drummer, do my introduction this time.

Michael was the first to introduce himself. He received a lukewarm response from the audience, but he was just a stand-in for me and not a part of Time Out. Next up was Macy Richards on keyboard, and she really threw down. She had a few standing ovations. But it really came down to a tie between our bass guitar player and our electric guitar player who both took it home, then challenged each other side by side.

"I have the pleasure to introduce a cat who has been play-ing the drums since his freshman year at Murray Wright High School," Michael said. "Some of you may have seen him perform at Baker's Keyboard Lounge and Burt's Place. He's performed in just about every venue in the Greater De-troit area, known as the Drummer Man and a Detroit fire-fighter, put your hands together for Porter Washington performing saxophone tonight."

I walked onstage wearing a floppy patchwork hat with dark shades, a fluorescent yellow crocheted shirt, black jeans, and a pair of black alligator cowboy boots, blowing the song I'd written, entitled "Travelin' Shoes," loudly through my tenor sax. The expensive outfit was sent overnight from Bev-erly Hills, California, by the songstress Keena and arrived with the price tags still attached. The shirt alone was $8,600. The jeans cost $1,500. The boots were $15,000 and the hat was $992. Danzo Barron, her manager, called on behalf of Keena to see if I'd received my "housewarming gift." When I questioned what she meant, Danzo said she had bought me the outfit mainly because she was a generous person and she wanted me to wear something nice and funky when I opened for George Benson and Al Jarreau, but also because she was confident that I had found a new home with her band. I accepted her gift, partly because most celebrities don't pay for anything, especially not clothes, so I was sure these were items that had been gifted to Keena. And in fact Danzo confirmed that the designer was a good friend of Keena's. But I still hadn't made up my mind whether or not I was going to accept her offer. There were a few too many rumors floating around about Keena lately. I had to take my time to process it all, because if any of it was true, my gut told me it would be best to stay in Detroit and try to make it on my own.

Most of the crowd came to their feet as I continued to blow my tune. I was determined to succeed. I was almost thirty, but it wasn't too late to live out my dreams. I blew my saxophone like I was auditioning. Somebody out there who could make some decisions was listening. Somebody who could give me a deal so I didn't have to fly out to California to perform in the background with Keena's band. I wanted to have my own thing and release my own album. I was that good. I knew it, and judging by the overwhelming response I was getting from the audience, they did too.

Music was it for me and one day somehow I was going to make a living from it.

2 Winona

I drove up to the beige brick building with a green roof. A black-and-gold marquee marked the entrance of the Millennium Center and a black fence surrounded the property. Somehow, I'd allowed Gina to convince me to go to Hair Wars, which she described as a hair show and fashion extravaganza.

"If there's not going to be any styles that I can pick out for you to do on me, why are we here?" I asked Gina as I circled the lot looking for a good parking space. It was close to six on a Sunday and the place was packed.

"For entertainment and to show support to the hair community. After all, I am a stylist. I've been coming to these every year for the past fourteen years, and every year I enjoy myself. And mainly I'm here to see what Kevin Carter came up with this year. He is known as the king of fantasy hair."

"Well, I've been out of Detroit for almost twenty years, so I don't know anything about hair wars or Kevin Carter. I just hope they have some good drinks. I'm in the mood for Hipnotiq."

"Hip who? You're drinking now?" Gina asked.

"Socially . . . whenever the occasion calls for it. And judging by all these bright suits and alligator shoes," I said as I surveyed the patrons walking in, "it calls for it." I pulled into a space on the far right side of the building.

"I'm sure you remember DJ Hump the Grinder from back in our high school days."

I searched my brain for recall. "Sounds familiar."

"David Humphries is his name and he created this whole thing. I'm real proud of Dave. He takes this entire show on the road. This is big-time." I thought about what Gina had said about David Humphries. The fact that he had the vision to create something, anything, and stick with it for all those years was admirable. I wanted to do something. Something more than what I was doing now, which was working in corporate America. "Don't party-poop this, okay?"

"I'm not. Any opportunity I can get to buy new clothes and show them off, I am grateful for. Do you like my new outfit?" I asked as we got out of the car.

"I love it," Gina said as she scanned me from head to toe. "But I'm sure you spent too much money for it."

"I spent too much money for this," I said as I swung my Dior handbag. "But I make it, so why not?"

"I'm so proud of you, girl. Remember when we used to be eating peanut butter and jelly in the dorm room and calling each other with our stolen calling cards dreaming about adulthood and being rich. I'd say we've made it."

"I remember eating Spam and sleeping through my classes. As far as stolen calling cards, that was you, not me. And I'm going to get you straight now before you tell that lie around my kids."

We took our seats a few rows from the arched stage minutes before the production started. A few minutes later stylists marched the stage with their striking models parading flamboyant hairstyles. A large screen was suspended over the stage so the audience could view a close-up of the hairstyles. The music boomed through the speakers. LaToya Pearson, who Gina said was a retired hairstylist—I mean, hair entertainer—provided the commentary, and often used the phrase "You go girl."

The most outrageous hairstyles I saw that evening were a giant beehive that unzipped to reveal champagne service for two and the hairycopter, a toy helicopter perched on a model's head. Then came Kevin Carter's creation of a spiraling web of hair with a spider dangling on the side of the model's face.

It was three hours of hair, fashion, and dance, among plenty of competition. And when it was finally over, I was ready to go. Because tomorrow I had to go to work, and the day before I had gone to Porter's jazz concert. Today it was this. I wasn't used to being out so much, and it would probably take me a month to recover.

Gina wanted to stay for the reception in the lobby and

mingle with her stylist friends, but I refused, and since I was driving she had to do what I said.

"Okay, but this is a good way to find a new hairdresser. I'm not going to be doing hair forever."

"Maybe you won't be doing hair forever, but you will be doing my hair forever." I picked up a hair magazine from a vendor booth on my way out, and looked through it as we walked toward my car. "This is Porter's father," I said. I stopped in my tracks and turned toward the building. "I didn't even notice if anyone was standing there. Did you?"

"There was a man standing there. A fine, tall, distinguished-looking older man, who, come to think of it, looked just like Porter."

"Come on, let's go back," I said as I grabbed Gina's hand and pulled her toward the building.

"Oh, now you want to go back. See how people are. When they want to do something, it's time to do it, but when you want to do something—"

"Just come on. I just want to see him."

Gina and I walked back inside the building and positioned ourselves so that we were in clear view of Porter's father's booth, Millennium Hair.

"You're not going to speak. You're not going to introduce yourself. You're not going to say that you're his son's fiancé."

"Should I?"

"Yes," she said, nudging me.

I walked up to Porter's father's crowded booth and waited in line. A young black female with a red Vegas showgirl costume made of human hair approached me. "If you're looking for a hairstylist, you can search by criteria on our Web site and we guarantee that we'll match you with the right one. We make love-hair connections."

"I'm waiting for him," I said, pointing to Porter's father.

She gave me a nasty look. "Uncle Richard, she wants you."

Porter's father walked up to me. "Can I help you with something?"

"Maybe. I hope, anyway. Do you have a son named Porter?"

"Yes," he said, hesitantly.

"Okay, well, I met your—his mother."

"My wife."

"Right. I'm Porter's fiancée and I just wanted to say hello."

He nodded. "That's nice. Hello. Is he here?"

"No, he stayed at home."

"Can you do me a big favor and ask him to call me? Tell him it's really important. We have a new phone number." He wrote down the number on the back of his business card. "Stress to him the importance, okay?"

"I will." I took the business card from him and put it in my purse.

I made it home before eleven and Porter wasn't there, so I called him.

"Where are you?" I asked with concern.

"I'm at home."

"No you're not. I'm here and you're not here."

"I'm at my home, not your home."

"The studio? The home you're moving out of."

"The home I may be moving back into if you don't tell me when we're getting married."

"Soon, Porter. Very soon."

"What do you consider soon?"

"Porter, can we talk about something else for one second? I saw your father at the hair show."

"He goes every year and sets up a booth, so that's no surprise."

"I introduced myself to him and he asked me to have you call him. He said it's very important. They have a new number. He called your mother his wife so I guess they did get married."

"I'm not interested in talking to them."

"I have the number, Porter. Won't you at least take it down?"

"No, you can throw it away, unless you plan on using it."

It was five in the morning and I was heading for work. I turned on Alexander Zonjic's smooth-jazz morning show on 98.7. George Benson's "Turn Your Love Around" was playing, which made me think about Porter. Maybe that's what he expected me to do. How could I tell him that I'd changed my mind about marriage so he'd understand that it had nothing to do with him but about the whole idea of making a lifelong commitment to another person? I couldn't sleep the night before just thinking about it. I wasn't ready to marry him, but I was used to dazing into his bedroom eyes as he lay beside me, holding me in his muscular arms. He was so handsome, with a perfectly sculpted body that resulted from his rigorous daily workouts. I knew he loved me. And even though I did accept his proposal two months earlier, I did so without taking the time to think just how difficult marriage would be for us. I needed more time. I wished Porter could live by the saying *Patience is a virtue*, because that's what I needed from him right now. But that was very hypocritical of me because I didn't have that much patience.

I was thinking about too much this early in the morning. My brain couldn't function until I had at least sixteen ounces of caffeine in my system, but this morning I needed double that after hanging out over the weekend, and so far I had only taken a few sips. I had never been a coffee drinker but now I couldn't leave home without filling my travel mug with my freshly brewed Starbucks breakfast blend. My design job at DaimlerChrysler had become my scapegoat. I lived at the Tech Center, so if I were to really break down my six-figure income in terms of hours, I didn't make that much. . . . Well, I guess that's not entirely true, but what was true is that there was something more out there for me. Some people would call me a damn fool for not being grateful for what I had. I was grateful for my house in Sherwood Forest, for the company car, a black 300C with a Hemi, even for my designer clothes, because I had to admit shopping had become one of my passions—to the degree that I actually considered starting a shopping club the way others had started book clubs because I was tired of hitting the malls all by myself. There had to be other women out there just like me—women who spent their weekends at the mall, Somerset Collections being my favorite. I shopped to escape the harsh realities of my life. This year I even planned to add an exotic trip to the mix. Maybe a cruise. Just as long as it was someplace like St. Lucia, Antigua, or Belize, which reminded me to tune my desk radio to 98.7 when I got to work and listen for my name to be called for WVMV's trip-a-day contest that I'd registered for online a few days ago.

There was a void in my life that neither money nor a man could fill, because even though I had a good job, earned a decent income, and was engaged to a handsome man who was ten years my junior, it didn't really mean that much to me for one big reason—I was HIV positive. Living with that over my head was like living in hell on earth. Not a day could go by without thinking about how I contracted the disease. The what-ifs can kill you. I can what-if my life to death, but the fact of the matter is that it is what it is. My life is my life. Let me break it down even further in the words of Run DMC: It's like that . . . and that's the way it is.

I took the scenic route to work because the large gated homes in Birmingham and Bloomfield Hills, Michigan, always inspired me to want more from life since it was out there for the taking. When I stopped for a red light, I looked at my hair in the mirror. What was wrong with it? Why couldn't my hair look good for more than three days after it got done? Every week Gina did my hair, so bad hair days shouldn't have been something I even dealt with, but they were. And the more I thought about it, maybe nothing was wrong with my hair. Maybe it was Gina getting tired of doing hair in her basement when her husband was an executive at IBM and she was trying to get pregnant. She'd told me she was getting tired of massaging scalps, applying perm, roller-setting, crimping, weaving, and everything else her clients wanted done. She told me herself that she was giving me a hint to find a new hairdresser to go to. She even said she'd help, because one day she was going to put up her flat iron for good. I drove past Cranbrook Academy on my way to work. That's where I wanted to send my daughter, Sosha, for high school. Even though it was incredibly expensive and a boarding school, I wanted her to have the best; same with my son, Carlton, who was heading to college in the fall. I looked down at the book resting on the passenger's seat, *The Purpose Driven Life* by Rick Warren. It had been in my possession for three weeks and every day I promised myself I'd start reading it so I could figure out what on earth I was here for, since my time on earth was running out.

My life needed to change before it was all over. I was tired of being angry about my past. It was time to move on from all the hurt and the pain. But sitting in Sunday service with Porter and listening to a fake preacher try to inspire through words he'd stolen from others wasn't doing me any good. I was never the type to pretend I was moved when I wasn't. I wanted to be happy without being so skeptical about everything and everyone that entered my life. I wanted everyone in my life to be happy, even my sister Val who wouldn't rest until she won big either at the slots or MegaMillions. It just seemed to me that most people who I'd come in contact with these days were just going through the motions and I didn't want to be that way, which is why I bought the book.

At the next red light I picked up my book and flipped through the pages. *Could a book like this really help me?* I wondered. With all that I was dealing with in my day-to-day struggle with my disease, did it even matter anymore what on earth I was here for?

I knew it was probably too early to call Porter, especially

after his concert the night before, but I did so anyway. Before he had a chance to say hello, I said, "We're going to change our lives in forty days. Please tell me you'll do this with me. I need you to be my partner."

"Okay, Winona," he said, half awake. "I'll be your partner."

"And do me one other favor. Call your parents."

"That I won't do. Have a nice day at work."

3   Porter

The Next 40 Days

Winona was stretched across the lounge of her leather sectional reading her book. This would have been a perfect chance to tell Winona about my opportunity to join the band since Keena's live interview was about to air. After all, it was Winona who had brought up changing our lives in forty days. Maybe she'd understand how great an opportunity this was once I told her that music was my passion. With Keena, I had an opportunity to showcase my talents. Even though my passion was leaning a lot more toward being a saxophonist and away from drumming.

I'd signed the covenant on the inside of the book Winona was reading, but I was hesitant about the contents. I didn't think the author was saying anything differently from Bishop Coles. Yet Winona could sit up and read Day One aloud to me and expect me to be prepared to discuss it. Why should I? When she came home from my church, she was quiet as a mouse. If I dared to approach the subject of Bishop Coles' sermon, she'd change it quickly.

I interrupted Winona after she read the sentence that stated it wasn't a self-help book.

"I have to go into work tonight."

"Tonight on Day One?" she questioned as she rested the open book on her lap. "You can't leave before we complete the exercise and write our thoughts in the journal."

"I can't stop working so we can do an exercise in that book, Winona."

"I know that, but you've never gone into work at night. Your shift starts in the morning."

"True, it does, but I didn't feel like going in this morning, so I called in and told them I'd come in tonight."

"You didn't feel like going in because that's not your purpose in life. Don't you want to know what on earth you are here for?"

"I know what on earth I'm here for. I know exactly what I want to do."

Carlton, Winona's teenage son, came rushing down the stairs, grabbing the remote and switching over to the station televising the live interview with Keena.

"Damn, she's fine," Carlton said. "And she's got a body. Yeah, Keena baby, I'm getting your CD when it comes out."

Winona just shook her head at Carlton and then looked over at me.

"Do you think she's fine, Porter?"

"Turn it up," I said, after I heard the reporter ask her a

question about her drug use and so I could get out of answering Winona's question.

Carlton used the remote to increase the volume.

"For the record," Keena said as the camera zoomed in on her face, "I am not addicted to any drugs."

The camera zoomed out.

"I don't believe her," Winona said. "Look at her body language. The way she shakes her leg. She can't sit still."

"The media wants to typecast entertainers, especially singers, especially black female singers. We're not all alike. I'm Keena."

"Yes, you're Keena and your fans want to know why you disappeared after all of your success. What happened? Did it have anything to do with your relationship with the rapper Street Hype?"

"No, it didn't," she said curtly.

"He's on death row for murder. How has that affected you?"

"I didn't want to do an interview about Street Hype. I'm not here to discuss his business or ours. I'm not the only woman who fell in love with the wrong man. That's one chapter that I'm trying to close."

"Have you been able to close it?"

"Yes. I haven't been involved with Street Hype for quite some time. Let's talk about my CD."

"Your new CD is self-titled *Keena . . . living . . . learning . . . and loving*. How are you living? What are you learning? And who are you now loving?"

"I'm living large. I've come a long way from the projects of Detroit and I want little poor girls of every race to see what kind of life they can have if they believe in themselves and never give up, because that's what I did. And regardless of what happens with my second CD, no one can take away my Grammys—except the IRS—my AMAs and other awards too. I accomplished something that many dream about but few achieve."

"What have you learned?"

"To keep the media out of my business, so please don't ask me who I'm loving because I won't make the same mistake twice by telling people who my new man is."

"But Keena, the name of your new CD is *Keena . . . living . . . learning . . . and loving*."

Keena shook her head.

"Just tell us if he's in the business? Another rapper?"

Keena smirked. "He's a musician. I'll just leave it at that."

"Which instrument?"

"Nice try," Keena said, right before it cut to commercial. That's when I decided to leave for work so I wouldn't be late. I walked over to Winona and kissed her on the forehead.

"Be careful," she said. "And call me so we can do the exercise for Day One over the phone."

"I'll think about it," I said as I headed for the door.

The house was on fire. It seemed to be crumbling to pieces. I rushed in to do my job, which was save whoever was inside. And I did. At least I hoped that I did. I prayed that the little girl, who looked to be the same age as my daughter, Portia, around one, would make it, even though her body was badly burned. I walked past her mother, who was dressed like she'd just come back from the club: fishnet stockings and high heels and a low-cut dress that exposed her breasts and rainbow tattoo. She ran up to me screaming and shouting, trying to take her baby from my arms.

"Move back," I shouted. The dude she was with, what we used to call an old G for gangster, was wearing yellow gator shoes and a baggy black suit with gold pinstripes, and gave me a look like he wanted to kill me, and I gave him one back daring him to try. This wasn't the first house fire I'd been to where the kids were left home alone, and it wouldn't be the last. I was tired of the bullshit. Tired of trying to pick up the pieces from someone else's neglect.

"Where's LaShonda?" the mother said after I'd taken the child to the EMS workers. "My other daughter, where is she?"

"How old is your other daughter?" I asked.

"Seven. Where is she? Who got her?" she asked, running up to Conrad, another firefighter who worked on my shift.

"Ma'am," I said as I walked up behind her. "We were only able to get to one of your children. I'm afraid she probably didn't make it."

The woman fell to the floor, banging the concrete with her fist while she cried.

"This all could have been avoided," I said as I looked down at the woman in disgust. "You're the one who left your two kids home alone."

"What you say, nigga?" the old G asked.

"I said, she's the one who left two kids home alone. All this could have been avoided if she wasn't following after—"

"Hey," Conrad said, stepping in between the two of us. "I

know you're upset, but now is not the time to take out your frustration. Remember, the woman lost her child and she has another one who may not make it," he said quietly.

"And whose fault is that but her own?" I asked. "Children that age expect you to protect them, not leave them home alone."

"Porter, man, chill out. What's wrong with you?" Conrad asked.

"All for a man, a piece of one at that."

The old G pulled out a gun. "Keep talking shit now," he said.

"You're so bad that you're going to shoot me in front of the police," I said. "If you that bad, then go right ahead."

In the heat of things, I guess he didn't realize what he'd done, and by the time he tried to retract it, it was already too late.

"Put the gun down," one of the officers said as he stood behind the squad car pointing a revolver at the old G.

"All this for a night at the club. I sure hope it was worth it," I said as I walked back to the fire truck.

Conrad was walking behind me. "Man, you almost got shot and you were still talking shit. What's wrong with you?"

"Too much to explain to you," I said as I shook my head at the thought of my past.

Back at the station, Conrad and a couple other firefighters were playing spades in the kitchen, when the phone rang.

Conrad reached over to answer it.

"It's for you," he said.

"For me?" I questioned, wondering who would call me on the station phone when I had a cell phone. Maybe it was

Winona with her question to ponder from the book. I sure wasn't in the mood for that. Not tonight.

"It's a female with a nice voice."

I smiled as I took the phone away from Conrad.

"Hey, baby," I said as I walked into the other room with the cordless.

"Hey, Boo."

"Who's this?" I asked as I frowned from confusion.

"Who do you think it is? You said 'Hey, baby' like you knew and I was hoping you did, Boo. This is Vanity. Did you miss me?"

"I thought you lived in Chicago now," I said.

"I am in Chicago on my way to Detroit. Before we go any further, let me have your cell phone number."

I hesitated before rattling off the number because she was one of the reasons I had changed it in the first place. I was trying to get rid of all the people from my past that didn't mean me any good, and start over new.

"Man, you ready to start this hand," Conrad yelled into the room at me.

"You caught me at a bad time. I was in the middle of playing a game of spades," I said to Vanity.

"Spades? I'm calling you long distance and you're going to get off the phone to play cards?"

"Yeah, they're waiting on me."

"I guess I can just call you back later. Now that I have your number."

"Was there something you needed to talk to me about?" I asked. "You must've called for a reason. Were you trying to get in touch with my mom or something?"

"No, but how is she doing?"

"I don't know. I haven't talked to her. Haven't even seen her in two months."

"Porter, don't be like that. You only have one momma. The reason I called was to let you know that I'm going to be in town in a couple days and I wanted the two of us to get together. You won't recognize me. I mean, I know I was always beautiful and all, but I'm breathtaking now. Are you going to be able to spare a little time to see your friend?"

"I'll see. Call me back later."

I hung up the phone and walked back to the kitchen table, sat down, and picked up my hand, which was facedown. All I had were three trump cards and a bunch of hearts and diamonds.

"Who was that?" Conrad asked, but I never responded. "Whoever she was, she had a real sexy voice. Didn't sound like Winona though."

I threw down an ace of diamonds and was cut with a two of spades by Zeander, another firefighter.

"You don't have any diamonds?" I asked Zeander. "Don't renege."

"I'm a Christian."

"Oh, no, not that 'I'm a Christian' bullshit," Conrad said. "As if Christians can't lie, steal, and cheat. Porter's a Christian too, but he was on the phone whispering with some woman that wasn't Winona. Am I right?"

"That was an old friend. Just a friend, nothing more," I said. I took my cell phone from the case and set it on the table.

"You've got a message," Conrad said, "from an old friend."

"A message?" I questioned, because I never heard my phone ring but the red message light was flashing. I checked my voice mail and there were two new messages. The first was from Vanity. She said she was calling to make sure I'd given her the right number because she knew how moody I could be. The second message was from Winona, who'd left the point to ponder and the question to consider from Day One of her book. If I didn't call her back she'd be mad, but if I did call her back I'd be pissed because I'd have to sit through hearing her read the rest of the book and try to convince myself to participate. I just couldn't do it, so she'd just have to be mad. I couldn't even finish the hand of spades that had just been dealt. I was yawning. It was time for me to go to bed. The only point I wanted to ponder was how important it was for me to make the right decision when it came to joining Keena's band. The only question I wanted to consider was when I should tell Winona about the opportunity.

4 Winona

For some reason I was rushing while I was in the TJ Maxx dressing room trying on one of the six outfits that I was allowed to bring inside. I told the woman, who could barely speak English, that I had six items, but oh, no, she had to take the hangers out of my hand and count them herself. I wanted to ask her if she understood that the Christian Dior bag I had slung over my shoulder cost more than all the items in her hand and in the shopping cart parked outside the fitting room with a couple dozen more outfits I needed to try on, but instead I just rolled my eyes and snatched the plastic number six from her hand.

After I organized my clothes in the fitting room and removed the ones I had on, I started trying on outfits. I fell out of the skirt I was trying on and popped my knee, probably because I'd never bothered to take off my three-inch heels. Like I said, for some reason I was rushing. The pain was excruciating and caused me to fall to the floor and wait for a few minutes until it popped back into place. My knee was burning as I stood slowly to my feet, bracing the wall. It reminded me of a Lipitor commercial—a good-looking, well-dressed woman in her thirties going about her daily life suddenly falls down. It made me wonder if I fell because I was in a hurry or because I had high cholesterol. I shook my head because I'd had my wellness checkup at my job and my cholesterol level was normal. Life was too short to worry about all the things I worried about.

I looked at myself in the mirror of the dressing room and saw flakes around my hairline. Flakes. Dandruff was one thing I refused to deal with. Not when I had a best friend, Gina, who was a hairstylist by trade, and not when I earned enough to make sure that white stuff never surfaced, even if I had to wash my hair every day like a white woman. So I called Gina on my cell phone.

"Gina, can you squeeze me in?"

"Squeeze you in for what? I know you don't need your hair down. Not when you were just here on Tuesday."

"I see flakes," I said, pissed that she'd questioned me. "Can you squeeze me in or not?"

"That's what I'd be doing, squeezing you in, so don't get mad at me if you're my last and you have to wait a while before I get to you."

"I'm on my way." She told me to wait a couple hours, and I knew by the time I finished trying on the rest of these outfits and stood in line to purchase the ones I wanted, a couple hours would have passed.

The weather forecast called for heavy April showers to begin in the early evening. I was in Gina's basement, which her husband, Mark, had converted into a hair salon. I grew tired of listening to the conversation two of her clients were having about Mayor Kwame Kilpatrick. One of her customers was sitting in Gina's chair; the other was under the dryer but lifted the hood to put her two cents in. I was sitting at the bowl with a plastic cap covering my conditioned wet hair, reading my book.

I jumped when I heard thunder strike.

"Let me see what it's doing out there," Gina said as she walked up the stairs.

"I sell real estate part-time, but I work for the city full-time," the woman under the dryer said as she raised the hood. "I'll quit before I take a ten percent pay cut and cut in benefits while he buys his wife a fifty-seven thousand dollar Lincoln Navigator. I can't stand him. But that's okay. I got some shit on him. My sister-in-law is a stripper. She told me all about the wild parties at the Manoogian mansion"

"The media got enough of their own shit on him," the woman who was sitting in Gina's stylist chair said. "And that story about the wild parties is yesterday's news. I voted for him and I'll vote for him again."

"That's because your job isn't on the line. And only an ignorant person would go to the polls and cast their vote for that hip-hop mayor after all the money he spent on a city-issued credit card for his own personal use."

"So I'm ignorant now just because I like him much better than the last mayor we had."

"Archer?" the dryer lady asked. "You must be crazy. Archer was a good mayor. One of the best. Not as good as Young, but right up there."

"Aren't you a real estate agent?" I asked the dryer lady. If there was one thing that would make a money-hungry Realtor change the subject it was certainly a potential sale. Personally, I could care less what Mayor Kwame Kilpatrick was doing. He was a Cass Tech graduate, which was my alma mater, so he was all right in my book.

"Yes, why? Are you in the market?" She took a business card from her purse and walked over to hand three of them to me.

"I'm thinking about selling my home in Sherwood Forest and building in Bloomfield Hills, but it's just a thought for now. I'd like to do something in the next forty days if possible."

"It's not raining yet," Gina said as she walked down the steps, "but it sure is dark out there."

"How much longer on me?" I asked.

"Don't ask me that when I already told you that you'd have to wait." Gina said, rolling her eyes. "You are my last like I told you on the phone."

I turned my attention back toward the realtor. "Okay, well, like I said, I'd like to build in Bloomfield Hills."

"Bloomfield Hills?" the Realtor questioned. "You'd like to build in Bloomfield Hills or Bloomfield Hills Township?"

"Bloomfield Hills," Gina answered for me. "Winona is rich."

"I'm far from rich," I said as I leaned back to rest my neck on the groove of the washbowl.

"I wouldn't say you're far from it," Gina said. "She's an auto designer for DaimlerChrysler. One of the lead auto designers, thanks to her recent promotion. I'm so proud of my girl. She has a concept car going into production. Tell them about the car you designed, Winona."

"Actually, Gina, I can't. That information is confidential."

"Well, just trust me, she can afford Bloomfield Hills. She doesn't need the Township or Pontiac or any of those other less expensive cities surrounding it."

"I'll check the developments in the area and get them right over to you," the Realtor said.

"Gina, give her one of my cards," I said without lifting my head.

Soon I'd fallen asleep at the sink and didn't wake until I felt Gina's hands massaging my scalp. "It's awfully quiet in here," I said.

"The chatterbox is gone and so is Miss Know It All. I want to hurry up and get you out of here because it looks really bad outside. You might want to stay over."

"No, I want to get back." I was looking forward to taking a long nap. "Porter's performing this evening. Sosha is with my parents and Carlton is probably studying with some friends. He's gone most of the time and I need to get used to it because he'll be away at college soon."

"Studying?" Gina asked. "He's studying all right."

"What, you think he's with a little girl?"

"Come on now. We're talking about Carlton, the one we found humping some little girl in your bed on his birthday."

"Why did you have to remind me of that?" I asked. "I'm just at the point where I'm getting over it."

"Sorry I said anything. So you have that big house all to yourself? What are you going to do, watch a DVD or just sleep the night away?"

"Just sleep the night away," I said.

Gina dried my hair with a towel and I followed her to the stylist chair so she could roller-set me.

"I have some good news, I think," she said as she handed me the plastic container filled with purple and red rollers. "And you should be one of the first to know," Gina said as she turned off the water. "I think I'm pregnant. I have a doctor's appointment next week so I'll let you know then, but I missed my last period."

"Good for you," I said. She and Mark had recently started trying to conceive, and over the past couple months all she talked about was having a baby. "Good for you," I said again, relieved my baby-having days were over.

"What about you and Porter?"

"You know we can't have any babies," I said as I looked at her through the wall mirror like she had lost her mind.

"No, not what about you and Porter having a baby. What about you and Porter getting married? What are you waiting on?"

"We just got engaged two months ago." I shrugged. "Why rush?"

"I was just asking. Don't be so touchy. I just think Porter is a real good guy and—"

"And what?" I asked as I interrupted. "I better hurry up and get him to the altar before he wakes up and changes his mind?" I waved my hand. "I'm not sure about the whole marriage thing, Gina. Look what happened to me the first time I tried it."

Gina scrunched her face. "That's because Derwin was a fool. You can't compare Derwin to Porter. I don't care if he is a doctor, he's still a nut." She shook her body from disgust. "I don't see how you did it. Ooh, I don't see how you did it. But then again, I did a whole lot during my high school and college days that I regret now. I'm a whole different person and so are you." And that she was. Because all through high school and the year that she went to college, she was wild, which is the reason she was kicked out of Hampton University. It's hard to pass your classes when you never go, not even at test time.

"I hope to God I'm pregnant because I really want this baby," Gina said.

"I'll pray for you," I said.

"Last couple times I've talked to you, you mentioned God more and talked about praying. What's gotten into you? Did you join Porter's church?"

I shook my head. "It's this book, I think. I just started reading it, but I feel really good about it. I'm anxious to see if my life really does change in forty days."

It had just started to rain when I pulled into my garage.

After I entered the house, I walked to the front door to check the mail. My box was filled with bills and there was a medium-sized box stuck between the screen door and the main one. I picked it up and tried to recall if I'd ordered anything recently, or if it was for Porter or one of the kids. The postmark was from New York. It dawned on me as I walked up the stairs with the box tucked under my arm what it must be. I smiled. Maybe this rainy day wouldn't be too bad after all.

He's my man and I can't even have him.

I was lying in bed, naked, playing with myself and fantasizing about Porter and how much I wanted to feel him inside of me.

With my eyes closed, I continued to imagine what real sex would feel like—sex with a man, with my man—instead of the Eroscillator, the vibrator I'd ordered online that arrived in the mail today.

Damn. Why did this have to happen to me?

I tossed the vibrator across the room out of frustration. Not only had the batteries died on the expensive thing, they did so right as I was about to come. I was so tired of purchasing adult toys online and buying sexy lingerie from Victoria's Secret so Porter could look at my body without feeling the warmth I held inside. There was only so much he could do to me with his finger. I wanted him just as bad as he wanted me, if not worse. And if I wasn't so worried that I'd give him HIV if we made love, we would have by now, but I was worried and he needed to be too.

I was thirty-eight years old with a seventeen-year-old son who was an exceptionally gifted golfer. He'd be attending college in the fall on an athletic scholarship. My daughter, Sosha, who her brother called super smart, was only twelve, but she'd be going to high school that fall because she'd been double-promoted twice. Aside from being a single mother of two, I was engaged to a man ten years my junior.

It wasn't fair. I was a good person, and I had always tried to do what was right. I just wanted to be happy. But now I wasn't sure what my happiness entailed. I knew I wanted my man. I wanted Porter. No matter how hard I tried to fight his love, I needed it. He loved me unconditionally. He could have had almost any woman, but he chose me. I also needed something else. What that something was I don't know yet. Hopefully I'd find out in forty more days, after I finished reading my book. In the past, every time I tried to think about what it was I wanted from life my mind got cluttered. Maybe it was the new medication I'd been taking: Truvada and Sustiva. So far, I hadn't had any of the wild dreams some of the people on the online forums I visited said they'd experienced, but my thoughts got wild at times. Maybe it was the medication or maybe I was crazy. Something like this could drive you there.

I needed to do something to release the feeling that was trapped up inside of me. That's why I'd been masturbating so much—to relieve some stress.

With my eyes closed, I imagined Porter making love to me. I started to touch myself as I visualized his hand stroking my breasts and lightly tugging on my nipples. I pictured his head buried in my chest while he devoured it like a Thanksgiving feast. I was aroused at how real my fantasy felt. I told him I love him and he lifted his head to tell me the same.

My eyes shot open and I sat straight up in bed when I heard thunder strike. My two nightstand lamps flickered and went out. I stood and walked over to the window to see if my neighborhood was in total darkness, but it wasn't— only the homes on my side of the street, and the streetlights. I stood still and listened to the heavy rain pour. The lightning in the sky brightened my entire street for only a few seconds. When it stopped, I was still looking out the window, and that's when I saw him strike her, in the bedroom window directly across the street, his fist pounding her face simultaneously as the lightning struck. And now I understood why she was always in her own world and barely spoke. Now it made sense to me why she wore large dark sunglasses. My neighbor was getting abused and I was a witness. The only thing I could think to do was make an anonymous call to 911. No, I needed to mind my own business because I had enough problems of my own.

5 Porter

I was in a hole-in-the-wall on the east side of Detroit sitting at the bar sipping my third glass of rum and Coke. I felt myself purposely slipping into a buzz. My relationship with Winona may have been in trouble, and I didn't like it. Winona and I had been together for almost a year. We met while I was on duty with the Detroit Fire Department. There was a major accident on the Lodge Freeway and I freed her son, Carlton, who was trapped in his car while a collapsed oil rig was in danger of exploding.

At the beginning of our relationship, things moved fast and seemed perfect, until everything came to a screeching halt once she confessed to being HIV positive. I needed to start my life over with Winona, so I decided that regardless of her HIV status I was willing to take the risk. I proposed to her and she accepted, but now that it was time to make the plans, she was dragging her feet. I wondered if our relationship was taking a turn for the worse. We rarely argued a few months earlier, but lately our voices seemed to rise and our tempers flared.

I'd lied to her. For the first time since we'd been together, I lied. There wasn't a performance at Baker's tonight. And if for some reason she drove to the jazz club, which was less than ten minutes from where she lived, or called up there for me, I had another lie prepared: I'd made a mistake when I said Baker's. That was next week. I'd performed at Flood's Bar and Grill on Saint Antoine tonight, which I had, but only one set. It was the risk I was willing to take once I made up in my mind that I needed companionship—sex. Something she couldn't give me. I'd held out for over a year. I couldn't have sex with Winona because of the disease, but before I met Winona I was going through a celibacy stage.

I felt a hand touch my back and I swiveled the bar stool around to see whose it was.

"Hello, Boo," Vanity said. She was an old friend who had pursued me for years and was in town for the weekend before she reported to work as a food and beverage manager at Carnival Cruise Lines. She had just one request before she left for sea—an evening with me, one she swore I would never forget. I decided to try something that I'd grown curious about and pray for forgiveness later. She was every bit a woman now. Even more attractive than the first time I'd seen her after her transformation, but not even the alcohol I'd consumed could help me erase the fact that she used to be a man.

"Are you ready?" she whispered in my ear. "This smoke is irritating my contacts. Her eyes were hazel naturally but blue today. Her hair was longer than I remembered it, and lighter and wavier. I wondered if it was hers or a weave, so I asked.

"You'll see later when you run your fingers through it," she said.

No matter what she was before she became Vanity, no one could deny that she was beautiful now, and it was that beauty along with her sexual confidence that aroused me.

"I need one more drink," I said to the bartender. "Let me have a Long Island this time." What was I doing? This went against everything I believed in. The bartender slid a drink in front of me and I didn't hesitate before I downed it. By this time, Vanity was sitting beside me with her shapely legs crossed. If it didn't work out for her in the food industry, I was certain she would make a perfect porno vixen. She took my free hand, the one that wasn't hugging the glass of alcohol, and placed it on her inner thigh.

"Come on before you change your mind. I told you this is our little secret."

"We have to drive separately," I said, laying down the ground rules. There would be no Eddie Murphy or Teddy Pendergrass moments for me. Even though I was sneaking, I truly believed that whatever was done in the dark would eventually come to light. I simply hoped that the light wouldn't shine on me for many years to come.

Vanity shrugged. "Fine with me. I'm ready to go." She leaned down and kissed me, but I turned so that she would touch my cheek instead of my lips. Kissing wouldn't be a part of tonight, and I still hadn't completely made up my mind what would. Maybe just oral sex. She could do me. Maybe. That way I'd have less to feel guilty for.

I decided to keep my car parked at the bar and ride with Vanity, but I drove her car. I stopped at a corner liquor store and bought a bottle of rum, a thirty-two-ounce bottle of Coke, plastic cups, and a three-pack of condoms. If this was going to go down, I had to be not only drunk, but well protected.

We went to a seedy motel a few blocks away from the bar, where we had to drive up and pay $29.99, which was the nightly rate. I requested a room on the first floor with parking close to the door, but what I received was a key tossed in the window.

As I drove into the parking lot, I allowed Vanity to rub the bulge that had formed in my crotch.

"I am without a doubt going to rock your world and mine too," she said as she sucked her teeth.

I parked the car in the only available space, which was three spots away from door 156, but before I could exit the car Vanity had unzipped my fly. I wasn't wearing underwear. Her eyes enlarged as she looked at my dick and up at me. "It's so big and beautiful," she said as her head started moving downward.

"Let's go inside first." I pulled her hair to lift her head just as her tiny lips almost touched the tip of my dick. She was a woman, soft and delicate, with no inhibitions. Anything I wanted to do tonight, even my wildest fantasy, I'm sure she'd be willing to accommodate.

I stumbled out of the car and staggered slightly to the

door, gripping the brown paper sack in my right hand like the zombies in the Cass Corridor.

Did this make me gay? Did this make me down low? My eyes focused on Vanity's tight round ass as she walked in front of me, pulling me by the hand. That was a woman. When you're gay and down low it's because you're with a man.

"Are you drunk, Porter? Because if you are this won't be any fun." She snatched the bag from my hand and inspected the contents. "No, you're not drinking this and we're not using those," she said as she took the condoms out of the bag and tossed them on the floor.

"Girl, you better pick them up. I can't be bringing no diseases home."

"Home to who?" Vanity questioned. "Who is at home that you're worried about giving a disease to that I don't have anyway? I've been tested for everything and my results always come back negative."

"No one's at home," I said, trying not to think about Winona. I didn't want to be one of those men who cheated behind their woman's back, and I swore to myself that after tonight I wouldn't be. I just had to release whatever this was that was pent up inside.

I fiddled with the key for several seconds before the motel door finally squeaked open. I bent down to pick up the box of condoms, and when I straightened back up I snatched the bag away from Vanity and walked inside the motel room, placing the bag on the table. I sat in the chair beside the table and poured myself a drink.

"Do you want one?" I asked Vanity.

"You've had enough of that shit, Porter. Why are you

trying to get drunk?" she said with an attitude. "I thought you wanted me." She took off her mink jacket and hung it up in the closet beside the front door. Then she unbuttoned her silk blouse. "Don't you want this?" she asked as she started squeezing her fake breasts. She walked over to me and sat on my lap. I started running my fingers through her scalp searching for tracks and felt none, which aroused me, because it made her seem even more feminine. I looked at her large breasts popping from her padded bra, and I wanted to bury my head between them and kiss and lick and suck. Instead, I took her by the waist and raised her off my lap.

"Get naked," I instructed.

"Okay. I will. Just give it a little time." She walked over to the light switch and turned it off. The darkness of the room disturbed me. Was she trying to hide something?

"Turn the light back on. I want to watch you as you get naked. I want to see your body."

I walked to the door, felt around the wall for the light switch, and turned it back on. Vanity was lying in the bed under the covers. Her clothes were in a small pile on the floor beside her.

I snatched the covers back. "Let me see you." Her breasts were exposed but she still had on panties.

"I will. Once you join me." I sat beside her and tugged on her panty line. "Stop, Porter. I'll take them off myself."

"Do it now."

"Can't we have some foreplay first?"

"I want to see your pussy," I said. She sat in the bed and

wiggled out of her panties, concealing her vagina with her legs. "Spread them."

"I don't want to," she said as tears streamed down her face.

"What's wrong? Why don't you?" I asked. "I can't do anything if you keep your legs closed."

"I want you so bad, Porter. I've wanted you so bad for so long."

"Then spread your legs and play with your clit. Can you do that for me?"

I watched as her legs opened slowly. My eyes were blinking rapidly to clear my vision. I wasn't sure if it was the alcohol I had consumed that was making her vagina look like something other than that and more like a hole. Whatever it was, I could feel myself getting sick from the sight of it. I ran to the bathroom, stuck my head in the toilet, and threw up. I must have temporarily lost my mind if I thought I was going to have sex with *that* tonight.

"I got to go," I said after I rinsed my mouth out with water.

"Go where?" she asked. "You're in my car, remember? I'm not ready to leave yet. You said we were going to make love tonight."

"I never said we were going to make love. Get it right, Vanity. I said we might fuck. Might. If a man gets drunk and horny enough, he might do anything. But I don't want you because, operation or no operation, I see now that you are still very much a man. What you have between your legs doesn't look like any pussy I've ever seen, which means it can't possibly feel like one either. Get dressed," I said as I picked her clothes off the floor and threw them in her lap on the bed.

"What did I ever do to you, Porter?" she asked as she put on her bra. "I break my neck every time I'm in town to track you down so I can hopefully see you. Finally you agree to, but once again all you do is tease me. I'm so tired of men playing with my feelings. I never thought you'd be one of them. I respected you more when you told me flat out you'd never be with me, but to come here, pay for a room, and pretend we were going to make love, fuck, or whatever you want to call it, is down low and I feel sorry for whatever woman is in your life, because not only are you confused, but if you ask me, you're gay and you might as well admit it."

I laughed because she was trying to make me angry and I saw all the way through it. "Just get ready so we can go." I picked the keys off the nightstand and headed for the door.

"This is it, Porter," she said as she stood and stepped into her panties. "This will be the last time we see each other. And don't worry, you will never receive another call from me, Mr. Christian Man. No wonder you go to Faith in the Word. That's the best place for you. Especially since your bishop is gay."

"My bishop is hardly gay. Nigga, finish getting dressed so we can go."

"Don't you ever call me nigga again," she said as she took the rum bottle and hit it on the side of the table. Glass flew everywhere. And I sobered up quickly. "Do you hear me?"

"What are you going to do now, kill me?" I asked. Maybe it was my time to die. The other day it was a gun. Now this.

"I don't know what I'm going to do now," Vanity said as she gripped the neck of the broken Bacardi bottle, blood dripping from her hand onto the dark carpet. "But I do know that I'm tired of men like you playing with me. I guess I should be thankful that you didn't stick your thing up me and then talk about me after you got what you came for. Men like you are so pathetic." Tears started falling from her eyes. "I thought you were different, Porter."

"I am different."

"You're no different," she screamed, her head shaking violently.

"What you gonna do? Are you gonna kill me?" I asked as I held my arms out. "Do whatever it is you're going to do. You don't intimidate me. You don't scare me. I'm sorry that I brought you here. I understand how you feel that I may have led you on. I'm sorry for that. But I still think that you're fucked up in the head. Anyone who could do what you did to your body has to be."

"So what's that make you? You were going to fuck me!"

I walked toward Vanity, unafraid. She wanted someone to understand her, but I wasn't that person because I was still trying to find myself. I squeezed her wrist until she dropped the bottle.

"You don't understand me, Porter. And you never will."

"You're right, I never will. Now let's go."

As I was driving Vanity's car back to the bar where mine was parked, my mind drifted back to the day my grandmother's house exploded. There was an empty bottle of Seagram's 7

Crown whiskey on the living room floor and a cigarette butt still burning in the ashtray sitting on the coffee table. My grandmother Florence must have been in a rush for work that morning. She always ran late, even though she worked at a dry cleaner that was less than ten minutes away.

"You sure," I whispered to my brother Richard as we tip-toed over to Florence's bedroom door. Richard peeped through the keyhole. "We gonna get it. Florence is gonna beat our ass if this plan don't work."

"Shh," Richard said as he held one finger to his lips. "He's sleep. Florence won't do nothin' 'cause she won't know. You got the key?" I nodded, took the dead-bolt key out of my pocket and handed it to him. Richard locked Florence's bed-room door with Uncle Ray inside. There were bars on the bedroom window, so Uncle Ray was trapped inside. The only thing left to do was to set the fire. Richard said he knew how to do something with the furnace to make it look like an accident. I wanted to go in the basement with him. I wanted to help, but he wouldn't let me.

"Just go outside and wait for me. It won't take long."

"I want to go with you."

"No, hurry up and go outside before he wakes up."

I ran out of the house and across the street to one of my friends' houses and started playing basketball. I remember turning my head for one second when I heard what sounded like an explosion. It was so powerful that it blew out all the windows to Florence's house and caused the homes on both sides to catch fire.

I ran toward the house, yelling out my brother's name. I

had to go back inside and save my brother. Either we were both going to live or we were both going to die. But before I could make it across the street, one of the neighbors grabbed me. He wouldn't let me go. I kept hearing the neighbors saying that the fire department was on its way, but it took forever for the fire trucks to arrive. My mother drove up before the fire department did. I hadn't seen her in a week, and then I remembered why she was there. That was the day she'd promised to come get us, but she'd broken so many promises that I never expected her to keep any of them.

When the firefighters did arrive, they stood around hopelessly. My mother's crying and pleading for someone to save her son didn't seem to faze them.

"It's too dangerous at this stage." They were trying to contain the flames from the outside.

"You just passed the bar," Vanity said. I looked over at Vanity, who was giving me a strange look.

"Why are you looking at me like that?" I asked as I made a U-turn and headed back to the parking lot.

"Why do you think, Porter? This is the second time you went off on me. I think you might be mental." She turned her body so that her knees were touching the passenger door, and her face was toward the window.

I parked the car beside mine and looked over at Vanity.

"I'm sorry, Vanity. You didn't deserve how I treated you."

"That's about the third or fourth time you've apologized tonight. I don't need your apology. I need to know why you acted that way." She kept her face glued to the window.

I took her hand and placed it inside of mine.

"You are a beautiful young lady and I'm sure you'll find a man who will accept you for who you are and love you just the way you are."

She slid her hand from under mine and used it to dry her tears.

"I want you to be that man," she said as she turned to face me. "Why can't you be that man? I'm not a man anymore, Porter. I was never a man. I know that's hard for most people to understand, but I truly believe that God made a mistake with me."

I shook my head for a moment, but stopped after I realized that it wasn't my place to disagree. I had to resolve within myself that we had a difference of opinion on the subject.

"Look, I let my sexual urges get the best of me. I didn't mean to lead you on."

She turned up her nose.

"Porter, are you gay?"

I shook my head. "No, I'm not gay. I don't desire to be with a man. The only reason I was considering sleeping with you was because you look so much like a woman that I forgot you weren't."

"I am," she said angrily and then sighed. "If you're not gay, what's wrong with you?"

"When I was a young boy, six or seven years old, I was sexually abused by my grandmother's boyfriend. My brother had been too. He died as a child—"

"How, Porter? How did he die?"

"I don't feel like getting into the particulars of that tonight. It's too sad for me to talk about. Anyway, the reason

I always stayed around you is because when I met you I thought about my brother. I always wondered, if he was alive would he have been gay and if he was would it have been his choice to be or would it have been because of his circumstances? So I wanted to know why you were, because the gay lifestyle has been a hard one to understand."

"You're confusing being gay with being a pedophile. Your grandmother's boyfriend was sick. He liked little boys. Every gay person was not abused. And you were abused and you're not gay, right?"

I hesitated for a moment. "No, I'm not gay. But why did I have to have that experience? Why did my brother have to?" I pictured the house exploding again.

"When I was growing up, I used to get beat because my mother said I switched my behind like a little sissy. She said she wasn't raising no punk bastard. I love my mother, but you and I both know that wasn't right. Some children have good memories from their childhood and others have bad memories and others, like you, have tragic ones. But I learned that no matter what happened in our past, somehow we have to move on." Vanity put her hand on top of mine. "I forgive you. I knew something was going to happen tonight anyway. I knew my fantasy wasn't about to happen after all this time, because some things are just too good to be true."

I leaned over and kissed Vanity on her cheek. "Take care of yourself." I opened the driver's door and stepped out, walking toward my car.

Vanity let her passenger window down. "I know you probably don't want me to, but I'm keeping in touch. Just as friends. Okay?"

"Okay, Vanity. Enjoy your time at sea."

"And, Porter, even though you never said anything, you obviously have a woman at home."

"Why do you say that?"

Vanity rolled her eyes. "Come on now. No man can resist the seduction of Vanity, so she must be one hell of one."

I nodded and smiled. "She is."

"Then I guess I can't be too mad at you," she said as she slid over to the driver's seat. "I get another break in a month. I'll call you. Tell your mom I said hello."

My mom. I needed to break down and check on my parents. See if they really did decide to renew their vows.

6 Winona

"What the hell is this?" I said when I noticed a black late-model Mustang parked in my driveway as I drove up from a long day at work. There was a temporary license tag affixed to the back of the window. My son, Carlton, was all smiles as he stood beside his father, Derwin. They both waved when they spotted me. I blew my horn but not before my eyes rolled. "I know he didn't," I said as I slammed on the brakes and shifted into park.

"Mom," Carlton said as he rushed over to the driver's side of my Chrysler 300C. "Dad bought me the new Mustang—fully loaded."

I opened my door calmly, then slowly walked over to Derwin, who was smiling as I approached him.

"Don't you think you should have consulted me first?" I asked.

Derwin looked puzzled. "Consulted you about what? It's my money."

"For one, he already has a car, or had you not noticed?"

"I did, but he didn't like it and you of all people should know I'm a Mustang man, at least I was when I was his age. Now I'm a Cadillac man." He looked over at his black STS parked in front of my house.

"That may be who you are, but I am a designer for DaimlerChrysler so my first instinct when I see a competitor's car parked in my driveway is to slam into it. He doesn't need your car. I get three free cars a year through my company and I already have a Crossfire on order for him."

"You do?" Carlton asked, shocked. He held his chin as if contemplating. "Honestly, Mom, the Mustang is more of a muscle car and I think I'd rather keep that."

I eyed Carlton first and then Derwin, who had the nerve to just shrug.

"I give up. I'm not arguing anymore. Now I guess I have to sell the Liberty and take the Crossfire off order."

"Not really," Carlton said. "The Liberty can be my everyday car and the Mustang can be my leisure vehicle. The Crossfire doesn't really thrill me so you can go ahead and take that off order."

"Everyday car? I'm an adult who designs cars for a living and I have only one of my own. You're a teenager without a job and you think you're going to have two? If you're keeping the Mustang, I'm selling the Liberty."

"If you're selling it," Derwin said, "I'd like to buy it for a young college student who needs some reliable transportation. She just had a baby—"

"Your baby?" I interrupted.

"My baby? No," he said, shaking his head. "Not my baby. I just know this young lady. I'm not involved with her or anything like that."

"Not that it matters," I said. "That's your business if you want to rob the cradle."

"You should know all about that, huh?" Derwin asked. I started walking away from him. My neighbor across the street pulled up in his Ford 500 and I rolled my eyes because they're copying the Chrysler 300 and not even trying to hide it. I didn't bother waving at him because he has the same mean scowl on his face every time I see him, which I now know is because he's beating his wife. I walked toward my front porch. "And that's a shame when you could have me," Derwin said.

Have him? I couldn't believe what I was hearing, and I couldn't believe that at one time, even if that one time was a long time ago, I actually used to want him.

When I walked through my front door, my phone was ringing. "Miss Fairchild, this is Diane Schaeffer from Dr. Gant's office. I'm calling to confirm your nine o'clock appointment tomorrow morning with Dr. Gant."

"I'll be there," I said and hung up the phone before saying good-bye. My mind started racing. I had to remember the questions I needed to ask. It was so hard to keep track because there was always so much I wanted to know, but then when I was at my doctor's office, I'd forget half of it. That's why I needed to take Kelly Townsend's advice and keep a journal to take with me to my appointments. Speaking of Kelly, tonight was the first support-group meeting at her house and I promised her I'd be there, but I really didn't feel like it. It was one of those days when I wanted to go straight to bed, but I probably wouldn't be able to get any rest. Derwin had blown that for me.

I sat down at the kitchen table with a large bag of barbeque Baked Lays, a glass of crushed ice filled with white grape Diet Rite, and pulled out the latest issue of *O Magazine* along with the *Detroit News*.

"Mom," Sosha said as she ran down the stairs into the kitchen, "can we please have a talk?"

I couldn't help but smile at the sight of Sosha. In just a few months, she'd started to mature. She still had her ways—smart-talking, eyes rolling, or moments of acting just plain spoiled—but those were few and far between. The main issue with her now was her excessive talking on the phone.

"Talk about what, Sosha?"

"High school, what else?" she said as she raked her fingers through her long wavy hair caused by the braids she'd let down, and not by genes. "I know that you don't want me to go to school with boys, but instead of sending me to Mercy can I please go to Marion?"

"Marion is right next to Brother Rice, an all-boys school, and that would defeat my purpose. Where I need to send you is to Cranbrook Academy."

"Oh, why? Are you trying to get rid of me?"

"No, I'm not trying to get rid of you. Why would you say that? Cranbrook is one of the finest schools in the country."

"And it's a boarding school. Mom, what is your purpose?

To shelter me, put me in a position where I'll be vulnerable when I go to college, because that will be my first experience with being around the opposite sex. Do you honestly think that will solve anything?"

"Is Baxter going to Brother Rice?"

"Maybe." Baxter was a boy from one of her classes who was crazy about Sosha, but honestly, in my opinion, the boy was just crazy. They were both eighth-graders, but he was getting ready to turn fourteen whereas Sosha was only twelve. He professed his undying love for my daughter as he stood in my living room beside his mother and in front of me. He told me that he and Sosha were like Romeo and Juliet and they would be together one day because she was going to be his wife. He came over to get permission to talk to her on the phone because every time I picked it up and heard a boy's voice, I'd make her get off. And his visit with his mother didn't change things. In my eyes, she was still too young to talk to boys on the phone, and I was upset that his mother couldn't see that. "Nothing's wrong with a little puppy love," she said to me when I pulled her off by herself.

"Mom, please consider letting me go to Marion. I'll turn out a much better child. Please, Mom," she whined.

"I'll think about it, Sosha. That's the best that I can do right now." And all that did was gave me one more thing to think about. I was already thinking about Porter and what he had done the night before. He came home close to three in the morning with the smell of alcohol all over his breath. I didn't even bother to ask how much he had to drink or where he'd been. I can still remember my maternal grandmother saying that they can't take it all—the other woman, that is—but I hadn't had any of it yet so the very thought of Porter being with another woman tore me apart. I'd be a fool to think that he was being faithful when I could do very little to satisfy him sexually. I'd be an even bigger fool to believe that a marriage between the two of us would work. Just thinking about saying I do made my head pound. I walked to the cabinet and removed the super-strength Tylenol bottle. Took two with water and tried to think up a good enough excuse for why I couldn't attend Kelly's support-group meeting tonight.

I couldn't think of an excuse. So I went. This was the first Sisters Living Positively support-group meeting that I had attended. I walked in with two other ladies who smiled but didn't speak. Not that I minded any because I wasn't up to socializing. Kelly had a nice home with original African art displayed throughout the main rooms.

The three of us were the first to arrive. Kelly had mentioned that it was a small group. After being introduced to Kelly's husband, I sat on a bar stool in her great room and took out my miniature book of *The Purpose Driven Life*. I think I was obsessing over it. I'd even ordered the audio series from work so I could listen to it in my car. It would be so much easier if Porter agreed to read it with me, but half the time he was either at the station or falling asleep in front of me when I did start to read.

Day Three talked about what drives your life. I read the Thomas Carlyle quote that started the chapter: "A man without a purpose is like a ship without a rudder—a waif, a nothing, a no man."

"Okay, we're going to get started," Kelly said after two more ladies entered. "We're only missing three more, and my husband and Carla's husband are going to sit in with us today so this will be our first official coed meeting, which might not be a bad idea. We could rename our group Sisters and Brothers Living Positively." I slid off the bar stool and sat on the love seat beside another lady. "I'd like to start by introducing a new member, Winona Fairchild."

We all smiled at each other.

"Winona, can you please tell the group about yourself?"

"Is it okay if I stay seated?"

"Of course," Kelly said. "We keep our meeting as informal as possible."

"Hello, everyone," I said as my mind raced trying to figure out how much I should say and even what. "I'm here because Kelly invited me and because I think a support group for people living with HIV is needed. My family tries to understand what I'm going through, but only someone who is living with HIV the way we are can understand how hard it is sometimes. But lately, I've tried to change my attitude and become a much more positive person."

"Who is your support system now?" a member asked.

"My fiancé, Porter, who isn't HIV positive and my best friend, Gina. I have two children but I haven't disclosed my illness to them yet."

"Why not?" Kelly's husband asked.

I shook my head and sighed. "I just don't want them dealing with that. I don't want them worrying about me." I looked at each of the members for some sort of approval, but most of them stared back at me with blank expressions.

"Winona," Kelly said, "we meet every month, sometimes twice a month depending on our agenda, and we discuss different topics. We also exchange ideas, medical information, motivation, and always offer encouragement. Whoever hosts provides the food, but tonight I cheated. Usually I make something but I was tired from work so I stopped and got a tray from Lou's Deli."

"That'll work," the other woman's husband said.

"Tonight, let's just talk about whatever we feel like discussing."

"Well," I said, "I'd like to recommend this book." I said as I held up my miniature copy. One of the ladies squinted as she looked over at the book. "It comes in a regular size and you can also buy a journal to go along with it. Even though I just started the book, I feel really good about just the prospect of change. I'm really expecting something drastic to happen to me in the next thirty-six days."

"Whatever works," one of the ladies said. "But personally I have read every self-help and faith-based book on the market and none of them helped me. I have come to realize that every day is a work in progress." She shrugged. "For me anyway."

How I could relate to that statement—every day truly was a work in progress. And that's what I was trying to do, work on myself to be a better person, because sometimes I got on my own nerves. I had to laugh out loud as I thought about the things I did sometimes.

Before the meeting ended, Kelly announced a special meeting that was going to be held in a couple weeks with an invited guest, a doctor, whose name I'd forgotten just as soon as Kelly mentioned it, who would be speaking about alternative medicine.

"I hope everyone can attend. I'll send out reminders on e-mail unless you'd rather me call."

I walked up to Kelly on the way to the door. "Don't e-mail me a reminder. Just call. I'm not yet at the stage where I'm open about my status."

She nodded. "Maybe that will be something else to change in the next thirty-six days. Think about it. It's nothing better than coming to peace with where you are in life. You never know who you might touch."

7 Porter

performed at Baker's the night before as a solo saxophonist. Usually when I performed there I was on my drums, but I needed to take every opportunity I could to showcase my other talent, try out some of my material from my demo, and judge the response I received from the crowd. So last night was a big night for me and I wanted Winona to come lend her support, but I didn't put too much pressure on her to go. And I wasn't playing a game. I had put my request out to see what she said.

Winona was rushing to get ready for work, and I was sitting up in bed watching the madness unfold since she'd woken me up with the noise of her opening and closing dresser drawers and closet doors. And once she flicked on the switch and the light above me began glaring, I knew my morning had prematurely begun.

She was still angry. I could tell from her facial expression. The way she slung her right eyebrow and refused to look at me. The dry way she answered my questions and told me to have a great day.

"Is something wrong?"

"The better question is, is anything right? I'm pissed at Derwin for buying my son a Ford. And I'm mad at you for last night."

"Baby, that wasn't anything for you to get upset about." This all stemmed from the night before, which was another disappointment. I tried to make love to her but of course she wasn't having it. She kept apologizing and I kept accepting like a true sucker in love, which is what I had to be. Otherwise I wasn't sure why I hadn't booked from this situation months ago. This must have gone off and on for close to thirty minutes until finally, after I heard the first snore escape her mouth, I quietly left the bedroom, went down to the basement, and used Winona's computer to log on to the Internet. I wasn't any different from most men out there. Every now and then I watched a little porn. Even though I hadn't done so in a while, the night before I felt compelled to go back on that Web site Conrad bragged about at the fire station. He said they let you view so many free clips that you could essentially get off without charging a dime to your credit card. I was a man used to getting most women without waiting too long. Now waiting was all I ever did, so every now and then I'd sneak downstairs, log on to Winona's computer, watch several porn clips, and jack off. I never forgot to delete my cookies and clear my history so Winona wouldn't be able to backtrack anything I'd done. But last night, what I hadn't suspected was her waking in the middle of the night and coming downstairs to find me with my hand between my legs, tugging on my dick while I watched a man and woman having anal sex.

I heard a gasp. My instinct had me turn before I even thought to close down the Web page, and that's when I saw her standing behind me with her hand covering her mouth.

"Baby, wait," I said as I grabbed her wrist with one hand and used my free hand to guide the mouse to the top of the open window to close it out. "What are you doing up?"

"What am I doing up?" Winona looked down at my penis. "I'm not the only one up. What are you doing watching that filth? You get on me every week about going to church, make me out to be the worst person living, and you're down here jacking off to this shit. I don't believe this."

I took offense to that. No, I definitely didn't want Winona to find me down there that way, but what did she expect for me to do? I was a man and I had needs, wants, desires, none of which she was willing to satisfy. I wasn't in the champagne room of some strip club letting one of the dancers give me a hand or blow job. I wasn't roaming Woodward or Eight Mile for a prostitute. And I wasn't at some bar or club trying to pick up a one-night stand. I was in the basement looking at two people have sex and letting my mind pretend I was one of them and Winona was the other.

"I didn't do anything wrong," I said.

"You didn't do anything wrong? Do you really believe that?" She snatched her wrist free.

"What did I do wrong, Winona? Tell me. I'm a man."

"I'm the only one who needs to be asking questions right now. Do you think what you were doing was right? Whether you're a man or not." She shook her head. "You've just been acting real different lately. Just like the other night when you came home smelling like someone had poured a bottle of alcohol all over you. You were drunk. Filthy drunk, Porter. What am I supposed to think about that?"

"Don't judge me right now."

"You judge me for not going to church, but you can come down here and do that." She pointed at the computer screen that was now displaying the Windows welcome screen.

"Okay," I said as I stood. "What other options do I have to satisfy myself? I don't want to cheat on you so I have to fantasize. I have to do what men serving time do, because that's how I feel, like I'm locked up and can't get access to any pussy," I said with anger. "How long are you going to deny me?"

"After seeing that, probably forever," she said, then turned and stormed up the stairs.

I waited fifteen minutes before I went to bed. I tried to apologize for masturbating to porn, the way she tried to apologize earlier that night for not having sex with me, only mine went unaccepted. She left for work angry, but I was determined for her not to stay that way.

As I drove to the DaimlerChrysler Tech Center to personally deliver two dozen red roses and to tell Winona again that I was sorry, I asked myself what really was the point of all this. I had already told her that once; now driving out there with flowers made it seem like there was a whole lot more to my story. Maybe I was trying to apologize for more than she knew, like the other night at the motel with Vanity. It was bad enough that I was starting to realize how my life was becoming a series of bad decisions on my part. I should be so far ahead from where I am now. Michael Einstein, a saxophonist out of the Detroit area who came on the scene a few months before I did eight years ago, struck a two-disc deal with Warner Brothers last year. His first CD was released a week ago Tuesday, and when I went to Best Buy trying to support the brother they had already sold out. I'd be lying if I didn't admit to being a little envious. Now I'm at the point of my life that I want a whole lot more than what I have right now and somehow, some way, I intend on getting it. Keena is the only way. It can be a start to hopefully something bigger and better.

My cell phone rang just as I pulled into the visitor parking lot at the DaimlerChrysler Tech Center.

"I would like to speak to my drummer please," the woman's voice said.

"This is Porter." I was hesitant because even though I assumed it was Keena on the phone, her voice didn't sound anything like it did on television.

"Well, hello, Porter. I'm tired of trusting Danzo to convince you to come to California to join my band so I decided I would call you myself. What's taking you so long to decide, baby?"

"California for one. I asked around and the cost of living would really kick my ass."

"You can stay with me. A couple of my other band members do."

"I can't put you out like that."

"My house is so big I don't even know how many rooms I have. You won't be putting me out."

"Let me think about it."

"You think too much. I'm going to help you make your decision a little quicker. You need to come out here, spend a few days, see the area, spend some time with me and the other band members in the studio, and let me present the offer to you. I'll pay for the trip. Put you up in a real nice hotel in Santa Monica. I'm very generous to those people in my life, especially when I want them to be there. And I want you to be there. So when can you come out here?"

"I have some engagements planned so probably not until next month."

"Next month? Okay, you do know I'm going on tour in the fall. You need to make your decision by July. Next month is May, and I need an answer soon," she said and hung up without saying good-bye. I just took it as her diva complex.

When I walked into the Tech Center, there was a guard standing behind a post at the entranceway. He stopped me to ask for my name. I waited while he called Winona.

The guard spoke my name into the phone and then said, "She'd like for you to leave those with me."

"May I speak with her?"

"He'd like to talk to you," he said into the phone, and then held the receiver toward me.

"Don't be like this," I said as I turned my back to the guard. "I'm trying to say I'm sorry."

"Okay, leave the flowers with the guard and I'll see you tonight and you can tell me then."

"Tonight I have a gig to go to at Baker's."

"Why is this the first I'm hearing of it?"

"I thought I already told you. I know I did because I'd like for you to come."

"I can't. I'm working late. I have to go," Winona said. "We can't hold up security with a personal call. Call me later if you want to talk."

"Why can't you ever do what I ask you to do?" I asked.

"Why can't you ever do what I ask you to do?"

"What haven't I done, Winona?"

"You signed that covenant in our book and you promised to commit forty days with me. You can't even commit forty days with me so how are you going to commit the rest of your life?"

"You can't even compare the two."

"Yes, I can. I expect when a person promises me that they'll do something that they do it. So no, I'm not going to promise you that I'm going to Baker's tonight. Enjoy yourself." She slammed the phone down.

I tried her later, after five, but she didn't answer. I tried her again a little after six, and she still didn't answer. I'd even called her cell phone but it was turned off and went directly to voice mail. Each time I called I left a message but none of them were returned. I went onstage at Baker's Keyboard Lounge, just me and my saxophone, wondering whether or not a relationship was something I needed right now. Maybe what I was doing tonight, playing my music, was all I needed. Just like I could tell that Winona's momentum toward our relationship had dropped off, so had mine. Why else would we be almost into May and not married, when back in February we planned to be married within a matter of days?

I kept blowing my horn with my eyes closed. Okay, so my life wasn't perfect. Winona wasn't perfect and neither was I. I'd worked all that out in my mind. Now if I could just decipher what I needed to do with all this imperfection we'd be fine. As I blew out my final note, I stood and slowly opened my eyes to a standing ovation. It felt good—better than sex—and for now, it was what I had to do in place of it. Something more than California was in the near future. I could feel it in my bones.

8

Winona

This is totally inconvenient, I thought to myself as I drove around the Detroit Medical Center's parking structure looking for an available space. Every month I had to see Dr. Gant and I was sick of it. And today's appointment was going to be a long one. It was time for him to take my CD4 count and check my viral load; these were tests he performed every four to six months. So far, my CD4 count was above two hundred and I was very thankful for that, because I'd been told anything below that level is when illness sets in. Dr. Gant explained CD4 count by saying that it provided a gauge of how much damage HIV had done to an immune system. It was a viral-load measure of how much HIV was in the blood and told how fast the damage was happening. Often, my HIV level was undetectable, but the trick was to try my best to live stress-free. I noticed that whenever I let things bother me and build up inside, if it was close to my doctor's appointment, I'd see a drastic change in my blood test results—a change for the worse.

On my last visit, Dr. Gant had checked my health chart and determined that I was in need of a complete blood count, liver function test, renal profile, hepatitis B screen, rapid plasma regain test, toxoplasmosis filter, and tuberculosis screen. He also noted administering vaccines for hepatitis B, diphtheria tetanus, pneumonia, and influenza. I was expecting at least a two-and-a-half-hour visit.

I sat in my car for several minutes, unable to move or maybe just unwilling to. If I had to come here every month, how would I ever be able to forget? Sometimes I wanted to forget that I was a person living with HIV and just be a person.

This time I didn't have to wait at all. As soon as I signed my name on the patient sheet, I was told I could go back. I followed Dr. Gant's assistant to the door leading to the bathroom.

"We need to get a urine sample so we can check for OIs," she said as she opened the door for me and closed it after I entered. I tried to focus on letting my urine flow. I felt a tiny drop, and then another. Nothing was coming out. I left the bathroom and sat beside the water dispenser, drinking several tiny cups. "Did you leave your sample for us?"

I shook my head. "No, I'm trying."

"Come on. We'll take your blood first, and then after that maybe you'll be able to urinate."

I followed Dr. Gant's assistant to the lab and stood outside the glass-encased room awaiting my turn. When the door opened and the patient inside exited, I was the next to enter. The technician replaced his latex gloves, took out three syringes, and filled them each with my contaminated blood. When I left, I was ready to empty my bladder, so I walked back to the bathroom and filled the cup. I checked my watch. I was making good time—only forty-five minutes had passed. Maybe I'd be out in an hour and a half, if not sooner.

Dr. Gant's assistant placed me in a room at the end of the hall. I sat on the examining table and waited for Dr. Gant to enter.

After several minutes, I heard voices outside the door and it sounded like they were discussing a patient, perhaps me. I quietly hopped off the examining table and tiptoed to the door.

"That patient was diagnosed with 3-DCR HIV two months ago, now he has full-blown AIDS. He was resistant to every drug we put him on. He was a heavy crystal meth user and he was also very promiscuous with other HIV-positive males so he probably received multiple reinfections," Dr. Gant said as he opened the door. He was startled to see me standing so close to it.

"Hello, Winona. How are you?" Dr. Gant asked as he walked in with his assistant.

"I guess I'm okay."

"You have to have a more positive attitude than that."

After seven years, I still felt like I was living through a bad dream. Every month I came here, which was excessive. Most of the ladies in my support group only saw their specialist twice a year and their gynecologist three times a year. I still didn't have a gynecologist.

I listened to Dr. Gant explain the next steps he wanted to take once the results from all my blood work were received. If anything seemed abnormal, I could expect a call, but in the meantime he wanted me to schedule another appointment in two months. "Why do I have to come here so often?" I asked.

"You don't, but I prefer to see my new patients more often than most."

"I'm not new anymore. I've been coming here every month for over a year, and now I want it reduced to twice a year."

"If that will make you feel more comfortable, that's fine."

"I'd feel a lot more comfortable if I didn't have to come at all."

"How are the meds working?" Dr. Gant asked. "Are you experiencing any side effects?"

"No, my shitty attitude is not a side effect. My sleepless nights, the night sweats, the anxiety I feel, I've had ever since I was diagnosed."

"Has any additional stress been added to your life?"

"Being HIV positive is stress enough."

"How are your personal relationships with your family?"

I sighed. "I really don't feel like talking. The best thing you can do for me is find a cure."

I was lying in bed on my stomach wearing only a thong. My arms were spread out to my sides. The only light was coming from the eucalyptus spearmint aromatherapy candle that I'd bought from Bath and Body Works nearly a month ago for the massage I gave Porter, and now I was finally being repaid with one of my own. That's what he said he'd do so that I'd forgive him, and forgive him I would if he kept rubbing me this way for another hour. How could I refuse that type of spa treatment?

"Did you say something, baby?" Porter asked. I shook my head. "You sure? Are you relaxed?"

I nodded. I think I had fallen asleep from the relaxation of having his hands firmly rub my tension-riddled back for nearly thirty minutes. And I still had an hour left before he could quit. It was so nice to lie still and rest while my man massaged me. Not once had I thought about my kids or work.

"I think you're working too hard," he said as he pressed down on my shoulder blade.

"Ooh," I said as I shifted my body. "Not so hard."

"I know what I'm doing. You need a deep-tissue massage because you have a lot of knots in your back from the tension and stress that you're under."

"That's okay. Leave my knots alone. They're not bothering anyone."

He kissed the back of my neck. "Is that better?"

I nodded. "Much. Hand me my book so I can read Day Five."

"Not the book. Not tonight. Please. We'll double up the chapters tomorrow. I promise." He took his lips and went down my spine with his kisses. "Damn, you have the sexiest ass," he said as he grabbed hold of it and started squeezing my butt cheeks like they were Nerf balls, even though I'm sure he was too young to know what that was. "Winona, make love to me." I felt the weight of his body as he climbed over mine. "I've been wanting you so bad, baby. Just let go and let's do this. You know you want it just as bad as I do." I opened my eyes and turned my head to the side so I could watch him stand over me completely naked and erect. The T-shirt and jeans he was wearing when he started the massage were in a small pile beside the bed. "Baby, it's going to feel so good. Trust me. Everything is going to be okay. I've done my research."

"What kind of research, Porter?"

"I went online last night and did my research."

"Are you sure you were online last night to do research?" I said sarcastically.

"Yes, I'm sure. I went on thebody.com."

"Thebody.com, huh? Sounds kind of sexual to me," I said, jokingly. I was well aware of the Web site, but I wanted to give him a hard time because I still didn't appreciate catching him masturbating the other night.

"I read some of the forums posted for mixed-status couples and we could definitely be having sex with condoms at the very least. Did you know that a lot of mixed-status couples are having sex without condoms if their mate is undetectable?"

I shook my head.

"And I remember that your last few tests were undetectable. I told you I would research it and find out my risks. Seems like I have very few."

I closed my eyes and pushed my body up on my knees. I was almost ready to give in to the temptation when I heard some loud banging at the front door.

"What's that?" I said as opened my eyes and grabbed hold of the footboard. "Do you hear that? It sounds like it's at our front door."

"Carlton probably has the TV on."

"He better not have it on at one o'clock in the morning. Go see what's going on, Porter."

"I'm not answering the door at one in the morning. I'll call the police, because if I go downstairs to answer the door I'm shooting first and asking questions later."

"Do something," I said.

He climbed off of me, stepped into the clothes that he had just taken off, and walked over to the window to look out. "I don't see any cars in the driveway."

"Someone's still banging," I said as I stepped out of bed.

"So," he said as he turned around and stared at my partially naked body. I grabbed my silk robe off the footboard and wrapped up in it. "Let the fool bang. It's probably some drunk who wandered from off Woodward. I'll just call the police."

I walked over to the window and peaked out. Porter stood close behind me, kissing on my neck.

"Shh. Don't you hear that? They're arguing."

"Who?"

I shrugged, but as I listened closer it sounded like my neighbors from across the street—the flight attendant and her pilot husband. The woman I saw getting beat by her husband.

"I'm not good enough for you because I don't fly now, huh?" the man yelled. "What happened to for better or for damn worse? You didn't marry me because you loved me." I heard some commotion, possibly shoving, and then a woman screamed.

"Ooh, call the police," I said as I rushed out of my bedroom and down the stairs.

"Where are you going? Don't answer that door," Porter said. "I'm calling the police. Don't open the door, just wait until I get down there."

I turned the porch light on and saw my neighbors standing in our doorway. I'd spoken to the wife only a few times and I'd seen the husband a couple times pulling in or out of their driveway. I couldn't remember either of their names.

I turned the light off and ran back upstairs. Sosha was standing at her bedroom door.

"Who is that?" Sosha asked as she rubbed her sleepy eyes.

"Go to bed. You have school in the morning," I said as I ran into my bedroom. "It's the neighbors," I said to Porter. He was on the phone with the 911 operator giving them our address. When he hung up the phone he walked to the closet and reached for his gun box that concealed his nine-millimeter.

"You don't need that thing. I said it's our neighbors."

"Those crazy fools on the news are somebody's neighbors too. That fool that pulled a gun on me the other day while I was trying to do my job was somebody's neighbor."

"Somebody pulled a gun on you?" I asked. "Why didn't you tell me about that?"

"I was trying not to stress you out."

"Porter," I said as I followed him down the stairs, "don't open the door holding that gun. Somebody pulled a gun on you?"

"Drop it, Winona. That slipped out. It was no big deal."

"Okay, but please don't you open that door and pull a gun on somebody."

"Oh, so you'd rather me open the door and get shot? Let me handle this." Porter stepped in front of me, turned on the porch light, and opened the door with the chain on. "Is there a problem? Because the police are on their way."

"See, what did I tell you?" the man said to his wife. "Just get back in the house and leave these people alone."

"I'm not going anywhere with you. Sir, is your wife home?" I peaked around Porter's body. "Can I please come in? I can't go home with him. He's crazy. Ever since he lost his job—"

"Yeah, let's talk about ever since I lost my job. That's why you're leaving me, because I got laid off and shit's getting a little tight, but for eight months while I was on furlough and all the bills were paid, things were fine. I guess my unemployment isn't good enough for you." He grabbed her arm and started pulling. She struggled with him and they both fell against our glass door.

"What unemployment, Frank? You're not getting that anymore because you're a drunk and they fired you."

I moved around Porter, took the chain off the door, and let the woman in. She was barefoot and wearing a sheer nightgown. When her husband tried to enter, Porter held him back.

"Stay right there," I said to her. "And you stay in there," I told Porter. I walked to my entry closet and took one of my raincoats off the hanger to give to her.

Her husband was banging on the door.

"The police are here," Porter said.

As I walked into the den, I looked out the window and saw two Detroit police cars driving slowly down the street. They stopped in front of our house. "Put that gun up," I said to Porter.

"I got a license to carry one so I don't have to put it up."

"Well, put it away."

He tucked it in his waistband and cut his eyes at me. He was pissed, probably because I didn't listen to him and I let the woman in our house. Maybe he couldn't understand what she was going through the way I could, since I'd been exactly where she was with Sosha's father. I knew full well what it felt like to be scared to death of the man you were living with.

I sat beside her on the love seat.

"Would you like some tea or something to drink?"

She shook her head.

The doorbell rang and I stood to answer it.

"It's the police. I'll get it," Porter said. "Why don't you go upstairs and put some clothes on? I'm not letting them in here while you have your robe on."

I stood there while he looked at me and sighed. "Can you do one thing that I ask you to?"

I nodded. "I'll be right back," I said to my neighbor. "I'm sorry, what is your name?"

"Andrea."

"I'll be right back, Andrea."

I ran upstairs, put on some jeans and a T-shirt, and hurried back downstairs.

"What's going on?" Carlton asked. He was standing near his door looking down the stairway.

"Go to bed," I said as I jogged down the steps with my breasts bouncing.

Porter and two police officers were standing in the den. One of the officers was talking to Andrea. When I walked in, Porter and the other officer who was standing beside Porter looked down at my chest. Then Porter looked at me with his mouth twisted in disgust. I discreetly looked down and saw my nipples sticking out against the fabric. In my excitement, I'd forgotten to put on a bra and I was so embarrassed.

Porter stood beside me. "Go upstairs and wait for me. I'll handle this."

"But—"

"But nothing. You're just trying to be nosy. Go upstairs."

I guess he was trying to run me, I thought as I stormed upstairs. Did he think I was going to be the submissive type like my mother was to my father? I hoped not, because if so he'd be disappointed. I was going upstairs because it was almost two and in two and a half hours I'd have to get up and get dressed so I could head to work. Not because he told me to. That's why this whole marriage thing was making me wonder whether or not I'd be able to do it.

Porter

9

I looked at the clock. It was almost four a.m. Winona had closed her eyes about an hour ago. After the police left she wanted to stay up and talk about what happened as if she hadn't heard everything from the stairway. I accommodated her for about twenty minutes and then told her it was time for bed. Now I had a flash of Winona in that shirt with her nipples standing at attention and I got excited. If our neighbors hadn't interrupted we probably would have made love. *So why can't we start now?* I wondered.

"You sleep?" I asked as I snuggled my body up to hers.

"Yes, Porter," she whined and turned her back to me.

"I want a quickie, okay?" I asked as I rubbed her butt cheeks. She just didn't know how badly I needed this. I reached for the condom that was lying on the nightstand and tore it open with my teeth. I slid it on, turned her over from her side onto her stomach, and climbed on top. I was struggling to get her legs to open.

"No," she whined and smacked my hand away from her. "I want to go to sleep. Don't be selfish."

Some of the things she said to me really had me wondering if she loved me at all. I was a patient man, at least I considered myself to be, but how much could one man take?

"I think you're the one being selfish," I said as I tried to get something started. "Just a quickie is all I want." I brought my hand around her body and fondled her breasts.

"Then masturbate," she said as she pushed my hand away. "That's what I do."

"Oh, that's what you do, huh? And women wonder why men cheat," I said to hurt her the way she'd just done me.

She flicked the cover from over her head and sat up.

"Oh, so you're going to start cheating?"

"I didn't say that. I just said women wonder why men do."

"Well, I don't need a doctorate degree to figure out what you meant by that. You know, Porter, I really thought you understood what I was going through, but how can you when you're not HIV positive? Do I need to apologize because sex isn't exactly the first thing running through my mind, especially since it was sex that got me in my predicament to begin with, so maybe I have some hang-ups and maybe ... just maybe"—she was really putting on the dramatics—"sex turns me off."

"Well, if you're masturbating, I'd say sex doesn't turn you off. Now does it? But if you think you and I will never have sex, that could be a problem, Winona, because I want us to be in a loving relationship and that has to include sex. So if you don't plan to make love to me, I need to know that now."

"Of course I plan to and one day we will . . . but definitely not unprotected. It's late right now and I'm tired and irritable so please just have a good night."

"A good night? It's a little too late to have one of those. I had on a condom. It was going to be protected."

I lay awake thinking about our relationship, with the Bee Gees' lyrics floating through my head: *How a love so right can turn out to be so wrong.* That's what Winona and I were—so right yet so wrong.

All the women I'd met since I'd been with Winona. All the numbers I'd thrown away. I thought I could fight temptation with love, but what's love got to do with it? Besides, there are some women who just want a warm body next to them for a few hours with no strings. Maybe that's what I needed too—a woman, a real woman. Not someone like Vanity. Maybe if I stopped pressing Winona for sex she'd eventually give in on her own. Right now, I needed to release what was building up inside of me. I had a phone number of a woman I'd met while I was performing at Baker's. Her name was Angie. It was the only number I hadn't thrown away since I'd been with Winona. The woman was forty-four and divorced with four kids. She wasn't looking for anything serious, just some good sex from time to time, which is exactly what I wanted. And then there was Judge Dash, who I'd see riding downtown in her Mercedes CLS500 every now and then, looking real fine to be in her fifties. It was times like these that I kind of wanted to take her up on her offer of a threesome with her and her girlfriend.

"I'm sorry," Winona said as she rolled over and kissed me. "I just need a little more time, okay?" She snuggled in closer to me and wrapped her arm around my chest.

"Take all the time you need, baby. I'm not going anywhere," I said as I kissed her arm. I closed my eyes. My mind was pretty much made up. If I couldn't fight my temptations, I knew one of these days I was going to give in to them.

10 Winona

It's bad when you walk into the house of God and the church members look you up and down like you don't belong. What happened to making a guest feel welcomed? That's how it was for me every Sunday I visited Porter's church—Faith in the Word. His coworker Zeander and his wife were pleasant enough. They sat next to us during service. And out of the ten thousand or so that the church held—I surely couldn't account for everyone—many were giving off evil vibes, especially the bishop.

I knew the sermon sounded familiar, but I couldn't place where I'd heard it until the bishop said, "Bud, blossom, fruit." That's when I knew he was stealing from Bishop T.D. Jakes. He'd change a word here and there, but for the most part it was almost identical.

"Touch someone and say, 'I've been carrying this burden for such a long time,' and then shout, 'Overnight!' " The bishop paused for a second and then said, "Faith in the Word family, God told me to tell you He's going to do some things overnight, so when I tell you things are going to change for you overnight, that's exactly what I mean. Get ready . . . get ready . . . get ready, because you're about to get blessed overnight," he yelled.

"He took that," I said to Porter. "That's T.D. Jakes's. He stole that."

The more Porter's bishop talked, the more I heard him taking not only from Bishop T.D. Jakes but Bishop Eddie Long and Bishop Noel Jones. *What's he doing, a remix?* I wondered as I looked around at the overly excited congregation jumping to their feet. Surely I wasn't the only one who knew those weren't his words. I wasn't the only one who watched TBN.

"I want you to count off one, two, three, four, five and when you get to the sixth person I want you to say, 'Overnight!' "

"That's not right," I said as I turned toward Porter. "He's taking from other bishops."

"Maybe they took from him," Porter said.

"No, he's a fraud," I said passionately. "Can we go?"

Porter looked down at his watch. "In another hour."

I folded my arms, crossed my legs, and shook my head while I watched the bishop put on his show. I looked at his wife standing on the pulpit. She was a very attractive fair-skinned woman with short bleached-blond hair. She had her arms raised upward and her head leaning back. I glanced at her and then back at the bishop and then back at her. I was trying hard not to judge them, but the first word that popped into my head to describe them was "charade."

As his sermon was winding down, the bishop wiped his forehead with a white handkerchief and said, "We're raising miracles up in here. Are you a miracle?" he shouted. "Do you want to believe in miracles? Do you need a miracle? Do you need a blessing? If so, it's time to turn your life back over to Christ. Those of you in the congregation who would like to have a relationship with God, whether it's to renew the one you already have or to start to develop one, please come forward. Give your life to Christ. The Lord is calling on you," he shouted. "He's calling on you," he shouted louder, and then the praise team stood and sung the verse that the bishop had just said. "He wants you."

"He wants you," the praise team sang.

"Are you going to give your life to Christ?"

"Give your life to Christ and you will see it renew," the praise team sang.

Dozens of people walked down the aisle.

"If you're visiting for the first time or the fiftieth and you feel as if you've finally found your church home and you want to become a member, today is the day. It's your day. Come forward. Come on forward," he said as he extended his arm. Porter nudged me and I nudged him back. Did Porter really think that I was going to walk to the front of *this* church to join? Dozens did, but I wasn't among them.

"Go in peace," the bishop said. And as soon as I heard those words, I sprung from my seat, because until I left this church I wouldn't have peace.

On the ride home, Porter was unusually quiet. When he stopped at a red light, he played the first track from his "Travelin' Shoes" demo. It was my first time hearing it.

"Is that you?" I asked with excitement as I listened to the instrumental jazz track. I turned toward him after he didn't respond. "Is something wrong?"

He let out a loud sigh. "Church is very important to me if you didn't already know."

"God or church?"

"God and going to church and worshipping. But I shouldn't have to beg you to go and when you get there I shouldn't have to listen to you complain about my bishop."

"I wasn't complaining. I was simply stating a fact, which is, he was pulling from other sermons. Bishop T.D. Jakes for one. I have Bishop Jakes' tape series where he talks about God changing your life overnight. I can let you hear it if you don't believe me."

"No. I don't need to listen to it. Maybe they both said something similar."

"No, it wasn't similar. It was pretty much exact."

"Winona, stop making excuses for why you don't want to go to church. We have to have God in our lives with all that we're going through. And I love my church so if you're going to be my wife, you need to follow me wherever I am. You're still going to be my wife, right?" I didn't answer his question as quickly as he wanted, so he said, "Right?"

"Maybe we should do premarital counseling first just to be sure," I said.

"What can a stranger tell us about our lives that we don't

already know? The only way I will agree to premarital coun-seling is if we get it through my church."

"Then I guess we won't get any," I said as I leaned my head against the headrest and closed my eyes. I wanted to scream, I didn't hate church but I did hate his church. I opened my eyes and turned my head to face Porter. At this stage in my life with what I was dealing with I couldn't think about marriage. There was some reason this happened to me. If everything truly does happen for a reason, I had to find out what that was and make a bad situation a little bet-ter. I took my miniature book out of my purse and started reading.

"If you can read that you can read the Bible," Porter said sarcastically.

"Well, at least I read something," I snapped back.

11 Porter

I was at Belle Isle Park sitting on chunks of broken concrete behind the lighthouse and the abandoned hot dog stand. The small patch of wooded land nearby made this a perfect place to think and pretend that I was somewhere besides Detroit—somewhere far away, even though I'd never left the state. It was time.

My life was a lot more complex than I ever could have imagined. And now I needed to make a decision. Do I go to California and perform with Keena or not? And if I did, when should I tell Winona about the move and ask her if she'll come with me? I know in order for her to up and move she has to take a lot of things into consideration—her kids, her career, her house, and most definitely her health. But I felt like it was time to start living out my passion. Finally, after all these years, I got an offer to take my music to the next level. Not a solo act. I'm not Boney James yet. But if I accepted Keena's invitation to join her band as the drummer, it would be a step in the right direction, a chance to display my talent and see how far it could take me. You'd think the decision wouldn't be all that difficult, except there's always a catch in life. I'm scared. Scared that if I go, Winona may not go with me, and if I don't go, I give up on possibly a once-in-a-lifetime chance to pursue my dream. What if I fail? Or go there and get caught up in Keena's mess?

I love Winona so much that it hurts because I can't help her. Not in the way she needs it. I couldn't have imagined that loving her was going to be this complicated. I don't know what I thought and part of me wonders if I thought at all. It was times like this I wished I hadn't fallen out with my mother, because she always gave me good advice when it came to Winona. Now I only had myself to rely on.

I was sitting outside of my mother's restaurant in downtown Detroit. I didn't see her car, but that didn't mean anything because she could have traded it or she was back with my father. Maybe she was driving one of his, and I could never keep up with all the cars he was always getting.

I answered my cell phone on the second ring, and no, it wasn't Winona. It was Angie, the woman I met at Baker's Keyboard Lounge. She was trying to figure out what I was doing and when we were going to see each other again. I felt like telling her that we'd see each other the next time I was performing at Baker's and she came, but I didn't even want to say that because I honestly hoped I would never see her again. I was holding the phone up to my ear, but my thoughts were light-years away from Angie's weak conversation. She may have had a big ass but she had a small brain.

"Where are your kids?" I asked, because that's what I'm the most concerned about. Was she the type to leave her kids with anybody while she went out and got her groove on?

"With their daddy."

"Daddies? Right? Plural."

"Yeah, plural. Daddies," she said with a *tsk* as if I'd said something to piss her off.

"Oh, all of their fathers are in their lives?"

"I only have three baby daddies."

"Do you think having three baby daddies is a good thing?"

"What's wrong with you? You don't know me well enough to talk that way. I just called to say hey."

"Hey," I said as I felt myself slipping back into my old self. Sarcastic and rude—an asshole. I was angry because the woman I wanted was not the woman I was talking to on the phone right now.

She sighed and then her other line clicked and she told me to hold on. I hung up as soon as she clicked over and went back to my thoughts. If I could have my life the exact way I wanted to have it today, I wouldn't be working for the fire department earning pennies while I put my life on the line every time we were called out to a fire. I'd be in the music business playing the saxophone, because even though I'm known for drumming, it's something about the sax that I really love, and besides, you can't go solo as a drummer. I'd have custody of my daughter, Portia. I'd be married to Winona, only she wouldn't be HIV positive and she wouldn't be ten years older than me, because I still want more kids and her being thirty-eight, close to thirty-nine, and HIV positive has pretty much ruled all that out. I wouldn't even be living in Detroit. If I could have life my way I'd be living in Florida, maybe Jacksonville or Miami, because the California lifestyle doesn't exactly thrill me, too many wannabes out there. The longer my list grew of the way my life would be, the more I realized that I wasn't anywhere close to having what I wanted and now it was up to me to change it. Now Winona had me thinking about God's purpose for my life too.

12 Winona

There was a sea of arms swaying from side to side in every pew. Weeping filled the sanctuary, sounds of both sadness and joy. I closed my eyes, raised my arms, and stretched them outward as I prayed for my neighbor Andrea. It seemed that the bishop's words had touched many of those in the congregation as several went to the altar to throw down cash and checks. For a minute, I was actually feeling his sermon.

"If I may but touch," the bishop shouted. He'd already preached from Matthew 9, telling the story of the woman who had a flow of blood for twelve years who was healed by touching the hem of Jesus' garment. "If I may but touch," the bishop shouted again, his words stabbing my heart. *If I may but touch,* I thought as I closed my eyes. I could only imagine how much better my life would be if I could be healed by a touch.

"Where did he go?" I whispered in Porter's ear after I opened my eyes in search of the bishop.

"To change," Porter whispered back.

"Change what? His clothes?" I asked in disbelief.

"Yeah, his clothes. It's Super Sunday."

"You've got to be kidding me. And this is why I will stay Catholic," I said, my face scrunched together with confusion.

Porter shook his head. "Catholic?"

"Yes, Catholic."

"Well, while you're busy judging Bishop think about all the mess those priests do to little boys."

I rolled my eyes as the bishop floated back onstage. "People say I'm putting on a show," the bishop said. He'd changed into a burgundy suit with pink pinstripes and a pink shirt. "And I am. A show for the Lord." He made a loud screeching sound and jumped. The congregation went wild with screaming and shouting.

"Jesus," a lady in the pew behind us hollered, running toward the bishop. She was taken to the ground by two large male bodyguards.

"This is a true place of anointing and I feel the Holy Spirit in this place this morning," the bishop said, and then he began to speak in tongues.

The lady walked up to the pulpit and whispered in the bishop's ear.

"Glory be to God," the bishop said in response to the

woman. "May I share your story with the congregation?" he asked softly, his words amplified by the microphone attached to his ear. "Two years ago," the bishop emphasized, "this woman standing before us was diagnosed HIV positive." He paused and shook his head. "But last week, after I laid my hands on her, when she went back to the specialists for further testing, they told her that the virus was gone. Turn to your neighbor and say, 'Jesus is a healer, not a stealer.'" Porter squeezed my hand when I didn't turn my head or open my mouth. I couldn't move. My anger had paralyzed me. What the bishop had just said was the final straw.

I knew from the first Sunday I'd attended that I would never join. There were three people between me and the aisle, and one of them was Porter. I pushed by all of them so I could leave. As I was walking out I heard the bishop say, "Turn to four people and say, 'Weeping may endure for a nighttime, but *joy*"—he shouted the word at the top of his lungs—"cometh in the morning."

I snatched my car keys from my purse, marched through the church doors out to the parking lot, and sat on the passenger side of Porter's Magnum with my arms folded tightly across my chest.

"If he can simply touch people and cure them of HIV, he needs to work for the Centers for Disease Control," I said to myself. My anger grew the more I thought about it. I had been HIV positive for seven years and not a day went by that I didn't think about what it would feel like if a cure was discovered. Now some ballin' bishop wanted to tell me and thousands of others that he simply placed his jewelry-laden hands on someone and the virus was gone. *Please.* That was almost as bad as the woman who came up to the altar last Sunday and shared her miracle—her bankruptcy was dismissed and she no longer had to pay her bills because her debt was wiped clean. I know a little about bankruptcy since Keith, my youngest child's father, was always filing either a Chapter 7 or 13. When a bankruptcy is dismissed, the creditors can pursue the debt, so that was far from a miracle.

Porter knocked on the passenger-side window.

I turned a cold eye toward him before letting the window down.

"What was that all about?" Porter asked. "You need to come back inside. Miracles are being performed in there while we're out here."

I shook my head and rolled my eyes at Porter. "You're brainwashed. That man isn't performing any miracles. Can't you see through that?"

"All I see is how much my life turned around since I joined this church. I'm a different person because of Faith in the Word."

"But that's not even the same bishop. Your bishop retired, and you didn't like Bishop Coles at first, remember?" I shook my head. "I just don't get a good feeling about him."

"Winona, you need to try to open your heart and believe. I didn't like him at first, but he's growing on me."

"Believe? I know what I don't believe. I don't believe *that* man laid his hands on a woman who was HIV positive and now she's cured. I don't believe it and I won't believe it. You better watch out. He might be another Jim Jones."

"Another who?"

"Forget it. I'm not sure you were even born when that happened. Just please don't get brainwashed."

"If you're not coming back inside, you might as well take the car and go home. I can get a ride."

"I bet you can," I said as I climbed into the driver's seat. "I'm sure one of the sisters from the church would love to take you to their home since they can barely keep their eyes in their Bibles for looking at you and all the other attractive black men in the congregation." I put the gearshift in drive and sped away.

I raced into my driveway and slammed on the brakes inches from my closed garage door. I walked to the side of the garage with a dozen of the bishop's CDs I'd gathered from Porter's car and tossed them into the garbage can. As I walked around to the front of the house, I noticed my neighbor Andrea from across the street waving, so I threw my hand up as I walked into the house. I could have at least stopped to say something—after all, she was the woman I was at church praying for—but right now I had my own problems so the hell with her and hers.

"Mom, let's talk about graduation," Carlton said without allowing me a second of unwind time.

"Let's not," I snapped. "You kids don't even let me get in the house before you start working my nerves." I knew I had to take Carlton shopping for his graduation from the University of Detroit High School next month. He already had a custom suit being tailor made and he wanted a pair of green alligator shoes to match. The pair he picked out were close to a thousand dollars and I only agreed to go that high because he was graduating from high school with honors and had a full athletic and academic scholarship being offered by several universities. Among them was the University of Michigan, which I was hoping he'd select so my baby wouldn't be too far away from me. As much as he wracked my nerves with his disrespect and frequent use of profanity, he was still my firstborn. We'd hung tightly together for five years before Sosha was born and continued our bond afterward.

"How was church?" he asked sarcastically.

"It was all right."

"Mmm. Well, you might want to go back for the evening session because you definitely need Jesus."

I started laughing at Carlton's comment. Then for a moment, a quick moment, I started to get upset. But Carlton was right. I had a major attitude. "I'm sorry for snapping at you. I am very proud of you and how well you are doing."

Carlton felt my head. "You don't seem to have a temperature."

"Where's your sister?" I asked as I moved his hand away from my head.

He hesitated. "You're going to get upset because she's on the phone."

"She lives on the phone. Who is she talking to now?" I snatched the receiver from the kitchen wall and listened long enough to hear a young man's voice. "I know you're not talking to a boy on this phone," I shouted. "And I hope it's not you, Baxter." Everything went quiet and the next thing I heard was a dial tone. "Sosha, bring your fast ass down here right now!"

She took her time walking down the stairs, and when she did finally come she put her hands on her hips with attitude. I shook my head because today really wasn't the day for foolishness. Yesterday might have been, tomorrow could be, but today nobody better mess with me.

"Was that a boy?" I asked, trying to remain calm, even though I was practically hyperventilating.

"Did it sound like a boy?"

"Forget it." I waved her off with my hand. "But I do want you to tell that *boy* not to call here anymore. If you don't, I will."

"Mom," Sosha whined, "I'm getting ready to go into high school."

"You're twelve and therefore no boys can call my house before you turn sixteen."

"I'll be a freshman in college then. That's not fair."

"That really isn't fair, Mom," Carlton interjected.

"Maybe it's not. And if you haven't heard so already, let me be the first to tell you that life isn't fair, but that's the way it's going to be." The very thought of Sosha dating made me panic. I'd rather she not be around any young men until her mind caught up with the overdevelopment of her body. Her breasts were almost as large as my full D cup and her butt was larger than mine. A combination like that spelled instant trouble so I ran off an application from the Internet to the all-girls Catholic high school, Our Lady of Mercy.

"Where's Porter?" Carlton said. "Didn't y'all go to church together?"

"Mind your own, okay?" I followed Sosha up the stairs. "Who was that boy? Was it Baxter?"

"Maybe. Maybe not," she said and slammed the door.

"You're grounded. Do you hear me, Sosha?" I asked while I turned the knob to her locked door. "No phone. No TV. No going over to your grandparents either."

"So what?" she yelled back.

I stormed into my bedroom, slammed the door, and paced the hardwood floor for a while before I collapsed on the bed. This had to be one of the worst days of my life. Next only to the day I was diagnosed HIV positive. I felt like I was beginning to lose control of my life—like I could feel myself slipping.

Why did I leave my man at that church with a bunch of desperate church ladies looking for a man to call their own? And why did I have to go to that church at all and hear that preacher lie about curing someone from HIV? And then why did I have to come home and yell at my kids when they've done nothing wrong but put up with me and my shitty attitude?

I took my book off the nightstand and continued reading. Thirty more days before my change. *Please, Lord, let this work.*

13 Porter

Winona, Sosha, and I were sitting at the breakfast table with our square deep-dish pizza from Buddy's. Cooking was the one thing Winona did not do, which was something I definitely had to get used to because my family owned a restaurant and both my parents could burn in the kitchen. They'd taught me.

I guess I could have done all the cooking, but I firmly believed that was a woman's job. Just like women think it's sexy for men to be in the yard, wash their car, and fix things around the house, I thought it was sexy to see a woman in the kitchen making her man a meal. I saw that the first day I came over Winona's house, when she attempted to cook a roast that didn't quite turn out, but I hadn't seen it since.

Sosha was the only one talking, and it was about high

school and how she couldn't wait for eighth grade to be over so she could be a freshman. It was the only thing on her mind lately. That and boys. And she'd have plenty of them chasing her. In fact, they'd already started. I hadn't told Winona what happened the week before when I took Sosha to help me pick out a better engagement ring for Winona. I had been doing more gigs during the week so my side money was increasing enough for me to upgrade her ring to a larger diamond with more clarity.

I turned my back for a second, and when I looked around for Sosha I didn't see her. She'd left the store and was standing in the mall with some man who looked almost as old as me. Not quite, but way older than Sosha. I had to count to ten before I approached them—and I had to make it all the way to ten, because had I stopped anywhere before that number, I would have killed him.

"She's twelve." That's how I greeted him. He threw his hands up like I'd told him he was under arrest, and he would have been if he touched her. He apologized after he stressed how beautiful "my little sister" was. I didn't even correct him by saying she wasn't my little sister but was going to be my daughter. He told me that he was nineteen and thought Sosha was at least sixteen or seventeen. "Sixteen or seventeen?" I said as if he were out of his mind. But then I looked at her. For the first time I took a real good look at Sosha and I realized that she could easily pass for that age, if not older, which was scary. Sosha was going to high school with a woman's body and a child's mind—a frightening combination, especially when she couldn't talk to her mother about the facts of life, because all Winona did was freak. So instead she talked to me, and whenever we did talk, I gave it to her straight. I told her about boys and all the little games they can play. I told her how boys know girls better than girls know boys and probably better than girls know themselves, so they had you from every angle. "Whatever you do," I said to Sosha. "Don't have sex until you're married."

"Mom didn't do that," she quickly came back.

"I'm not talking about your mother. I'm talking about you. And I don't think I'd be speaking out of turn if I told you that she probably wished she had waited." Last week at the mall was our first conversation on the subject of sex and boys, but I was certain there would be more to come, and I'd be ready. The same thing I'd be telling Sosha would be the exact same thing I tell my own daughter, Portia, if her trifling mother ever lets me have a relationship with her.

"How was your day?" I asked Winona. She'd been quiet during dinner and that wasn't like her. Maybe she was still mad about church the day before. Last night, Winona told me straight out that she wouldn't be going back to Faith in the Word, and I believed her.

"Fine," she said, picking the broccoli off her pizza. There was something about Winona's facial expression that caused me concern.

"Are you sure your day was fine, baby?" I touched her hand.

"Baby?" Sosha said, giggling. "I wish I was somebody's baby."

Winona cut her eyes at Sosha. "I've given it some thought and you're going to Our Lady of Mercy. You want to be somebody's baby and you'll end up with one instead."

"I don't want to go to Mercy. You said I could go to Marion. Have a sense of humor, Mom. I was just joking."

"Your mother had a hard day," I said, interrupting. "It's Monday. Remember her rule."

"That's right," Sosha said. "No mess on Monday."

My cell phone started to ring. When I saw Reesey's name come across my cell phone's caller ID at first I wasn't going to answer it, but I didn't have a choice because she had my child. A man's child isn't something to play with but that's what Reesey always did, use Portia to get to me, even if she didn't think I realized it. I looked at Winona and watched her eyebrow rise.

"Baby . . . mama . . . drama," Sosha said softly and smirked as she bit into her pizza.

"What did you say?" Winona asked Sosha.

"Nothing," she said as she quickly straightened out her face.

"That's what I thought, and make sure I never hear that nothing again." Winona shooed me off with her hand. "Answer that in another room."

Once I said hello, Reesey sighed. I knew she wanted me to ask what was wrong, but I only cared if it concerned my daughter. "Portia's okay, right?" I asked.

"Portia's fine. But I do have a slight problem. I didn't realize that this weekend was get-together weekend with the Pistons wives—"

"Oh, you're a Pistons wife now?"

"I will be. You know I'm engaged to one so of course I get included. It's five of us and we're all real close friends."

I wanted to ask her to repeat what she had just said.

Reesey had some real close female friends? I didn't think that was possible.

"Friends, huh? That's a new concept . . . for you."

"Porter, I didn't call for your side remarks. I just called to let you know that this weekend is out for you to have Portia because she has a birthday party to go to on Sunday and then a picnic the following week."

"It ain't warm enough for no damn picnic."

"It's not warm enough here, but it's plenty warm in Orlando."

"Orlando? Why are you going all the way to Orlando for a picnic? Now, I'm trying my best to work with you, but every week there's an excuse for why I can't see my child. And your excuses are running out. If you keep this shit up, I'll have the court straighten it out."

"The first weekend in May would be good for us."

It was never about what was good for me. Why couldn't I have my baby every weekend since Reesey had her all during the week?

I held the phone in silence for a minute. I couldn't believe how powerless I was. "That's fine for now, but pretty soon I'm going to need more time. She needs to know who her daddy is, and how can she if you never bring her around?"

"We'll see," Reesey said. "But for now, plan on . . . the seventeenth."

If there was one woman I could say I hated, Reesey would be that woman. She was always dangling Portia over my head like some carrot. "Reesey, I'm not trying to argue with you."

"Then don't."

"I'm not waiting until the seventeenth. That's almost a month away."

"Well, I don't want *my* baby around that woman." Okay, so now the truth was coming out. "Your mother told me all about her. She's older than you. Were you that hard up that you had to go to an older woman with two kids?"

"*You* have two kids," I shouted.

"Yeah, and one of them is yours. I don't want my baby around that woman."

"Your baby around *that* woman? What woman? You mean *my* woman? You have her around *your* man every day and you don't hear me saying anything."

"Because what can you say? You're the one who up and left like some little punk."

Little punk? I was ready to seriously hurt some feelings when I heard that. "If I was a little punk you were a big wh—" Winona covered my mouth and shook her head before I could complete the word. I didn't even see her enter the room.

"Be nice," Winona mouthed.

"I can say plenty," I said, "if I want to be petty, but we're not together and you're not a nun, so the reality is that my daughter will be raised with another man, possibly the Piston."

"What you mean possibly the Piston? The Piston has a name, which is Dean."

"Well, once Dean finds out about you like I did, he's going to leave your ass too. You can't be faithful to no man. Let Ben Wallace or Rasheed try to holler in your ear. He'll see what I'm talking about."

"Please, neither one of them is my type, especially Ben Wallace."

"His money is your type."

"I'm getting off the phone now so I won't have to contend with your jealous ranting."

"Jealous ranting? I'm not hardly jealous. I don't want you," I said to a dial tone.

I was starting to realize that having an extended family was challenging, which was one of the main reasons I'd always said I'd never get involved with a woman who had kids. Although, I must admit, most of the drama involving the kids came from my end. Sosha's father wasn't alive so I didn't have to put up with any drama on that end. Carlton's father was trying to weasel his way back into the picture after eighteen years, which was pissing me off because I knew he had finally developed feelings for Winona. He was into her looks, her pretty face, and nice shape, something I assumed she didn't possess back in high school.

I dialed Reesey back.

"I'm picking my baby up Friday evening," I said to Reesey. "I'll bring her back either Sunday afternoon or Monday morning."

"Yeah, you can pick her up on Friday but she needs to be back Sunday by noon because she needs to go to her friend's birthday party."

"She can skip a birthday party. She's not even two yet so she won't remember it anyway."

"It's one of her best friends."

"You mean it's the daughter of one of your so-called best

friends, because Portia is too young to know what a best friend is."

"I'm through talking to you. You can pick her up Friday but she needs to be back Sunday by noon. If you can't accommodate that then don't come get her at all." And she slammed the phone down.

I pressed the REDIAL button and Dean answered.

"I need to speak to Reesey."

"She's busy right now."

"I just talked to her a minute ago and she's busy that fast?" He didn't respond. "Well, tell her to call me. Can you do that?"

"Who are you?"

"What does your caller ID say?" I asked.

"Unknown."

"Well, I'm not unknown. This is Porter, Portia's daddy. And don't you ever forget it."

He hung up the phone.

"I can't stand that bitch," I said as I threw my phone against the wall and watched the battery fly off.

"Calm down, baby," Winona said.

I shook my head. "You don't understand. That woman takes me out of my element. You know me, usually I'm very calm, but that woman there"—I pointed down at my cell phone—"she disturbs my spirit. I'm going to have high blood pressure if I have to deal with her until my daughter is eighteen."

"You'll probably have to deal with her much longer than that."

"When Portia is eighteen she can make her own decisions and I'll just deal directly with her."

"It really is a thin line between love and hate," Winona said.

"I never loved Reesey. I've told you that." In fact, it was hard to believe that I ever cared for that woman for so long—damn near twelve years, since I was a sophomore in high school until I was about twenty-seven—up until she had a child by another man and lied by saying it was mine.

"Is she going to let you get Portia?" Winona asked as she wrapped her arms around my waist and gave me a tight squeeze.

"She doesn't have a choice. I'm paying child support," I said as I kissed her forehead. "I just hope when I do go over there she doesn't pull no last-minute bullshit. You know how she is. Something always seems to come up. I really wish I could get full custody." I looked down at Winona. "Would that be okay with you?" She nodded. "Are you sure?"

She nodded again. "Of course it would. I just hope your baby likes me when we finally meet."

"She's only eighteen months, baby. She's going to like you. Just buy her a toy and she'll love you. And you're going to meet her on Friday so you'll see for yourself. Besides, you're going to be her momma one day."

"Her stepmother."

"No, her mother."

Winona

14

I'm on a mission, I thought to myself as I raced my shopping cart down the aisle and turned the corner so quickly that two of the wheels lifted off the ground. I glanced down at my watch. I had a couple hours to do what I needed before making it home to unload, and I still had to stop by a grocery store and get some juice because I remembered Porter saying that Portia loved Cran-Apple. I smiled when I saw the singing "I Love You" Barney stuffed toy. Sosha had the same one when she was a baby and loved it, so I threw it in the cart along with six other items from that aisle. A few things fell out because my cart was too full, which was my cue that it was time to check out. As I was unloading the items, I realized I'd gone overboard. I was buying more than most people buy their children for Christmas.

"It's kind of early for Toys for Tots. That's what all this is for, right?" the white male cashier asked.

"Toys for one tot . . . a little girl. It's too much, isn't it?"

"She's going to really like this," he said as he scanned the singing Barney. "I bought one for my daughter and she takes it everywhere she goes." I looked at the cashier as he was ringing me up. I wouldn't have figured him for a father. He seemed too young for that—probably Carlton's age or maybe a year or two older. How sad, a baby having a baby. I was twenty-one when I had Carlton and that was too young. If I could do it all over again, I'd wait until I was thirty. Something I hoped both of my children did. There was so much more to life than raising kids.

I started putting some of the items he hadn't rang up back in the cart. He was right. It was too much. "I changed my mind about this," I said every time I picked up a toy. At least fifteen items went back but my bill still came to over nine hundred dollars.

I handed him my American Express. Porter was going to think I'd lost my mind. No, he was going to think I was trying to buy his baby's love, when actually I was just trying to help. He was the one so concerned that she wasn't speaking as well as she should. He asked me how old Sosha was when she started talking. My answer of nine months didn't help matters. But Sosha was exceptional, not to say Portia wasn't, but nine months is definitely not the norm. It's just that my daughter is the type that catches on to things very quickly, which is why she was double-promoted twice. Carlton would be a much better benchmark. He was almost three before he stopped baby talk and formed completed sentences, but now look at him—

graduating with honors and getting ready to receive both an academic and athletic scholarship. I was so proud.

I requested help to my car and that's when I knew for sure I'd gone overboard. My trunk was practically filled with Toys 'R' Us bags. I even had to let the backseat down.

"I won't put all the toys out," I said to myself as I drove out of the parking lot. "Each time she comes over she'll have new toys to play with, or maybe that's excessive. Porter will say I'm spoiling her. I'm not going to worry about it. Porter's going to think I'm crazy when he sees all this. I'm just going to keep most of the bags in the car. . . . Oh, I'm getting like my mother." I stopped at a red light. "I said I'd never sneak around like she did and that's what I'm doing now. No." I shook my head. "I'm not going to do it. I'm not going to turn into her. I bought all this stuff with my own money. I don't have to feel guilty. Guilty about what?" I threw my hands up in the air and looked at the car beside me. They were looking over at me and laughing. When the light turned green, I hit the gas and sped off. "Maybe I should donate some of these toys to a shelter. I don't have to wait until Christmas to give to a needy cause."

I unloaded all but four of the Toys 'R' Us bags from the trunk of my car by myself. I didn't want the kids to help because they'd think I was crazy. The toys I left in my car were the ones I had planned to donate. I'd have to check with the support group, but there was probably a shelter for children with AIDS.

Sosha came downstairs after I'd taken everything out of the bags and boxes. Samson was walking around the den inspecting all the boxes with his nudging nose. "Why are you playing with toys?" Sosha asked as she walked into the den and sat beside me on the floor.

"These are for Portia. She'll be here tomorrow," I said as I stacked the lettered blocks on top of each other. Sosha picked up the Photo Fun Learning First Words book. "You're going to bore the baby. Why didn't you buy her some Barbies?"

"She's too young for Barbie dolls."

"You're never too young or too old for a Barbie doll." I was so relieved to hear her say that. Just when I thought she was starting to mature too quickly. "She can have mine. I don't need them anymore."

"Why don't you?" I asked. "I thought you could never be too old for Barbies?"

"I meant when you're a kid. I am getting ready to go to high school in the fall, Mom." She stood up and walked to the stairway. "Carlton, are you ready?"

"I'm coming in a minute so chill," he yelled out.

"Where are you all going?" I asked.

"He's dropping me over grandma's and then I think he has a date. Do you know anything about his girlfriend?" Sosha asked with a strange expression on her face.

"Is there something I'm supposed to know about her? I really didn't know he had one since Jill."

"He's had several since Jill, but this one—" Sosha stopped talking after she heard Carlton running down the stairs.

"You ready?" he said as he reached the bottom step and peered into the den.

"Yes, I've been ready," Sosha said.

I looked at Carlton's attire. It was more conservative than I was used to seeing. He was wearing a pinstripe dress shirt and a nice pair of black slacks with a pair of black dress shoes.

"Nice outfit."

"Head to toe Kenneth Cole. You like?" he said as he spun around.

"How did you buy all of that without a job?" I said. "I'm tired of you asking your grandparents to buy the things I won't. I've bought you plenty of clothes, so don't get greedy."

"I bought these but I'm not the one paying for it."

"Who is? And don't tell me your girlfriend because I didn't raise my son to take young girls' money, so I hope you're not like that."

"Well, if they want to give it to me, I'm not going to turn it down. But actually, my dad did. He got me an American Express card." Carlton whipped the green card from his wallet and waved it around. "Just in case you're wondering, Kenneth Cole," he said as he held out his wallet.

"So your father got you a credit card?"

"Not just any credit card, an American Express. Don't leave home without it," he said, chuckling.

I walked up to him and snatched the card out of his hand. "Well, you're about to because this is going straight back to him."

"You're trippin'. Give me my card back! It's not like you're paying for it."

"What do you need with a credit card?"

"Look, Dad said to try not to go over three grand a month. He also said if something comes up and I need to, just to let him know because the card has a ten-thousand-dollar limit. So if he's not sweating it, why are you? Just face it, my father's loaded."

Sosha's eyes popped out. "Well, can you buy your only sister some clothes?"

"Please, you better ask your only mother to," Carlton said.

I handed the card back to him. "Carlton, I don't want you even going over five hundred dollars a month—that's too much. I don't know what that man was thinking about when he got you an American Express."

"He was thinking he owes my ass some money."

"No, he owes *my ass* some money," I said as I used my finger to poke at my chest. "A whole lot."

"Mom, you're not paying for it so don't worry about what he was thinking. He told me he'd do a lot more for me if he didn't think you'd trip. Come on, Sosha. Let's go."

After I heard the door slam, I walked into the kitchen, picked up the phone receiver and dialed Derwin. He was always trying to outdo me lately and I was tired of it.

"Hello," Derwin said, answering in his happy voice. I figured his caller ID displayed my name, and since he'd been leaving voice mail messages on my work phone begging me to call him, I guess he thought this was a social call. Not.

I took a few deep breaths before I began to speak. "So Carlton needs an American Express? You didn't think a simple Capital One Visa with a two-hundred-dollar limit would do?" I remembered those so well because Keith, Sosha's father, had three of them. He called it rebuilding his credit. When they sent him one with a three-hundred-dollar balance he thought he'd arrived.

"I just wanted to do something nice."

"Something nice? When I think of doing something nice, I think of a dinner and a fifty-dollar gift card, not a ten-thousand-dollar credit card. You're trying to buy my son."

"Our son. He's my only child and my parents' only grand-child so he's going to be spoiled. My mother adores him and she buys him things. The credit card was actually her idea."

I laughed. "So you mean he's met your mother? I've never met your mother, but then again, I wasn't light enough to meet her, was I?"

"Look, I don't feel like arguing. If he spends ten thousand dollars on the card in one month, I told him I'd pay it off and close it out. I gave him his limit and I'm confident he won't go over it. Besides, it's teaching him responsibility."

"How, when he's not paying the bill? It's teaching him that he can go out and spend three thousand dollars a month on clothes or whatever and not have to pay for it. I don't want women to be into him because of the material things he has and not who he is inside. Plainly put, I don't want him to be like you."

"Oh, so the only reason women like me is for my money. Is that the only reason you liked me?"

"No, the only reason I liked you is because I was a fool and an insecure little girl who didn't think I could do better."

"I guess we were both fools because I never should have left you at the altar."

"Well, you did, and I'm so glad that you did."

"Why are you so angry, Winona?"

"I'm only this way when I'm talking to you, so good-bye," I said and then slammed the phone down.

I should have been glad Derwin was spending his money for a change. I guess I should have been glad that he was fi-nally a part of Carlton's life. I wanted to be, but for some rea-son I just didn't trust him.

15 Porter

After five rings and fifteen minutes of waiting for someone to answer Reesey's door, I pulled my cell phone out and called Reesey on her home number. I hung up when the voice mail service came on and dialed her cell phone. The original agreement was for Friday, but the day before she called and changed it to Saturday.

"Hello," she said. I heard the song, "My Boo" playing in the background, which reminded me of Vanity. I guess she was on her cruise ship.

"Reesey, I'm at your house to pick up Portia. Where are you?"

"I'm at the hair salon, but Portia should be there with Dean unless he took her over his mother's."

My blood was boiling. I was ready to explode. My child

was with Dean? "Why is my baby with Dean or his mother and not you? I don't know that nigga or his family."

"I'm getting my hair done. Besides, he's my fiancé so he's he's going to be her stepfather. He's the man she'll be around the most so you might as well get used to it."

"We'll see."

"Ain't nothing to see, that's how it is," Reesey said, smacking her lips. I shook my head. As refined as she'd been trying to sound these last couple weeks, I knew it was all an act. You can take the hood rat out the ghetto, but you can never take the ghetto out the hood rat.

"If you needed someone to watch my baby, you could have called me. I would have picked her up earlier. You knew I was off. Look, just because our relationship didn't work doesn't give you the right to be ugly about the situation."

"You think this is ugly? You ain't seen ugly yet. I'm being extremely nice to you considering you abandoned us."

"No, I abandoned you and your son who was by Dean even though you lied and said it was mine," I said for the umpteenth time because to this day I thought about how she deceived me, named a child after me, and would have still had me walking around thinking he was my son if I hadn't been told otherwise.

"Whatever," she snapped. "Hold on, I'll get him on the line and find out where Portia is."

"Yeah, you do that." *What kind of mother doesn't know where her own child is? A mother like mine.* As I waited for Reesey to click back over to my line, I tried to think of a plan. How could I get full custody of Portia? The only way the courts take the child away from the mother is when you can prove that the mother is unfit, but I wasn't going to be able to do that. Reesey didn't use drugs. She was living in a nice condo in Birmingham, a ritzy Detroit suburb, and she was engaged to a Detroit Piston. I wondered if Reesey would just let me raise our daughter. That would be one less child for her to deal with. It's not like she was really the mother type. But I knew her too well. She wouldn't give up Portia to me because that would be too much like right.

Finally, after about five minutes, she clicked back over to my line. "She's at his sister's."

"His sister's? You joking, right? It done gone from his mother's to his damn sister's. Just give me the fucking address. Is your son over there too?"

"He sho is."

"Give me the damn address!" I said as I walked to my car and sped out of the driveway. The Hemi was finally about to get put to use. "What side of town does she live on?"

"On the east side on Troester near Hayes."

My eyes bulged. "Troester and Hayes. You got my daughter in the hood? I don't even go over there." I was so upset I started to smile and then laugh. "I don't even believe this shit."

"What's so funny?"

"Your ass. You better be glad you're not in front of me."

"And if I was, what would you do? You want the address? Find it yourself," she said and hung up.

I redialed but she'd turned her cell phone off and the call went directly to her voice mail. But that was fine because I knew where she went to get her hair done. It was on South-field Road in Beverly Hills not too far away. She wasn't going to want to see me burst through the door of the mostly white salon acting the way *she* usually did—ghetto. Not in front of her snobby girlfriends, the Piston wives, which Reesey tried so hard to front.

I made it to the salon in fifteen minutes and told the gay Asian guy standing behind the counter that I needed to see Reesey. He took me to the dryer she was under. A *Vogue* magazine shielded her face. Her eyes bugged out when I took the magazine away from her and knelt down.

"What are you doing here?" she asked in a whisper.

"Either you give me the address right now or I'm going to act so niggerish that once you leave you will be too embarrassed to come back." I handed her a pen and piece of paper. "Write the phone number down too just in case they play *you* and don't come to the door."

"His sister is home. She'll come to the door. Please don't go over there acting a fool."

"Depends on what I see."

When I turned right on Hayes toward Troester, I wondered why this woman was living in a run-down neighborhood if her brother was a professional basketball player. I wouldn't do my blood like that, especially not my sister. But I had to remind myself that it wasn't like Reesey's man was Ben Wallace. Dean was a benchwarmer who had a relatively good performance during the 2004 play-offs, which led to more playing time this year. But with a woman like Reesey, even if he was Ben Wallace, he wouldn't be able to do too much for his family because the more a man had, the more Reesey would want.

When I passed the used-car lot on Troester and Hayes, I remembered that the owner, a woman, was in the news last year for using her nine-millimeter to kill an ex-con armed with a semiautomatic weapon after he forced his way into her home on Troester. And this was the area Reesey had my daughter in. I couldn't help but shake my head because it was so obvious to me that Reesey cared more about herself— her hair—than her own children. I turned on Troester and rode down to the block where Dean's sister lived. I parked in front of the well-kept home. It was the nicest on the block. There were a few abandoned homes a couple houses down and two more across the street. Then there were three dudes congregating near the corner house who were probably hustling drugs. I just wanted to get Portia and go.

A woman who looked to be in her thirties answered. She looked white, but so did Dean. I had to remind myself that they were mixed. Two kids ran to the door hugging on the woman's waist and leg.

"You must be Porter," she said as she widened the door to allow me to enter. "Gary, this is Portia's father, Porter. Gary is my husband."

"Gary Samuels?" I asked as I stared down the man sitting in the living room. "From Murray Wright?"

He looked away from the television, and when his eyes focused on mine he smiled and rose to his feet. "Porter Washington. Man, how you been?"

I shook my head. I was so relieved to see Gary. He was a good guy and Reesey could have saved me a whole lot of grief if she simply would have told me that Dean's sister was married to him. He was my boy back in high school, but we lost contact shortly thereafter.

"I been good," I said. "How about you?"

"I been okay. Things are starting to look up," Gary said.

I saw the keyboard against the wall and remembered we also shared a love for music. His wife left the room and returned seconds later with Portia in her arms.

Portia smiled and waved at me. She still wasn't talking and that concerned me. I reached to take her from Gary's wife.

"That's okay," the woman said. "I'll hold her while you all finish talking. She's no trouble at all."

"Thank you. I don't even know your name, I'm sorry," I said.

"Catrina."

"Nice to meet you."

I looked over at Gary and he was smiling as he looked at his wife. He turned to me and said, "I asked Reesey about you because I knew the two of y'all had been together for a while. She told me she hadn't talked to you in a long time and didn't know where you were. She didn't even tell me Portia was yours. I said to myself, that name sure is close to his, but okay, maybe she misses him or something. But now that I see the two of y'all side by side, there's no denying that she's yours."

He had just added more fuel to my fire. Reesey talked to me nearly every day about our daughter yet she tells a man who she knew I'd been trying to locate for several years that she didn't know where I was. That was evil. I didn't want to air our dirty laundry so I changed the subject. "Man, you still playing the keyboards?"

He nodded. "Yep. What about you? You still playing drums, and what was the other instrument?"

"The sax. I'm still playing both. In fact, I'm always performing at Baker's."

"That's good, man. I'm doing some things too," he said as he sat back down on the sofa. "I'm producing a young lady.

Have a seat, man." I walked into the living room and sat in the chair beside him. "Her name is Vikki Aires. You have to hear her voice—it has so much range."

"Well, you should know because your voice was full of range. That I do remember."

He shook his head. "I can sing, but she can *sang*. We're working on her demo right now and we have somebody in A&R for Sony real interested. In fact, man, she's performing in about a week. You should come out. She'll be at Seldom Blues. I know you've heard of that place."

"The jazz supper club downtown in the Renaissance Center. Yeah, I've heard of it. I've been trying to get in there to play."

"Yeah, that's where she's going to be. You're welcome to come. Bring your woman or your wife. Are you married?"

"Engaged to be."

"Congratulations. Why don't you bring her? Y'all will be able to hear a star in the making."

I nodded. "We might do that." I stood. "I better start heading back. Two weeks from this Thursday at Seldom Blues. What time?" I walked over to his wife, who was sitting in the dining room with Portia in her lap. I picked Portia up.

"Seven and ten. Come on out and support."

I nodded. "I will."

16 Winona

I had moved ahead of myself in the book. It was hard to keep with a regular schedule while reading *The Purpose Driven Life*, especially since I expected Porter to stick with his promise and read it with me. So sometimes I'd read ahead, like today, which was technically still Day Thirteen, but I'd moved ahead to Day Fourteen, but for the most part I read a chapter a day.

I heard someone fiddling with the lock at the front door.

When the door opened, I heard baby talk and it made me smile, but inside I was nervous because I wanted Portia to like me. I'd prayed on it all night and this morning.

I started walking toward the foyer but froze when Porter turned the corner and nearly bumped into me with Portia in his arms.

"Here, can you take her real quick? I need to use the bathroom."

"But," I said as he handed Portia over to me.

"I got to use it. You'll be fine."

"Hi," I said to her. She looked at me suspiciously. I felt like I could read her young mind. She wanted to know who I was and why I was holding her. She inspected my face, focusing on my lips. Then she started looking around frantically for her daddy. She didn't know if she should smile or cry. *Please smile.* "Can you say hi?" She shook her head. "I bet you can." I walked her over to the pile of toys, bent down to pick up the stuffed Barney, and handed it to her.

"Barney," she said as she took him in her small hand. She held him up to her mouth and kissed him.

"Ooh, kids know Barney." I put her down and then sat on the floor. My black Lab, Samson, walked from the living room into the den and over to her.

"Doggy," Portia said as she put her hand on his back. Samson sniffed her and then lay on the floor. "He seeping?"

"You can talk." She frowned when she looked over at me like she didn't trust me, then she started looking around for Porter again.

"He's coming back. I have a daughter too. Her name is Sosha and I can remember when she was little just like you. I wished she still was, in fact. You are the perfect age. I don't have to worry about boys or talking back." I sat down on my leather sectional with her. "Do you know that you look just like your daddy?"

"Look," she pointed. "He seeping. See Mommy doggy seeping, look doggy seep."

"She can talk," I said as Porter walked back in.

"She called you mommy. Did you hear that?"

"I heard it, but I'm not your mommy," I said to Portia. She nodded.

"Who's Mommy? Point to Mommy?" Porter said.

Portia pointed at me. "Mommy."

"No, I'm not Mommy. Say Daddy, Portia."

"Da."

"Daddy," I repeated. She laughed. "You're not going to say it?"

"Mommy," she said.

"Who's Mommy?" Porter asked laughing.

"That," she said, pointing at me. "Mommy," she said looking over at me. "Ju."

"You want juice, baby?" I asked. I looked at Porter. "Don't teach her that." I shook my head. "That's not right. I wouldn't want anyone teaching my child to call another woman Mommy. Don't do that. Seriously."

"I'm not teaching her anything. She did that on her own."

"Well don't condone it. You have to correct her when she does it. I'm not your mommy, Portia."

She nodded. "Jui pea, Mommy."

"She's trying to say please," Porter said. "My child has manners."

"I'll get you some juice, baby, but I'm not your mommy." I handed Portia over to him.

As I walked into the kitchen I heard Porter say, "That's your mommy. Say Mommy Winona."

"Mommy Wowa."

"Close enough," Porter said.

I poured the juice, walked to the den's entrance, and stood watching the two of them playing with the Little Touch Leap Pad. I rested the back of my head against the door frame and closed my eyes. I almost felt like crying. What if what we had didn't last forever? And marriage was supposed to be forever, which was a real long time. It didn't end and I was of the belief that love did and my parents could prove my theory correct. Not to say they didn't love each other, but I wouldn't want a marriage like theirs. I wouldn't want to be with a man who didn't communicate well and who spent more time sitting in front of a television set than he did with me. When I opened my eyes, I caught Porter staring at me. He winked and mouthed, "Are you okay?" I nodded, straightened out my back, and walked over to join them on the floor.

"You sure you okay?" he asked again.

"I'm positive. I wouldn't lie to you." That statement I'd just made was a lie, but sometimes a lie is better than the truth because the truth can hurt.

"We got our date next week at The Roostertail, remember?" he asked and winked. "You didn't forget did you? You're not going to stand me up for the prom."

"I didn't forget, and no, I'm not going to stand you up for the prom the way Derwin did me." Porter was taking me to a formal dinner dance that was being held downtown at The Roostertail. He'd had tickets for the event for over a month now. The attire was formal, and knowing me, I'd go all out trying to find the very best outfit. I'd even contemplated flying to New York, but that thought didn't last long because I hate to fly.

Porter kissed me on my forehead. "I got to go."

"Go where?"

"To work."

"But I thought you told Reesey that you were off this weekend?"

He nodded. "Yeah, I told Reesey that because I wanted to see my baby this weekend. Besides, I just work tonight. I switched with someone for tomorrow night."

I dropped my head. I didn't know how to tell Porter that I was afraid to be alone with his child. What if she started crying when he walked out the door and I didn't know how to stop her? "You're going to be fine," he said as if he read my mind. "If you need anything, just call me."

Porter

17

"**C**ome here, man," Conrad said to me, "and check out the ass on this woman." He enlarged the picture file on his laptop screen. "Now that there, that's what you call an award-winning ass."

We were in the kitchen of the fire station. I was standing at the refrigerator deciding what to eat. I laughed. "She's church-going and loves the Lord?" I asked after reading a small part of her online profile. "So why did she take a picture in her bathing suit, bent over with her ass the only thing visible?"

"Maybe that's how she prays."

"She's praying?" I asked.

"Yes, praying to God to send her a man. And with an ass like that I'm sure God's going to send her plenty because I, for one, am about to bookmark this page and send her an instant flirt and an e-mail. I just want to rub on it and make a wish. I wish I could have some of this ass tonight. Maybe I need to pray. "

"Why not? That's what she does. But can I ask you something though, man? Why do you even go online trying to meet women? Can't you meet a woman some other way?"

"How many times do I have to tell you I'm not you? Can a day go by without you meeting a woman?"

I nodded. "Plenty days go by . . . in fact, most of my days, because I'm not looking to meet women anymore. I'm getting ready to get married. I've been with my fiancée for almost a year and I really love her."

"Love, huh?" Conrad said with a smirk. "I don't believe in all that. When Scott and Laci Peterson got married, I assume they loved each other and you see what happened there." He scrolled through his list of profiles sorted by name. "I guess going online is no better. I'm sure a lot of these women posting their profiles are married and just online looking for a good time. I want a wife, but I don't want to get hurt because there's nothing worse in the world than a broken-hearted man."

I was on the sofa watching the Pistons play Philadelphia in the first round of the NBA play-offs. Conrad was sitting across from me reading.

"Oh, this shit is funny. Things to ponder," Conrad said. "How important does a person have to be before they are considered assassinated instead of just murdered?" Conrad began laughing uncontrollably. "Get it?"

"I'm trying to watch the game," I said.

"Here's another one. If money doesn't grow on trees then why do banks have branches?" Conrad paused after each sentence he read, waiting for my reaction. But I had none because as I had told him once, I was trying to watch the game. "Since bread is square, then why is sandwich meat round? Why do you have to put your two cents in but it's only a penny for your thoughts? Where's that extra penny going to? Once you're in heaven, do you get stuck wearing the clothes you were buried in for eternity? What disease did cured ham actually have? How is it that we put man on the moon before we figured out it would be a good idea to put wheels on luggage? Why is it that people say they slept like a baby when babies wake up like every two hours?" Conrad looked at me. "Where's your sense of humor?"

"I'm waiting to hear something funny," I said. "No, actually, I'm waiting for you to shut up so I can watch the game."

"Okay, this one is funny, I guarantee you. If a deaf person has to go to court, is it still called a hearing? You know that one was funny, Porter."

The Pistons went to halftime and I had just stood to pour a glass of Coke when the alert sounded.

Within minutes we were all dressed in our full protective gear as we rushed out to the truck heading for the old abandoned warehouses that were on fire. Upon arrival, I noticed that to the west of the warehouse district and the Jeffries Freeway a tower ladder had been set up on the off ramp in front of the burning complex. Our engine company was one of four engines, two ladder companies, a squad, and a battalion chief to be dispatched to the first alarm assignment at

11:22 p.m. We noticed a substantial amount of light smoke coming from the southeast corner of the third-floor windows. Just last month, our station had conducted a familiarization tour of the abandoned warehouse because we were aware of the risk of something like this—a large, out-of-control fire. The property had been abandoned and under the state's control since 1995, nearly ten years, and the city had plans for demolition in a few days. Abandoned building in the city of Detroit could be magnets for vandalism and vagrants.

Zeander, Conrad, and I forced entry through the front doors and made our way through an interior stairway to the fourth floor.

We found several small fires in trash cans that we immediately began putting out.

"Why do people pay to go up tall buildings and then use binoculars to look at things on the ground?" Conrad asked me. "These are just things to ponder."

"I'm going to give you something to ponder if you don't shut up."

I walked over to a window and dropped a rope, preparing to pull up a nose line. Suddenly, a large front of smoke and flames rolled over me. I heard a loud crashing noise and a voice said, "Jump!" so I did, straight out the third-floor window without giving it a second thought.

When I opened my eyes and realized that I was in Receiving Hospital, I was hoping to see Winona and my baby Portia standing beside my bed. Instead there was an older white nurse with a tray of pills she wanted me to take.

"I need someone to call my fiancée to let her know where I am," I said to the nurse. "Three-six." I could remember the first two numbers but nothing else. "Shit, what's the number. Three-six. That's all I know."

"I'm sure the fire department will call those you listed under your emergency contact."

I hoped not. I hadn't updated my emergency contact since I was with my baby's mother, Reesey, which meant they'd either call her or my mom and I didn't want either to know or to come see me. Not that I had to worry about a visit from Reesey. I was the furthest thing from her mind. She had enough problems of her own trying to keep up with her other baby daddy.

"Close your eyes and rest," the nurse said. "I'm sure someone will contact your fiancée for you."

I closed my eyelids, but I couldn't sleep. There was too much on my mind. For one, I was trying to make sure that a phone number was the only thing I couldn't remember. I'd lost my memory once before, after being jumped, and that was scary. To go to the mall and forget why you were there or to drive and not remember your destination. Fortunately it returned.

Three-six was the most of Winona's number that I could remember. I also couldn't remember what she looked like because I was almost positive that the woman's image that kept flashing in my head when I thought of Winona was actually someone else. Who that someone was I didn't know. But I did know that it wasn't Reesey.

I yawned. After an hour of racking my brain for more clues, I finally drifted off to sleep. When I opened my eyes,

Winona was standing over me and my brother was standing beside her. I couldn't believe that I was looking at my dead brother. This was the second time he'd appeared and I now wondered if I was crazy.

"Portia is with my mother. I didn't want to bring her to the hospital."

"Do you see him?" I asked.

"See who, Porter?"

"My brother, Richard. He's standing right beside you." She looked to her right and then her left.

"She can't see me or hear me," Richard said.

Winona walked closer to the bed and took my hand. "God was really with you. Do you know what happened?"

"The only thing I remember is that I was trying to fight a fire."

"You dove out a third-story window, struck a telephone post, and then hit the ground. But you just have minor scrapes and bruises."

"What about the rest of the guys? Zeander and Ross . . . Conrad too. Are they okay?"

"I heard that some of the firefighters were seriously injured," said Winona.

"Were any killed?" I asked.

She shook her head and looked down. "I'm not sure."

"Are you not sure or are you just not telling me?"

"I'm not sure. I overheard that there may be a few who didn't make it, but I'm really not sure at all."

I sat up in the hospital bed while Winona adjusted the pillows to fit comfortably against my back. "I want you to go find out. I want you to do that for me. Find out if there were any firefighters who didn't make it, and if so, get their names. Will you do that for me?"

Winona shook her head. "No, I don't want to do that."

"You're not going to do that for me, Winona? It's important." When I realized that she wasn't going to move, I tried getting out of the bed. She blocked me, and I didn't have the strength to do anything. "Are you sure I didn't get hurt? I feel like shit," I said as I held my head. I looked around the room for my brother. "Where did Richard go?"

"You hit a light post and fell three stories so you're not one hundred percent, but you didn't break any bones," she said, ignoring my latter question. "Obviously, we won't be going to the dance."

"Obviously, why not? We're going. I'm fine. No broken bones, remember? When I tell you I'm taking you somewhere, that's what I mean. I just fell out a window," I said with a shrug. "I'm a firefighter. That's what I do. No big deal."

Keena.

That's whose face I saw instead of Winona's. That's because it was time to make a decision about California, and after what happened tonight, I think my decision was finally made up.

18 Winona

I was sitting in my car reading my book in front of my daughter's school ten minutes before it was time to let out. I finished Day Fifteen and glanced at Day Sixteen. Day Sixteen was all about love. "No matter what I say, what I believe and what I do, I'm bankrupt without love," from 1 Corinthians 13:3, was the quote at the start of the chapter.

I stared at my hand resting on the steering wheel and the small diamond on my engagement ring. "I'm not ready to love. Not yet." I turned the radio off. I had a vision of Porter making love to me. And I wasn't ready for that or for marriage. What I wanted was more time. More time to get my mind right, but if it wasn't right after almost a year, would it ever be? That's what Porter asked me the night at the hospital. He seemed real groggy but he knew enough to question

me about our impending marriage and why I was refusing
to set a firm wedding date. At first, I lied and said I didn't
want a big wedding, but the other day he brought a bro-
chure home from the Precious Memories Wedding Chapel on
Livernois. For ninety-five dollars we could have the Whisper
Ceremony One, which included a predecorated setting, a
thirty-minute ceremony, a minister, recorded music, private
bridal dressing room, and six guests. *So now what is my excuse?* I shrugged. Maybe I was just confused, because how
could I think that I didn't love Porter?

I stopped daydreaming to look out for Sosha. She was
standing in front of Gesu Middle School with her arms
crossed, turning her head from side to side. On her next turn,
her long ponytail slapped a student walking out. I squinted
to see if Sosha's lips moved to say that she was sorry or to excuse herself, but she just kept her arms folded and didn't say
one word. I sighed. That was just one more example of the
type of behavior I didn't want displayed.

I blew my horn so she would look toward my car, but my
horn wasn't the only one blowing. I stepped out of the car
and started waving my arms until she saw me. When she
did, she started speed-walking in my direction.

"Winona," a familiar woman's voice said. I turned and
saw Kelly Townsend, the woman who was also living with
HIV who Dr. Gant had me talk to about her experience
with HIV medication. Kelly was also the president of the
support group I'd recently joined, Sisters Living Positively.
"You have a child that goes here too?" She was standing beside a girl that looked to be around Sosha's age. I nodded and

looked at Sosha, whose walk had slowed down to baby steps before she finally stopped two car lengths away.

"That's my daughter right there," I said, pointing to Sosha. "Come on, why are you stopping way over there? You see where the car is."

"I know," she said as she gave Kelly a strange look.

"Do you know her daughter?" Kelly asked her daughter, who nodded and cut her eyes in Sosha's direction. "Well, aren't you going to speak?"

"Hello, Sosha," she mumbled.

"Come on, Mom. Let's go," Sosha said, pulling on my arm.

"Don't be rude. Say hello," I said to Sosha.

"Hello," Sosha said quickly and then she ran to the passenger side of my car, jumped inside, and slammed the door.

"See you at the meeting," Kelly said.

"Okay," I said as my heart began pounding through my chest. I felt like I was about to have a stroke. I could have sworn I told the group that my children didn't know about my diagnosis. I'd just have to remind her at the next meeting that was coming up.

I walked to the car focusing on Sosha, who was sitting in the front seat with a frown on her face.

"What's wrong with you?" I asked as I closed the car door.

"Did you touch that woman?"

"Why are you asking me that?" I asked.

"Because, Mom . . . that woman that you were talking to has AIDS."

"No," I said shaking my head.

"Yes," Sosha said, nodding. "And we think Valerie does

too because she's always staying home sick and she's missed a lot of days this year. That's why nobody ever goes around her." I was getting ready to put my key in the ignition when Sosha said, "Aren't you glad you're not her?"

The keys dropped out of my hand. "Stop acting like that!"

"Like what?" Sosha said. "Aren't you? I know I'm glad I'm not like Valerie. Am I supposed to want to be sick? Am I supposed to want to have a mother who has *AIDS*?"

"Sosha, shut up. How many times do I have to tell you about that attitude that you and Carlton have? I'm tired of it. Thinking you're so much better than other people. You don't know what's going to end up happening to you in your life so you better count your blessings."

"I know I'm never getting AIDS."

I felt like I was ready to explode. "Sometimes in life shit happens, so just never say never."

Sosha knew when she heard me curse she need not say another word, and she didn't. I wanted to tell Sosha the truth. Explain to her that Kelly didn't have AIDS. She was HIV positive and that she contracted the disease the same way I did—from a man who was with her and also with men. And that man was Sosha's father.

I dropped Sosha off over at my parents', waited long enough to see her make it inside the house safely before I sped off. I wasn't going to let that little girl's comments worry me today. I told Gina I was having dinner with her and that's exactly what I was going to do.

We were at my favorite restaurant, J. Alexander's in the Somerset mall. I was using my fork to fiddle in my Caesar salad while I stared across the booth at Gina, who was eating what I thought to be her fifth croissant. I'd lost count after she'd eaten hers, then mine, and then asked our waiter to bring out a few more. What a way to count points. She'd been on Weight Watchers diet plan for almost four months. Initially, she had dropped ten pounds within the first thirty days. Her goal weight was 130 and she weighed around 160 now. Since she was tall, she carried the excess well. But at her rate, she'd be back up to 180 before summer started. "I know what you're thinking," she said as she looked across the table at me. "And I'm going to start a new no-carbs plan on Monday, so I can cheat a little now. Besides, I'm an emotional eater and my emotions are very high right now."

"What's wrong?" I asked.

"I was in Loehmann's yesterday and the woman working the fitting room asked me if I was pregnant. Do I look pregnant?" Gina asked.

What was I supposed to tell her? The truth when I knew the truth would hurt? The only reason I hadn't asked her the same question was because I already knew better. She'd already told me that her pregnancy test came back negative. Over the past several months, she'd tried everything from the rhythm method to an ovulation predictor kit to the low-dosage fertility drug Clomid—nothing worked for her.

She popped another bite of the croissant into her mouth. "Do I, Winona? Be honest?"

"If I didn't already know that you weren't, I'd probably think that you were."

She grabbed her stomach and dropped her head. Then tears came streaming down her face.

"Stop it, Gina. Why are you crying?"

She fanned her face with her hand.

"For so many reasons," she said.

"Well, name one of them," I said sharply because I was angry. She was not going to make me feel guilty for truthfully answering her question. At least that's what I was telling myself, In truth, it was too late. She already had.

"Physically, I'm falling apart. Back in high school I had the perfect shape. My self-esteem couldn't have been any higher. Everything on me back then was put together well. Now look at me. My hair is falling out." She put her elbows on the table and buried her face in her hands. "How can my own hair be falling out when I'm a damn hairdresser who specializes in hair care? I look pregnant when I'm not. And I'm starting to look my age."

"What's wrong with looking your age, Gina? Thirty-eight isn't old." I tugged at one of her arms.

"I turned thirty-nine last month. One year away from forty."

"Thirty-nine isn't old either. Oprah said her forties were some of her best years."

Gina rose up and gave me an evil eye. "Well, everyone doesn't live by what Oprah says the way you do."

"If you're self-conscious about your stomach, start exercising and stick to your diet. Take an abs class."

"An abs class won't help this." She slid around the circular booth so she could be right beside me. "This isn't fat." She took my hand and placed it on her rock-solid stomach.

I pulled away. "What is it?"

"A tumor—a fibroid tumor that I've had ever since I was

nineteen. Eight of them, only back then they were the size of a pea. Now my doctor said that my uterus has expanded to the size it would be if I was four months' pregnant." She shook her head looking dazed. "I never wanted a baby as bad as I want one now—now that I probably can't have one."

"Rattlesnake pasta?" the waiter asked as he lifted the plate from the serving tray. I stuck up one finger and he set it in front of me. "So you must have the aged prime rib?"

Gina looked at the plate the waiter set in front of her and burst into tears.

The young black waiter looked at me. "Is something wrong with the meal? I can call over a manager."

"She's fine. Nothing's wrong with the meal," I said. He stood holding the empty tray for a second and then he left.

"Gina, snap out of it," I said to her as our waiter was walking away. "As bad as you may think you have it, your girlfriend right here has it ten times worse. Fibroid tumors aren't that big of a deal. My sister Colleen had hers removed surgically about five years ago."

"My doctor doesn't want to do it since she knows that I want to have children. The only procedure she does is called a myomectomy and she said that can sometimes turn into a hysterectomy. I don't want that."

"You don't have to have that if you don't want it. Go online and do your own research. Find a doctor who specializes in removal of fibroids."

"I have a sonogram scheduled for next week. Will you come with me? I'm scared. My doctor said once she can see the size and location she can tell me if I can get pregnant. I want a baby."

"And you're going to have one, but if you don't, I have two you can have. They're almost grown so the hardest part should be over."

"Stop playing, Winona. I want to have my husband's baby." She paused. "If I can't, I think he might leave me for someone who can."

"Don't have a child to keep the man. If a man's going to stay, he's going to stay regardless. There are some men who leave because their wives *had* children."

"Mark wants children and so do I."

"Go online and do your research. I'll do some too. You're going to have a child. Just don't make a hasty decision. Weigh all of your options and find the very best doctor."

I looked down at our plates, which were still untouched. "Let's wrap this stuff and take it to go."

"Good idea," Gina said. "My appetite is shot anyway."

19 Porter

The nightstand lamp was on. I was sitting on the edge of the bed staring at myself in the large mirror affixed to the burgundy walls. I was over Judge Dash's house for the second time, but the first time this year. We'd had sex before over a year ago, and for a woman in her fifties, she looked good and felt even better. She knew about my relationship with Winona because I told her, but she said she wasn't trying to interfere with that. She wanted what she wanted, which was to have sex with me from time to time. I turned and stared at her. Most of her makeup had rubbed off on the pillowcase. I had just finished taking a shower and I was sitting on the edge of the bed getting dressed. I felt bad, sick, like I'd slept with my mother. Not because of her age—fifty-five or -six, the exact number I can't remember especially since she could pass for a woman in her thirties—but because she knew my parents, probably slept with my dad, and my mom couldn't stand her.

"Why do you have to leave so soon?" Judge Dash asked as she touched the small of my back. She was still lying in bed on her side, in the fetal position, with her head resting in her hand.

I jerked away and shrugged. "It's just time for me to."

"That was the best two-hour sex I've had with a man in a long time. I'm ready for some more." She rubbed my back and it sent chills up my spine. "Hand me my cigarettes, baby." I shook my head. "What's wrong, baby doll?"

I shook my head. "I feel kinda bad. I shouldn't have done that. I have a woman that I love, waiting for me."

"So do I, but if you're going to cheat, please don't feel guilty. The only way your woman will find out is if you tell her because I damn sure won't. Don't worry. I'm not looking for a husband. Every now and then I get the urge to be with a man, but if you don't want to be that man, I can find someone who does." She looked at me for confirmation. "Porter, baby doll, there are things that the two of us can do together that won't leave this house. We can get as freaky as you want." She sat up and raked her fingers through her spiked hair. "Don't you want that?"

I shrugged. "I'm not sure what I want right now."

"Mmm. Please hand me my cigarettes."

I took the pack of cigarettes off the nightstand and tossed them over to her. "Wait until I leave to light up. I don't want to go home smelling like smoke." I stood up buckling my belt.

She snatched a cigarette from the pack and lit up anyway. "You sure are fine but you're not fun at all."

"Lord, please forgive me," I said as I looked up.

"Lord, please forgive me," she said as she belched out laughter. "I know you're not one of those. Sinning and always repenting. If you're going to be a dog, you can't worry about the consequences." I snatched my shaving bag off the counter. "No kiss good-bye?" she said as I was walking out the bedroom.

"I'll talk to you later."

"I know you will. And probably sooner than you think."

I couldn't compare cheating on Reesey, who didn't know how to be faithful, to cheating on Winona, a good woman who I trusted. I didn't feel guilty about what I did while I was with Reesey, but Winona didn't deserve this. Why couldn't I have been stronger? How was I going to be able to look into her big innocent eyes and lie about where I had been when she asked about my night? At least I wore a condom. And switched it three times to make sure it wouldn't dry out and break. When I got in the car, I turned on my cell phone and saw the red light blinking. Five new messages. I didn't want to listen but I had no choice. I needed to know what she said so I'd know how to respond.

"Porter, it's almost two in the morning and I haven't heard from you. I called the station and they said you were there but then I got disconnected. Three times that happened. I've felt like this before and I know what this means. And you wonder why I don't want to get married."

I skipped through three others, all from Winona, and listened to the last one.

"I'm not calling you anymore. This is my fifth message. Don't bother to come home."

Think . . . think . . . think . . . think. I hit the side of my head with my hand. "Okay," I said and nodded.

When I arrived home and entered the bedroom, Winona was sitting up in bed reading her book. "Are you ready?" she snapped.

I was prepared to explain my whereabouts, not listen to her read a chapter from *that* book, but I knew she was pissed and that I needed to appease her.

"I'm ready." I sat on the edge of the bed and bent over to untie my gym shoes.

"You're not going to take a shower like you usually do? Or have you already had one?" she asked.

"No, I was going to wait until after we completed the chapter since it's so late."

She shrugged. "That's your choice." She opened the book and began reading aloud. "Day Twenty-six—growing through temptation."

"Wait a minute. Is this Day Twenty-six already?"

"No, it's Day Seventeen."

"So why are you reading Day Twenty-six?"

"Because you need to hear this," she snapped. "Happy is the man who doesn't give in and do wrong when he is tempted, for afterward he will get his reward, the crown of life that God has promised those who love him."

I had to sit through the longest eight pages in history, feeling nothing but guilt as I tried hard to play it off. Now I believed in women's intuition because Winona's was working overtime. The worst part was the exercise at the end of the chapter. I had to name a Christlike quality that I could develop to defeat the most common temptation I face.

"Is that a hard question to answer?" Winona asked as she sat with her arms folded and the book resting in her lap. "What is the most common temptation you face?" She gave me a moment to respond and when I didn't she said, "Fornication?"

"Not really." Then I blurted out the first thing that came to mind. "The way I'd like to live my life is to do unto others the way I would like them to do unto me. If I can live that way, I'd be doing fine." I yawned. "I guess I better take my shower. Are you all done with that chapter?"

She nodded. "Porter, is there something that you want to tell me?"

"Just that I love you." I kissed her forehead, walked into the bathroom, and turned on the shower. I allowed the water to run for fifteen minutes while I sat on the toilet stool and reminisced about the time I'd spent with Judge Dash. It was going to be hard to stay away from the judge as long as Winona was denying me.

20 Winona

While Gina and I were sitting in the waiting room of the medical center, I was reading my book and periodically looking at the patients walking in and out. It was an OB/GYN office so it wasn't much surprise that there were several pregnant women coming in and out. At one point, while we sat waiting, I looked over at Gina and watched her eyeing the women with envy and it saddened me. But I understood it so well. It was the same look I gave her from time to time. Same look I gave Porter. How I would love not to be HIV positive.

After a relatively short wait, Gina's name was called. She stood and walked to the door. I stayed seated reading more of my chapter.

"Winona," she said softly. I looked up. "Come back with

me." I nodded and walked over to join her, with my head looking down at the book pages, reading as I walked. According to the book, God expects me to help those in the Body of Christ. And I needed to be sympathetic to what Gina was going through and let her know that I understood. "Can you put that book down for a minute and come on?"

I closed the book and focused all of my attention on my friend. I held her hand as I walked with her to the room with the big machine in the corner and a blond-haired white woman bent over milling through her briefcase.

"You can come in and get undressed from the waist down. Throw the sheet over you," the technician said as she picked up her briefcase and walked out of the room.

I closed the door.

"Are you nervous?" I asked Gina.

She nodded as she stepped out of her skirt. "Very."

Gina sat on the examining table after she wrapped the thin sheet around her waist.

"It's going to be okay. You're going to have a baby and you're going to name her after me." She smiled. I shook my head. "No, don't do that to the child. For the life of me I don't know what my mother was thinking when she named me after that small town in Texas."

There was a soft knock on the door and then the technician walked in.

"Ready?" the technician asked as she walked over to Gina and turned on the machine. "Lay back." She spread some gel over Gina's stomach and moved a wand over it. "I can't find your uterus."

I studied the monitor, squinting to bring the screen into focus.

"We're trying to have a baby," Gina told the technician.

"Mmm," she said as her eyebrow rose. "Let me see if I can even find your ovaries. How long has your stomach been like this?"

"Like what?" I asked with attitude.

"Put your feet in these stirrups. I need to give you a vaginal sonogram." She inserted what looked like a plastic penis inside of Gina's vagina and looked at the monitor, marking off one section. "Okay, here are your ovaries, up near your hip bone.

"We want to have a baby," Gina repeated.

"This is a very large fibroid. So large it's hiding your uterus. The doctor may want you to get an MRI so we can determine if this is just one large fibroid or a mass comprised of several." She shut off the machine.

"Will I be able to get pregnant?"

"Oh, I don't know, honey. You'll have to ask the doctor that question."

Gina's head dropped hopelessly and her eyes started to water.

"Yes, Gina, you're going to get pregnant," I said as I eyed the technician.

"Let's see what the doctor says," the technician said as she walked out the door, closing it behind her.

"I don't care what the doctor says," I said to the closed door.

The technician returned a few minutes later, apologizing for the doctor because she was seeing other patients and wouldn't have time to talk to Gina.

"She'll call you," she said. "As soon as she looks over the sonogram results. What number should she use?"

"Can she just talk to me for a few minutes? I want to know if I'll be able to have a baby."

"She can't talk to you now, but she'll call you as soon as she finishes up. I promise. I'll make sure of that."

Gina's head collapsed in my chest and she started crying uncontrollably. "She'll be staying with me tonight," I said. Mark was out of town on business, and in her present condition I didn't want her to be alone. I gave the technician our numbers and walked Gina out of the examining room. "It's going to be okay," I told her. "When we get back to my house, we'll go online and figure this whole thing out. You're going to be fine."

I stayed up late at my computer. Ten open windows cascaded my large monitor. I was determined to find help for Gina. Just because I couldn't be cured didn't mean she wouldn't. The problem I was running into with fibroid research was that all the Web sites looked good and sounded even better. There were too many choices. After spending several hours searching and reading various sites, I decided that the procedure Gina needed to strongly consider was uterine fibroid embolization. There were risks with this procedure as well as most of the others I read up on, the biggest one being that it could interfere with pregnancy.

I walked into my bedroom with several sheets of paper that I'd printed out on fibroid surgery.

"I hope I'm not running Porter off tonight," said Gina.

"No, he'll be at the station all night." I sat on the edge of the bed with the papers in hand. "You know, if you get the fibroid removed you're risking a lot. I think what you should do—and this is just my opinion obviously—but I think you should try real hard to get pregnant, and if after about six months you don't, then go to a fertility specialist and see what they say."

Gina closed her eyes and sunk down in the pillow. "I'm so tired, Winona. I just need to hand it over to God because I'm so tired."

I put the comforter over her shoulder, kissed her on the cheek, and turned off the light. I waited until I heard her snoring and then I returned to the basement to do some more online research.

21 Porter

I drove by the Soul Station again, but this time I got out of the car to go inside. When Mom saw me, she'd probably shit herself. Her stubborn son finally breaking down. There was a note affixed to the door.

TEMPORARILY CLOSED. WILL REOPEN SOON.

That was strange. Will reopen soon with no date? Sometimes my parents really knew how to ghetto things up. How did they expect to maintain their clientele doing some unprofessional mess like that? I shrugged it off and walked back to my car.

I rode down East Jefferson, listening to my demo while I tweaked it in my mind. An incoming call came from Danzo Barron, Keena's manager, and I almost had an accident reaching for my cell phone. I had to quickly swerve into the right lane to avoid rear-ending a vehicle that had stopped suddenly. I pulled into Kentucky Fried Chicken's lot to park and talk business.

"Danzo, brother, what's going on?"

"That's what we want to know. Have you heard the new single 'Messin' Me Over'?"

"The only way I couldn't is if I didn't listen to the radio."

"It's number one, man. We're getting ready for this three-month West Coast tour. We need you, man. I know Keena has already mentioned flying you down here to talk business and give you a chance to look around. When do you think you can come down?"

"Why me, man? I'm just a drummer."

"I don't know. Keena is insistent upon having you as her drummer," Danzo said with his British accent. "Perhaps she thinks you're her baby daddy." I laughed at the way he said baby daddy. "All I know is she told me to make this happen. So when can you come out and meet us all in person?"

"Let me check my schedule and get back to you."

"The tour starts in September, Porter. This is a comeback. We need you here by June at the latest. She has a few summer festivals she's co-headlining. One is at the Essence Fest in New Orleans. The other is in Florida. All I'm saying is, get back to us ASAP. We're offering you a chance to do what you do best, Mr. Firefighter. Now, if you'd rather stay on a truck, by all means—"

"If you can get me two tickets, I can probably come next weekend. Can you check on that for me?"

"I can get you two tickets. I don't need to do any checking for that."

After I hung up from Danzo, Winona called me from work in a panic. She'd forgotten that today was her mother's Red Hat society meeting and therefore she wouldn't be able to pick up Sosha from school, and of course neither would Winona because she'd be working too late. Which left me, but I was way on the other side of town.

"Maybe I should call the office to let them know to have her wait for you there?" Winona said.

"That might be a good idea."

"How long is it going to take you, Porter?"

"I'm all the way on the east side, so it's going to take a minute."

"She gets out in twenty minutes."

"Why did you wait so late before you called me?"

"Porter, I took a late lunch and when I came back my mother had left the message on my voice mail. I don't know why she didn't just call my cell phone. Can you hurry up and get there?"

"Winona, the fastest I can get there is thirty minutes. I'm on East Jefferson, almost to Grosse Pointe."

"What are you doing all the way down there?"

"I went to visit my mother, and then I went riding."

"Riding?" she said suspiciously.

"Don't start acting like that. Yes, riding. Are you going to start putting a tracking device on me?"

"Do I need to?"

I didn't bother responding, and I guess she got the

message because she changed the subject back to Sosha, and I assured her that I'd get there as quickly as I could, which ended up being thirty minutes later. The school was practically empty with the exception of a few cars and a handful of children scattered throughout. I saw one of Sosha's little friends. I couldn't remember her name, but I did remember she was fast because she was only thirteen and already having discussions about liking older men because there wasn't anything a young one could do for her. She even told Sosha she was going to take me away from Winona. When Sosha first told me that, I laughed, but whenever the little girl came over, I noticed the flirtatious way she'd look at me.

"Are you looking for Sosha?" the little girl asked as I approached her.

"Yeah, I am. Is she in the principal's office?"

She shook her head. "She walked home with Baxter."

"Walked home with Baxter? Which way did they go?" I asked, concerned.

"It'll be easier if I showed you," she said, taking my hand. "And you can take me home on the way. I just live on Fairfield. That's not far."

I removed her hand from mine. "Why didn't you walk home with them then?"

"They wanted to be alone and my dad is supposed to be picking me up."

"Alone, did they? Well, I'm sure your father will be here any minute. Which way did they go?" She shrugged. "I'm sure you have some idea. Just point in that direction."

"I can't remember. But maybe if I'm riding with you that will help me recall some things."

"Don't worry about it. I'll do what I can to find them. Would you like me to call your father for you to make sure he hasn't forgotten to pick you up?"

She shook her head. "He's right there," she said pointing.

Now how would it have looked, I wondered, *if he pulled up and saw his little girl getting into my car? Not good, I'm sure.*

I rode around the area, up and down several streets, and didn't see them. I expected to find Sosha at home when I got there, but she wasn't, which made me worry, so I called Winona at work and told her, and she left work two hours before she'd planned. When she arrived, she walked in the house with Sosha, who was in tears.

"Where were you?" I asked Sosha, who ran to her room.

"She was over that boy's house. I called his mother and she said that Sosha was over there and had been there when she came home from work at five thirty. Do you know how much they could have done in two hours? I should take her to the doctor to get checked."

"Don't do that," I said, shaking my head.

"Why not? That's what my mother did to my sister Val."

"Okay, but you told me that your sister Val was very wild. Sosha's not. She just has a crush on a boy. At that age, it's all innocent," I said, not even believing all of my own speech. In my heart, I didn't think that Sosha had done anything. Maybe kiss, but that's about it.

"It's my fault," Winona said. "I need to keep a tighter rein on her. Moving to Detroit didn't mean taking a break from raising my children. When I was living in Texas, I didn't have the luxury of having them at my parents' every weekend and nearly every day after school."

"They're just making up for lost time with their grand-parents. Nothing's wrong with that." She sat at the kitchen table, kicked off her pumps, and looked off into space as if deep in thought. "Are you okay?"

She shrugged. "I guess." She looked over at me. I gave her a look to let her know I didn't believe her. "It's Day Nineteen and I've been reading that book. I expected to feel a little better but I don't, and I'm almost halfway through."

"If you can't read the Bible and feel any better, what makes you think you can read that book and feel better?"

"The Bible is too hard for me to understand."

"We can read the Bible together and study it." She stood, picked up her shoes, and walked toward the stairs. "Where are you going?" I asked as I lightly grabbed her arm.

"To bed. I have that meeting tomorrow and it always drains me."

"What meeting?"

"*That* meeting," she said and kissed me on the cheek. "Good night."

22 Winona

The Sisters Living Positively meeting didn't start until seven p.m. but I left work at five thirty and arrived at Deborah Hudson's house thirty minutes early. I rode around the North Rosedale Park neighborhood and listened to my Lyfe Jennings CD. I'd replayed track three, "Must Be Nice," four times. I'd much rather sit here listening to music and thinking my own thoughts than try to think up small talk with Deborah while I watched the minutes pass by slowly.

Today's meeting was slated an emergency. We had an honored guest, a doctor. Someone Kelly said she'd been trying to get for months but due to scheduling conflicts was unable to. I didn't know much about him other than he was a HIV/AIDS specialist out of southern California.

I pulled up to Deborah's house on Westmoreland at ten

minutes before the hour and was surprised that mine was the only car in the driveway. I noticed a piece of paper affixed to the door, flapping in the wind, which I assumed was a note. Hopefully, it was canceled, because even though I was off the next day, I was tired now. Not so much my body, but my eyes. Those long hours at work designing on a computer screen were catching up with me.

I got out of my car and walked on Deborah's porch to read the note on the front door.

MEETING TONIGHT AT THE COMMUNITY HOUSE 18445 SCARSDALE. TAKE THE SOUTHFIELD FREEWAY TO EXIT #13 TOWARD MCNICHOLS ROAD. TURN RIGHT ON PURI-TAN STREET. LEFT ON GLASTONBURY AVENUE. TURN RIGHT ON SCARSDALE. LIMITED SEATING. PLEASE ARRIVE PROMPTLY AT 7:00 P.M.

My heart started drumming in my chest. I was nervous. First, I was going to be late and I hated being late—even a minute. I hated to adhere to the stereotypical CP time and so I always made it a point to arrive early for everything I at-tended, but the time wasn't as big a deal to me as the fact that the meeting was going to be in an open forum. There were only eight members in our support group, so why would the seats be limited unless others were invited? What if someone was there that I knew? I sat in my car for a few minutes. Not even Lyfe's music could relax me. I wanted to hear what the doctor would say because I remembered Kelly saying he knew of a cure. I guess the other seven ladies didn't mind that we'd be exposed to the public. Kelly, Deborah, and Monica were HIV activists and the other four ladies came twice a month to complain about how doomed their lives were.

There was a park surrounding the Community House, and unfortunately for me, it was an unseasonably warm April day and families were out in full force.

"How do you like that Hemi?" a man with long dreads and chiseled features said as I got out of my car and fumbled with my purse and keys.

"I like it most days, except when I have to fill up."

"I can definitely understand that," he said. "Would you like some help?"

"No, I can manage. Thank you." He stood beside me and smiled. "I'm okay. I've got it."

"Are you going into the community center for the support-group meeting?"

I hesitated. It felt like a trick question. "Are you?"

"I'm Dr. Bryce Johnson, but you can just call me Dr. Bryce. I would say you could just call me Bryce, but after all those loans that I just paid off, I earned the right to be called doctor."

"Oh, you're the guest speaker," I said as I extended my hand to shake his. My purse and half of the contents fell on the ground.

"Now you definitely need some help," he said.

"We're running late," I said as I looked at my watch.

"I'm the guest speaker. The meeting doesn't start until I

arrive." He smiled, revealing his perfectly straight white teeth. He picked up a bottle of my meds. "Do you like taking these?"

I shrugged. "I like the fact that I only have to take one of them a day."

"What if you didn't have to take any? That's what I'm going to be talking about. Man, you're pretty," he said. I snickered. "What's so funny?"

"Man, you're pretty. It sounded white."

"Sounded white? I never could get with the idea of sounding like a certain race. Maybe because I'm a mixture of both, but don't hold that against me. My dad couldn't help that he was a white man."

I smiled. "So are your dreads to further accentuate your ethnicity?"

"No, I wear them because I look sexy with them," he said and then winked.

I shoved the contents back into my purse. Dr. Bryce and I started briskly walking toward the Community House across the park. When we approached it, Kelly and Deborah were waiting outside.

"We have a full house," Deborah said to Dr. Bryce. "Seventy-five people are waiting to hear your speech."

"Hear it they will," he said arrogantly. "Let's hope they receive it."

He handed us each a purple flower out of his large bushel. "Hold on to these, ladies. You'll find out why real soon."

I sniffed the flower and watched Dr. Bryce stride confidently through the front door as we followed behind him.

"The room is at the end of the hall, doctor," Deborah said.

"I assumed it would be where the open doors were with all the people entering," he said as he kept marching. "Looks like I'm just in time," he said as he walked through the door. I looked at my watch. It was a quarter after seven. He waited for the three of us to enter before he shut the door. "We have a full house, but not as full as we should considering the message I'm delivering today." He walked down the aisle passing out flowers. He left a stack at the front. "If I missed anyone, please come to the front before I begin and take a flower."

He waited several minutes as over a dozen people came up to take a flower and went back to their seats.

"I'm here not to encourage you to keep living with HIV and AIDS. I'm here to fire you up about not only stopping the spread of the virus but curing those who already have it. The flower you are holding is a Prunella vulgaris. The extract from that plant is said to inhibit the HIV virus. And that's not the only herb being studied for the cure and prevention of HIV/AIDS. Now that I still don't have your attention. Now that I still have most of you giving me that crazy look like I'm your preacher asking for another love offering—" I laughed, and when I realized that I was the only one, I covered my mouth, but oh, how I could relate to that statement. "What if I told you I'm not just an HIV/AIDS specialist? In fact, what if I told you I have just as much at stake for a cure as you do because I'm also HIV positive. Then would I have your attention?" He looked directly at me and nodded because he had mine. "I'm HIV positive and I've been so for three years. Imagine going from treating HIV and AIDS patients to becoming one.

Overnight my life changed and it will never go back to the life I had. I was married with three kids and was working as an HIV/AIDS specialist with Kaiser Permanente of southern California, where I was involved with education, research, and policy issues. I was also on faculty in the department of medicine at UCLA. That was my life after I graduated from Cass Technical High School in 1980 and left Michigan to attend Stanford University. That was my life before the dreads, when I had a big bush of sandy brown curls. I was a nerd, and maybe I'm still a nerd just dressed up to fit in, but this nerd is about to do something that's going to change all of our lives. All I'm asking each one of you to do is simply believe."

He spoke for another hour and told us of some of the drugs currently being tested. He talked about the pharmaceutical market and how it's a multi-billion-dollar industry that benefits from those who are sick and dying. "So why should they find a cure?" he asked. "If someone tells you that no one profits from sick people, call them a liar because that's a bald-faced lie. You can put a price on life, which is why preventive medicine is so expensive. But people, believe me when I say that HIV is a manmade disease and if a man can make it, surely another man can find a cure for it."

After his speech, he had a long line of people waiting to talk to him and ask him questions. I stood to the side, contemplating if I should wait my turn to step forward and talk to him. I just wanted to tell him how much I enjoyed listening to him. He had passion behind his words, but the line was just too long.

As I was turning to walk away, Dr. Bryce raised his hand

and said, "Young lady, can you wait just one minute." I stood near the door as he excused himself from the crowd and walked up to me. "Can I walk you to your car?"

"But what about all of them?"

"They can wait, but I can't," he said with a smile. "What's your name?"

"Winona."

"Winona? What kind of name is that for a black woman?"

"My mother named me after a small city in Texas that she rode through on her way to Shreveport when she was pregnant with me."

"Is your mom from Shreveport?"

"No, she's from Lake Charles, Louisiana."

"That explains your beauty because there are some very pretty people in Louisiana."

"I don't look like my mother though. I look like my father and he's from here."

"Do you think we could talk?" he asked.

"Talk?"

"On the phone. In person. I'm hitting on you. I don't go to these events trying to meet women. I haven't dated since my divorce two years ago, but when I saw you, I thought, *That's a beautiful woman. I sure hope she's going where I'm going, because if not, meeting me would just complicate her life. But if she is, meeting me will be the best thing for it.*"

I smiled the biggest one ever. I liked him, but "I'm engaged," I said.

"I really don't care as long as you're not married." I couldn't believe how blunt he was being and I told him so. "I'm a very direct person. I don't have time to waste. No one really does."

"Do you have something to write with?"

"I have my Treo 650. Best thing on the market. I don't need a pen with this." I smiled again. "You like me, don't you."

"I think you're neat," I said as I took one of my business cards from the holder and handed it to him.

"Neat? That sounds like something a white person would say." He looked down at my card. "You design cars. I've never met an auto designer. That's neat. Do you mind?"

"Mind what?" I asked as his face approached mine. I drew back.

"If I kiss you on your cheek."

"Yes, I do."

He held his hand out to shake mine and held on to my hand a minute too long.

"Dr. Bryce, it was very nice meeting you," I said as I jerked my hand away from his. "But I have to go now."

"I'm going to call you. Real soon."

I nodded, unlocked my car, and stepped inside.

I was sitting on the bed, flipping through TV channels and thinking about Dr. Bryce when the phone rang.

"Is your name Winona?" the woman asked loudly.

I looked down at my caller ID but the number was unknown. I felt like this was someone's wife calling and I was the other woman, even though I knew that wasn't possible, but it was too late at night for some woman to call my house with that tone of voice.

"Who's calling?"

"Is this Winona? Just answer my damn question."

"Not before you tell me who you are."

"Reesey, Winona."

I started to hang up or lie. I didn't want to deal with her, and since Porter was taking a shower, I couldn't hand the phone to him.

"Yes, this is Winona."

"Bitch, did you teach my child to say your name and tell her that you're her mama?"

Bitch? "Excuse me, but did you just call me out my name?"

"No, and since you like teaching *my* baby to say your name, next time teach her to say bitch since that's what you are."

"First of all, you don't know me like that. I've never even met you for you to come on me like this."

"Did you or did you not tell my daughter to call you mama? Just answer my damn question."

"I taught Portia to say my name, but no, I never told her that I was her mother. I wouldn't do that. I have children of my own and I'm not like that."

"*Mmm hmm.* Well, I hope you really do know you're not her damn momma because I know how some of you psycho women like to get when you start dating a man with children. She don't need a substitute. She already got a mama."

The mere fact that Porter was with that type of woman for so long was turning me off. That he could be such a bad judge of character made me wonder.

I laughed and that really set her off.

"What you laughing at? You think something funny? I bet Porter ain't gonna think it's funny when he don't see his child no more. And let me tell you something, bitch. Just because you're temporarily with *my* baby's daddy don't mean you're *my* baby's mama. Believe me, there's gonna come a time when Porter's gonna leave your ass and that time will probably be sooner than you think, because Porter can't commit to shit. Not even his damn music. And besides, the only woman he's ever loved is Pamela Dunlap. And you're far from Pam."

I hung up the phone.

"Who the hell is Pamela Dunlap, Porter?" I shouted as I hung up the phone. "And you better tell me the truth since she's the only woman you've ever loved according to Reesey, and by the way I don't appreciate being called a bitch over and over again by your baby mama. I don't need this shit in my life with all the other shit I'm dealing with so if you want to get with Pamela Dunlap go right ahead because I'm sick of this shit . . . the baby mama drama and all the other bullshit. I don't need it!"

The shower water stopped running. "Did you say something, baby?" he asked as he walked out of the bathroom with a white towel covering his lower half.

I took a deep breath and let out a long sigh. The way he said baby always made me weak. "No, that was the TV."

He kissed me on the lips. "I love you."

"I love you too, but you have got to talk to Reesey. She called here acting a fool and calling me a bitch."

"Calling you a bitch?" he said angrily. "For what?"

"Evidently, Portia's saying I'm her mama."

Porter smiled. "Good." He laughed. "I'm loving that."

"Who is Pamela Dunlap?"

"What?"

"Who is Pamela Dunlap?"

He looked around the room nervously. "Someone I dated in high school."

"So why did Reesey say that Pamela Dunlap was the only woman you ever loved?"

"Why do you think? To get at you."

"Me? I did nothing to that woman. But I guess just being with you is enough." He climbed in bed and turned his back toward me. "You take showers every morning so why do you have to also take them at night?" I asked.

"I like to be clean."

"But you don't need to take a shower twice a day to be clean. I find it strange since you just recently started doing this."

"Why do you think I do it, Winona?"

"I don't know. I'm not sure."

"Good night. I'll deal with Reesey in the morning."

"We're moving your stuff out of the apartment in the morning."

"I can still deal with her too."

I sat on the edge of Porter's bed folding his underwear when I heard a loud knock at his apartment door. I stared straight ahead wondering who it was and praying it wasn't Reesey. I'd never been in a fistfight before and I certainly wasn't going to start now.

I marched to the front door, looked through the peephole, and sighed after seeing the FedEx man. I opened the door and signed for the package. Going back inside the tiny studio, I sat on the edge of the bed and stared at the Airbill affixed to the envelope. PLATINUM ONE ENTERTAINMENT, BEVERLY HILLS, CALIFORNIA. *What could this be all about?*

The door opened and Porter walked in. He was coming back from giving his thirty-day notice to Mr. Fortier.

"This came while you were out." I held the envelope out to him before he had a chance to close the door. "What is Platinum Entertainment?"

He took the envelope from my hand, tossed it on the kitchenette counter, took a suitcase from the closet, and set it on the bed.

"Mr. Fortier said I don't have to pay for this month, so everything worked out. He said he figured I had moved any-way when he hadn't seen me for the last couple of weeks." Porter unzipped his suitcase and started packing his clothes.

"Porter, answer my question."

"What question?"

I narrowed my eyes in disgust. "What is Platinum Enter-tainment? Why are they sending you an overnight package like it's important?"

"I was going to tell you."

"Tell me what?"

"I'm thinking about quitting the fire department and do-ing my music full-time," he said matter-of-factly.

I sat in silence. I needed a few minutes to take in all that he had just said. "And when were you going to tell me this?"

"I tried to the other day, but I know you and I know you wouldn't take it right."

"Why wouldn't I take it right?"

"I might not even do it. And I'm only going to go if you and Sosha can go to California too."

"You're moving to California? Is that what I'm hearing?" I asked as I slipped off my engagement ring and handed it back to him.

"Put it back on. I'm not going anywhere. I was going to ask you what you thought about it. You, me, and Sosha would be going together. And hopefully Portia too. Carlton will be in college."

Me and Sosha? Like I was going to up and move my child to California. Did Porter really think I was going to leave my secure job as a designer with DaimlerChrysler Corporation to go to LaLa Land with a bunch of wannabe stars? Not even on my worst viral-load and CD4-count day would I consider that.

"I can't do that," I said.

"So you're telling me you can move to Texas from Detroit with a man you barely knew but you can't move to California with your fiancé?" He continued removing clothes from his dresser drawer and throwing them into the suitcase. "I don't understand that."

"Well, understand that that was twenty years ago and there's a big difference between the mind of a twenty-year-old and the mind of a woman close to forty. But since you're still in your twenties maybe you can't understand that. I refuse to go backward."

"There you go. Why is it backward? I'm your man. Don't you want to be with me?"

He threw a pair of balled-up underwear on the ground.

"I'm too old for you. We just don't see eye to eye."

"I'm tired of hearing that so don't bring it up again," he demanded.

"And if I do, what you gonna do?"

"Do it and see," he said as he gave me a stern look.

"Do what, talk about how you're a little baby?" I said in a soft, playful voice.

"Yeah, that, keep it up," he said, calming down.

"Talk about when I was walking across the stage getting my high school diploma you were just learning your times tables. Is that what you want me to keep up? And when I had my first child, you weren't even in middle school." I stroked the back of his ear. "You're still wet behind the ears."

He picked me up. "I'm wet behind my ears? Well, let's see where you're wet."

"Stop, Porter. Put me down. I'm sorry. I was playing."

"Oh, no. I told you to keep it up. Keep on talking shit."

"No, I'm through talking shit, I promise."

"No, keep it up. How old was I when you had your second child?"

I thought for a second. "Sixteen—just getting your driver's license."

"Oh, I was a little older then, almost out of high school . . . almost legal."

"Put me down, baby."

"Don't be trying to sound sweet," he said as he placed me back on the floor.

"All I'm saying, Porter, is that I can't go with you to California. I have my doctor here, my job, my kids. I can't just up and move for a man again. My past experience proves that doesn't work out."

"Skip your past experiences. I'm not just a man. I'm going to be your husband, baby."

"Porter," I said, extending my hand toward him as if I was a crossing guard. "Stop and listen to me. I will never stand in the way of a person's dream. Regardless of my insecurities, if that's what you decide to do, I think you should do it. By all means, do it. I just can't go with you because I have my own dreams."

"What kind of dreams do you have?" he asked as if insulted by the very notion. "You're an auto designer. You just got a damn promotion and now you're making six figures. What more do you want?"

"More than what I have. I want all there is to get and there's plenty out there to get. I want to travel and be free. I want my dream job. I just haven't figured out what it is yet."

"Maybe a change of atmosphere will help you figure it out. We're moving to California. I'm signing the contract, taking the bonus, and moving us to California, so you might as well put your house up for sale now."

"Who is Platinum Entertainment? Are they a record label? Are you going to be in a band? What? Tell me more about it."

"Do you remember the singer Keena . . . Keena Jackson?"

" 'Do Me' Keena Jackson? 'If Love Ain't All There Is' Keena Jackson?

"She dropped Jackson and she's just Keena now. She wants me for her band."

"How does she know about you?"

"She's from Detroit. She had her people get in contact with me. When I did that benefit concert and opened for Al Jarreau she was there."

I laughed. "Hmm."

"What?"

"She wants you for more than her band, I'm sure."

"Winona, why do you think *every* woman wants me? I mean is it really like that?"

"Yes, it's like that," I said with attitude. "And that's the way it is."

"Do you want me to stay in Detroit and keep working for the fire department? I'll do whatever you want me to do. I'm serious. Whatever you want me to do." He sat beside me on the bed. "I'll stay miserable and risk my life for twenty-seven thousand dollars a year."

I felt bad for being so self-centered but I wanted what I wanted, which was Porter to stay with me in Detroit and not go to LA to play drums for some pretty singer who was a few years younger than him instead of ten years older like me. I didn't want to stand in the way of an opportunity for him, but I had a strange feeling at the pit of my stomach that if Porter left for LA he wasn't coming back to Detroit unless it was a stop on Keena's tour.

"I'm not sure what I want. Besides, it really is your decision," I said.

"I could try to stay here and get my career going. In fact, there's something going on at Seldom Blues tomorrow night. Do you want to go?"

I sighed. "No. I don't feel like going out again this week."

23 Porter

"**B**ring your woman with you," Gary said when I called him for directions to Seldom Blues. "You don't need no temptation and believe me when I say that Vikki can be one." He laughed. "Wait until you see her. And she's a little on the free side with her sexuality."

"You've been with her."

"Man, I'm married. I don't get down like that."

"Well, I feel like I'm married and neither do I," I said.

"I hear you, man. Well, at least bring your drumsticks so you can show us why they call you Drummer Man. Besides, the drummer we have right now we're not really happy with. He ain't shit."

"I'll bring 'em but I don't know how another drummer

would feel about me beating on his drums. That wouldn't be cool with me."

"I bought those drums, so the hell with what he might think. I know you know how to get to the Ren Cen. Just go to Tower 400 and it's on level one. There's valet parking if you need it. The shows are at seven and ten. And I'll have a table up front reserved for you."

"I'll see you at seven but I can only stay for one set."

I walked into the main area of the restaurant and noticed the tall cinnamon brown–skinned woman standing onstage introducing her next song. I assumed she was Vikki because she was indeed very attractive and she knew how to dress to show off her best assets—her long, slender legs, toned arms, and sexy shoulders.

She used her hand to play with her short, curly Afro.

"I'm influenced by a lot of artists, but one of my favorites is Chaka Khan. If I'm ever blessed to meet her one day, I want to tell her how much her music inspired me, so in tribute to her, I'd like to sing a few of her songs. Any requests?" She looked around at the silent crowd. "Somebody must want to hear something."

" 'Ain't Nobody,' " I said.

She smiled and nodded. "That's one of my favorites too. And your name, sir?"

"Porter Washington."

"Welcome, Drummer Man." A few people in the audience clapped. "You have some fans, I see." I shrugged. "Okay, well, 'Ain't Nobody' at your request." She closed her eyes for a few moments when the music first started and opened them right after she belted out her first note.

Vikki focused most of her attention in my direction as she sang and danced. I felt like she was singing the song only to me and that we were connected to each other through the music. When she belted out one of the highest notes I'd ever heard, I knew I wanted to be her drummer. It became Keena who? And when she finished the song I stood and clapped. Something I'd never done for any singer known or unknown.

"Thank you," Vikki said. "Is everyone ready for the next Chaka classic? I don't need a request . . . just a guess of what it may be." She looked at me.

" 'I'm Every Woman.' "

"Mmm, you are really good. Let's say we invite Drummer Man onstage for this one. Is that okay with everybody?"

The audience started applauding.

Vikki put the microphone in the stand, walked over to the drummer, and whispered in his ear. He threw his hands up in her face, said a few words, and walked off the stage.

"Drummer Man, are you going to join us? You have to join us now because I don't have a drummer at the moment."

I stood, grabbed my case off the table, and walked onstage.

"Oh, my God, he is so fine," a woman yelled out from the crowd.

"Ditto," Vikki said and winked at me as I walked past her. "Drummer Man, just let us know when *you're* ready. We'll wait. Won't we, ladies?"

"Yes, Lord," the same lady yelled out.

I hit a cymbal with one of my drumsticks to let them know I was ready.

"Here we go. I'm every woman and if you feel like you're every woman . . . *and* every man, stand up and dance to this," Vikki said. She danced over toward me and started singing. When she really started feeling the music, she also started really feeling me by rubbing on my face. "I can cast a spell / With secrets you can't tell."

Afterward, she mellowed out the crowd with one of my favorite Chaka Khan songs, "Every Little Thing." My original plan to stay for just one set turned into staying for both shows and an hour after to talk to Vikki and Gary about joining the band.

"I'm excited because you have a lot of talent," I said. "I'm surprised that I've never heard you perform before. You are hands down better than any singer out right now and possibly out ever. Your voice is incredible."

She smiled. It was interesting to see her personality change when she got off stage. She became a lot more reserved when the spotlight was removed and the microphone was out of her hand.

"Thank you," she said in a soft tone as she sat across from me at the table for two.

"So are you going to join us?" she asked.

"Hell, yeah, I'm going to join you. . . . Well, I don't want to speak too soon. I do have something in the works but it's been going on for a while and I'm not sure what's going to become of it. So what I can do is perform with you and if the other project doesn't come through then we can start talking some real business. Mainly how to get you out there so you can be discovered."

"Thank you," she said. Her eyes looked into mine again before dropping to the floor.

"Are you shy?"

"A little bit."

"Well, you sure aren't onstage."

"Porter," Gary interrupted. "Can you take Vikki home?"

"Home?"

"If you don't mind," Gary said. "I would but I have to stay to talk to the manager and she's tired."

She yawned. "I am. I'd really appreciate it if you took me home. I live right at the River Place."

"Oh, that's right down the street. That's no problem. No problem at all."

It was so quiet in the car that I almost forgot I was driving. I didn't hear the engine, the tires on the road, or anything. My Magnum seemed to float down Jefferson like it was a boat cruising the Detroit River.

"Did you want me to turn on the radio or put in a CD?" I asked her.

"No, I'll be out of your car before I can get into the music."

I stopped at a red light and opened my center console, pretending to look for a CD when I was really checking out her shapely legs. They were almost as nice as Tina Turner's and I couldn't take my eyes off of them. She may have caught on because she crossed them right as I sneaked my first peak.

"The light's green," she said. I could tell that she knew she looked good. She'd probably been told plenty of times just how good. Her face wasn't all that beautiful, but she had one hell of a body. And even though Reesey always accused me of being a breast man, I was a leg man for sure.

"Don't take this the wrong way," I said as I stared at her legs unapologetically. "But you have some beautiful legs. I'm sure you know that, don't you?"

"I think they're pretty nice," she said with a smile. "You can make a right at this light coming up. I live in one of the brownstones at the end of the street."

I drove down Jos. Campau until she told me to stop. "I'm right here." I stopped in the middle of the street. "Would you like to come in?"

"No, I better get home."

"Are you sure?" She turned to look out her window. "There's a parking space right across the street." She placed her finger on the glass to point toward it. I shook my head. "Well," she pulled her keys from her purse. "If you change your mind you can ring my bell." She sang, "You can ring my bell, ring my bell." She smiled. "I'll let you in." She leaned over and kissed me on the check and then she turned my face toward hers and kissed me on the lips. "Thank you again for taking me home."

I watched her legs step out of the car and then back in.

"Can I ask you a question?" Vikki said. "I'm a fairly direct person."

"Sure you can. What's on your mind?"

"What's on my mind is making love to you. How do you feel about that?"

What happened to being so tired? I wondered. "Why is that on my mind? I mean your mind," I said.

She smiled. "It's on yours too." And it was, but I didn't want to admit it.

"I'm involved with someone."

"I'm just talking about some fun. Not a commitment."

"I thought you were so tired."

"I am tired . . . of seeing something I want and spending too much time trying to negotiate to get it. Yes or no."

"No. It really wouldn't be right and I'm trying my best to live better and to make the best choices."

"I understand." She pulled her keys from her small hand-bag that was resting on the floor of the car. I watched her legs step out, walk to her front door, and then disappear inside.

I hadn't made it to the corner when my cell phone started ringing. I thought for sure it was Winona trying to figure out where I was, but it was Vikki telling me she'd left her purse in my car.

"Are you sure?" I asked, after stopping at the red light on the corner of Jos. Campau and Jefferson. I stretched my arm across the passenger seat and felt around for her purse. "I've got it." I picked it up and placed it on the passenger seat.

"Do you mind bringing it to me? I would come out and get it but I'm already dressed for bed."

"No problem." I made a right on East Jefferson and pulled into the Harbortown strip mall. I needed to go to Rite Aid to buy some condoms. A man can only take so much tempta-tion. Now I felt like I needed a release.

I sighed. "Are you sure about this?" I asked myself. "Yes," I answered, after seeing a flash of those legs. I was in and out of the store and back in front of her place in less than ten minutes. I thought about calling Winona first but that's what guilty men do. She had an opportunity to come and she turned it down. She told me to enjoy myself when I left and now that's what I was about to do.

I rang the doorbell once and Vikki answered. She was standing behind the door, and when I entered she closed the door and revealed her nude body.

"You're dressed for bed?" I asked.

She nodded. "I sleep in the nude." I got an erection as soon as she said that. She must have known because she started rubbing it. "Is that all for me?"

"Yes, but listen—"

"You have a woman. I already know. Don't spoil my mood." She placed her hands on my chest and gently pushed me out of her foyer and into her dining room.

"Have a seat."

"Do you have a man?"

She shook her head. "No, my lifestyle is way too busy for that. As long as I can get serviced from time to time, I'm fine."

"Serviced," I said, smirking. "That's what this is?"

"That's all it is." She unbuckled my belt, unzipped my pants, and slid them down to my ankles. Then she turned her back to me and sat down on my erection. I hadn't entered her yet. She bounced her ass on me a good three times, and on the fourth time I felt a warm sensation that sent my mind in orbit. She was bouncing up and down on my dick like she was working out. In the excitement, I'd forgotten to put on a rubber. I'd pulled two out of the package before I left the car, but both were still in my pants pocket.

"Put your hands around my neck," she said. I looked at both of my hands and slowly moved them up toward her neck. "Strangle me."

"Do what to you?" I asked as I took my hands from her neck.

"Do you want to know what I really want you to do to me?" she said as she bounced off of me.

"What's that?" I asked as I watched her walk up the stairs. "Come up here and I'll tell you."

"I followed her up the stairs of her brownstown and into her master bedroom. She walked over to her bed and positioned herself so that her butt was hiked up and in full view. She spread her cheeks and said, "Take my ass. Put it right there in the middle. Do it!" she shouted.

"Nah, I don't know you like that."

"Okay, then grab that empty Coke bottle off the dresser and stick it in me."

"In you where?"

"In my ass." I wasn't sure I'd heard what she said. I'd never had a woman ask me to do that. I once had a woman ask me to strangle her while we made love until she passed out, but I never did because I always imagined it going too far and her ending up dead. But no woman had ever asked me to stick a plastic bottle in her. "Do it," she said as she looked back at me with her butt cheeks spread wide apart.

"I got to go."

"Go where?" she asked as she stepped off the bed

and walked toward me. "Most men like a freak and that's what I am."

"Well, I'm not most men."

I fucked up. She had a great voice and wonderful legs, but all that stuff she added on—strangulation and bottles up the ass—all that wasn't something I was trying to get myself into. I cursed myself on the ride home, and then realized that I couldn't go home, not smelling like sex. I'd have to get a hotel room, call Winona, and tell her I'd been drinking and didn't want to drive. I took my HIV test, finally got up the nerve last week. The results came back negative, and I was so relieved to know that all the sex I'd had didn't count against me. But now it was like I'd thrown my gear in reverse. My condoms were right in my pants pocket and I hadn't even taken them out. She didn't even ask me to use one. She gets serviced, she said, and I could only imagine how often. *Damn, I fucked up.*

24 Winona

It was pitch-black inside the two-story loft, except for a tiny red power light coming from the stereo system and the streetlights from Woodward Avenue shining through the open blinds. I could see a partial view of downtown Detroit from the wall of large floor-to-ceiling windows I was facing and for the first time in almost twenty years, I realized that Detroit had a halfway decent skyline. It wasn't a bad place to live, despite the fact that *Time* magazine had recently named Kwame Kilpatrick, known across the country as the "hip-hop mayor," as one of the three worst mayors in the nation, criticizing Kilpatrick for using the city's money to lease a cherry red Lincoln Navigator for his wife while the city suffered from a $230 million budget deficit.

Dr. Bryce and I listened to Kem's "This Place" and briefly talked about how inspirational the singer's story was, how he'd overcome drug and alcohol addiction as well as homelessness to sign a five-disc deal with Motown.

I'd been at Dr. Bryce's place for several hours and I knew that it was time to leave, but I didn't want to. Porter was obviously cheating on me. His behavior was strange lately. The showers twice a day. The call I received from him late last night saying he had to sleep at a hotel. That was the last straw. When Dr. Bryce called and asked me to dinner I not only accepted, but asked if he could be lunch. I had a day off that I was supposed to use for a doctor's appointment, which I canceled. Dr. Bryce said I could pick the place so I chose La Cuisine in Windsor, Ontario, just across the bridge. My cell phone was turned off, and for once Porter could wonder where the hell I was. Yes, I was getting even, but I wasn't taking it as far as I was sure Porter had. I wasn't going to have sex, but I did want Dr. Bryce to touch me even in a nonsexual way. Tap me on the shoulder with his finger. Even nudge me. I needed something. Anything. So I could feel his skin against mine.

The room darkened naturally as the hours passed. He was sitting across from me in an art deco black leather chair with his feet resting on an ottoman. He stared at me in silence. I was stretched out on the chaise portion of his black leather sectional, so into the music that I didn't realize he'd moved until I felt his hand wrap around the back of my neck. The crinkling sound of leather let me know that he was moving closer. I felt his lips against my cheek as they made their way down to my lips. I didn't resist.

It's sad to love someone in your soul while still knowing in your heart that the two of you will never work, that the pain each one of you feels is too unrelated for you to come together. Porter and I would never mesh because neither of us could fix the other.

"I'm trying to respect the fact that you're in a relationship and that you're engaged. But it's hard, baby. It's so hard." I sat in silence with my mind running rampant. "Since I can't see you, can you please say something to let me know you heard me?" I stood and he took my hand, pulling me back down beside him. "Don't go yet," he said.

"I have to. This isn't right."

"So much in life isn't," Dr. Bryce said. "We both know that."

I stood again, leaned down, and kissed him on the forehead. "Talk to you soon."

"Why are you leaving, Winona?"

"I'm dealing with too much right now."

"You're dealing with the same thing I'm dealing with—HIV."

"We barely know each other," I said to Dr. Bryce.

"I know people who've been together for ten years who barely know each other. I knew you from the first time I laid eyes on you."

I smiled. "I really have to go."

"No, you don't really have to go. You really could stay. If you wanted to."

"Dr. Bryce. Let me explain something to you. I am in a relationship with a man who loves me very much. I shouldn't be here."

"You know why you are? Because he loves you very much, but do you love him at all?"

"Like I said, I really have to go." He turned on a lamp so I could see my way out. I took my leather jacket from the closet and stood by the door. "Is that how you're going to act toward me? You're not even going to walk me to my car?"

"Look how you're acting toward me," he said as he stood and walked over to me. He put his hands on my hips and pulled me toward him.

I wiggled away from him. "I'll be fine going to my car alone." I held the door open by the handle.

"Don't go, Winona. Stay just a little while longer." I felt something with him that I didn't with Porter—that perhaps I couldn't with Porter—a sense of freedom with who I was and what I had. "Kiss me some more," he pleaded. He placed the palm of his hand flat against the door and closed it shut. His lips touched mine and I didn't want to let go.

25 Porter

Winona held up the *Detroit News* Metro Section with a smile. "The Soul Station is in the paper." She started reading the article but stopped a second later, her smile disappearing. "Oh, no," she said, looking up from the paper and staring at me in silence.

"Oh, no, what? I saw the headline: POPULAR SOUL-FOOD RESTAURANT CLOSES DOORS. I've been telling my parents forever that they needed to change with the times. You can't keep the same hours and the same menu for fifteen years. They had a nice run at it. Now my mom can go and do something else. I don't even know what else my mom wants to do."

Winona's eyes locked with mine. "You need to call your mother, Porter."

"And say what? Mom, sorry to hear that you failed?" A single tear dropped from Winona's eye. "What's wrong with you? It really isn't that serious. Mom was tired of the restaurant business anyway. It consumed too much of her time. This is the best thing for her."

"Read the article," Winona said as she slid the paper in front of me.

"Yada ... yada ... yada. Nothing I don't already know." I read halfway down the article and stopped as I came across a paragraph that disturbed me. I read aloud, "Several reasons were cited as to the owners' decision to close the doors of the well-known and highly trafficked restaurant, the main one being the failing health of co-owner Jolene Washington, who was recently diagnosed with stage IV breast cancer and is recovering from surgery." My body sank down in my chair. I was in total disbelief. The last time I saw my mother I told both her and my father that it would be the last time they either saw or spoke to me again. Now I was praying that I could take back those words.

Winona stood and walked to the cordless phone hanging on the kitchen wall, removing it from the base. "Call her, Porter." She handed the phone to me.

I looked at the numbers on the keypad, trying to remember my mother's number, which hadn't changed in nearly fifteen years. After dialing the seven digits, I expected to hear her voice on the other line but instead I received a prerecorded message stating the number had been disconnected.

"Nobody bothered to call me?" I asked as I stood, snatched my keys and wallet from the kitchen table. "Let's go."

Winona drove because I was too upset. My mother's house

looked abandoned. There were no window treatments. No lights on inside the house. And when we walked to the porch and peaked through the windows, we saw the house was completely bare.

"I don't understand what's going on," I said as I snatched my cell phone from the holder that was attached to my belt and called my father. The phone rang five times before it switched to voice mail. "This is my fault." I felt the energy slipping from my body. I sat down on the porch step. The only person that I wanted to see at that moment was my mother. The only person who mattered to me right then was her.

26 Winona

It was going to be a long day. I could tell by how much time I took getting ready this morning. I was dragging because I was so worried about Porter's mother, mostly. He still hadn't made contact with his father and I'd asked him to start checking with the main hospitals in the area. I called the Detroit Medical Center but she wasn't a patient there. *Were long days even worth it?* I wondered. *Why? So one day I could become a top executive and have a reserved parking spot, if I even live that long.*

I drove my car into the structure, rode past the executive section, and pulled into the first available space on the main level. I read a little of my book, but opted to listen to the radio. I turned on 105.9 to listen to The Scoop, a prerecorded gossip show.

"You didn't hear it from me," Porch Lady said, "but a certain young R&B singer whose album stayed at number one for over fifteen weeks on the *Billboard* charts is trying to make a comeback. Maybe if she could keep the powder away from her nose long enough to lay down some tracks in the studio, she'd be able to prove that she's more than capable of repeating her success. And I did my research after seeing her live interview. The musician she's involved with is no other than our local favorite Porter Washington, also known as Drummer Man from the band Time Out. Can anyone guess who this is? Her initials are KJ and she's dropped her last name for the comeback along with forty-five pounds, but I'm sure her habit had more to do with the weight loss than anything. Oh, but remember. You didn't hear this from me. Ah, did you say Keena? You might be right."

My cell phone started ringing. After I saw Porter's name on the display, I turned the volume to the radio down and answered.

"Hello, honey," he said as I stuck the headset in my earlobe.

"What are you doing up so early? You must have heard what they said on the radio."

"What who said?"

"Porch Lady."

"I don't listen to that mess."

"Well, I'm glad that I do because otherwise I never would have known that you and Keena are having a fling. You're her man, Porter?"

"Her man? What are you talking about?"

"I'm telling you what I just heard on the radio. You're Porter Washington, aren't you? Also known as Drummer

Man, right? In the band Time Out? I hate you," I shouted
and hung up. I was too tired to even call back. I took a deep
breath and grabbed the door handle. My problem was life
and trying to deal with it when each day seemed tougher
than the one before. It's like I've always heard people say.
Without your health you don't have anything. I don't care
how good I looked on the outside. I knew exactly how bad I
felt in the inside.

I pushed open the car door, dropped my pumps on the
concrete floor, slid off my riding shoes and into my three-
inch black heels. I grabbed my briefcase from the passenger
seat and got to stepping. I was on my way to the design center that was located on the third floor of the DaimlerChrysler
Tech Center. Before I heard that mess on the radio I was excited about today because the product executive committee
had approved the last quality gate several months ago, which
meant the project was in line and within the budget for production of my concept car. The next step would be manufac-
turing a test model. When I was leaving the building the
week before, I saw one of our cars out on the test track
camouflaged with a black tarp stuffed with Styrofoam to distort the actual shape. It was the NG model T, a spin off of the
GXT concept car I'd designed that was displayed at Detroit's
International Auto Show. Even though I'd just been designing for a few years, all I needed was one hit like the Magnum
or the 300 to skyrocket my career, even if I was still trying to
figure out if it was a career that I wanted.

Porter called me back on my cell phone but I decided not
to answer. I had someone to think about now, just like he
did, so the hell with him.

* * *

I yawned.

My head was resting in the palm of my hand and I rubbed my stinging eyes and yawned again. The only light on in the design center was the one from the overhead in my cubicle. I had been fiddling around on the computer with one of my virtual models working on our next exciting Hemi-powered vehicle. I could barely keep my eyes open as I stared at the twenty-seven-inch flat-screen computer monitor. I was tired. It had been a long day and it was already past ten p.m. I slid my engagement ring off, placed it on my desk, and started twirling it. It was time for me to leave the office and go home, but I really had an urge to see Dr. Bryce.

The phone rang and I answered hoping it was Dr. Bryce, but it wasn't. It was Porter. I talked to him because he was talking about his mother and how bad he felt, which made me feel bad because I'd been selfish that morning when he had a lot on his mind, but still, I couldn't believe Porch Lady had said my man was Keena's man. As we talked on the phone, he assured me that it was just gossip, like all the lies they'd told on Oprah in the past. He had to use someone I could relate to. I knew firsthand the rumor mill had missed the mark on her.

"Well, I guess that means you're becoming big-time," I said. "Now that you're name is associated with rumors."

"That's one way to look at it."

"Porter, we don't have to go to that dance. I'm sure you don't feel like it. I know you're worried about your mother."

"We're going. I promised and I don't break promises. Mom's going to be fine. I just have to get my dad on the

phone and find out more about her condition. I've been trying every hour."

I ended the call with Porter, turned off my overhead light,
and shut down my computer. I realized I needed to make it
to Somerset Collections before it closed. I was looking for a
pair of black evening shoes to match my dress. Porter and I
had big plans. He was taking me to a formal dinner and
dance at The Roostertail, which was on the banks of the Detroit River and featured live entertainment by Norma Jean
Bell. Porter had searched for months for someplace nice to
take me after I admitted that I was stood up for my high
school prom. I described for him how I waited for hours in
the living room in my peach dress that my mother had made
me before it finally clicked that he wasn't coming. Derwin
had stood me up, the same man who would also leave me
standing at the altar on our wedding day two years later.
Once shame on you, twice shame on me.

The phone rang and I let it transfer to voice mail. A few
seconds later, it started to ring again.

"Hello," I said, sounding slightly rushed but mostly irritated. I didn't even bother to answer with my normal
Winona Fairchild, design team, greeting.

"Is this Winona?" the woman asked softly. "Winona
Fairchild?"

"Yes, it is. How may I help you?" She took a deep breath
and sighed. "Hello," I said, when the woman remained silent.
"This is Winona. And you are?"

"Lorna," she said softly. "Just give me a minute. I'm trying
to find a way to say this. I called to introduce myself," she

said, pausing again. I impatiently looked at my desk clock. Time was ticking away. The malls would be closing soon.

"Is this a sales call? Because if it is I'm not interested," I asked. I should have listened to Porter when he told me not to fill out any of those drawing forms at the home and garden show we'd attended last month. Even though I don't gamble, I'm a sucker for a free chance to win anything, especially twelve mortgage payments and a brand-new Hummer. But now I see Porter was right—they just take that information and sell it.

"No, this isn't a sales call. Let me just come out and say what I need to—I'm your sister."

"Val?" I asked, even though it didn't sound like her. But that was probably because she was down at the MGM Grand drunk out of her mind and heavily in debt from blackjack. "I don't have any money, Val. It's Friday so call your husband. He got a paycheck or have you already spent that?"

"I'm not Val. I'm Lorna."

"Who? Lorna? I'm sorry but you obviously have the wrong number," I said as I rolled my eyes. I didn't have time for this nonsense. Those black Manolo Blahnik satin shoes at Neiman Marcus were calling my name and I needed to leave the office in less than five minutes so that I'd have enough shopping time.

"No, I don't have the wrong number. But I probably never would have used it if today hadn't been such a fucked-up day, excuse my language. I made up my mind that I was going to make some changes and that included contacting my family. Winona, I *am* your sister."

"My mother didn't have a daughter named Lorna."

"No, your mother didn't. But *my* mother and *your* father did."

I repeated in my mind what she'd said. Her mother and my father. "Who do you think my father is?"

"Our father is Donald Fairchild. I know that you don't know about me."

"Wait, before you say another word, I just heard you say your mother and my father. You're telling me my father had an illegitimate child."

"He had three by my mother. I have a twin sister and a brother. And I'm assuming outside of you and your siblings, those are all the children he has, but I don't know, just like you didn't know about us."

I shook my head. This couldn't be right. "How old are you and your brothers?" I asked. The question was important because maybe he had these children before he married my mother. Even though I really didn't think that was possible because they married so young, but I wanted anything to be true other than him cheating on my mother. A revelation like that would shock the hell out of me. It would distort my view not only of him, but of men and my own life.

"I'm thirty, my sister is thirty-eight and my brother is thirty-five." I gasped and grabbed my chest hoping it would calm my heart, but I still had to sit down in my office chair just to gather my thoughts. "Are you there?"

"I'm the same age as your sister, which means our mothers were pregnant at the same time." I shook my head.

"I know that it's not really fair for you to find out this way. Especially since the only reason I called you is because my life is turning upside down. But for years I wanted to know you . . . wanted to get to know you, but my mother always told me no."

"Please explain to me how you are my sister."

"I already told you that we have the same father."

"I don't believe any of this. It's not possible. You expect me to believe that my father had three illegitimate kids while he was married to my mother when he was always home?"

"Well, obviously he wasn't home all the time—"

"He was my father so I should know. He was home all the time, except when he went to work."

"Well, then I guess he wasn't always working."

"Excuse me?" I said with a serious attitude.

"Look, he's my father too."

"I don't know if I believe any of this. I don't know who you really are—"

"Who I really am?" she said, raising her voice. "I am who I say I am. How else would I know your name, and that you have two sisters, Val and Colleen, and a brother, Trent. My father lives in Palmer Woods on Burlington. He just bought a Pacifica."

"That's my mother's car."

"If you want, I can send you my picture. I'll e-mail it to you right now. You and I favor."

"I'm not interested in seeing your picture. I'm not interested in getting to know you or your brother and sister. With all that I'm dealing with right now, this is one added piece to my life puzzle that I wish would have been left out." I looked at my desk clock. "The mall is getting ready to close and I have to go."

I slammed the receiver down, signed off my phone, and sat still for a moment. Dad always faulted me for any little thing I did wrong, and look how much he had done. I had to tell my sister Val. I logged back on my phone and pressed the first outside line. While I was dialing my sister's number, the second outside line started to ring. Surely that woman wasn't calling back. "Hello."

"Winona, just hear me out for one second. For years, I wondered when I was going to meet the rest of my family. I didn't even find out that Dad had other kids until I was thirteen and my mother got mad at him on Christmas and called him a liar and a cheater after he told her that he wouldn't be able to come over. What my mother and your father did was wrong and I'm not trying to justify it, but I didn't have anything to do with that. I've always wanted another sister, because my sister thinks her shit doesn't stink and her life is pretty good so maybe it doesn't. I called you after I realized that my so-called girlfriends aren't shit. My man ain't shit. My job ain't shit. My life ain't shit. And the way our father talks about you, I've always had the impression that you had your life together. I figure you're where I'm trying to go."

I took a moment to digest all that she'd said. I might as well forget about going to the mall and picking up my shoes tonight. If I still felt like going to the dance tomorrow, I could go to the mall in the morning.

"Well, I don't. I don't have my life together. I'm not mad at you for calling because you're right, what your mother and my father did was on them and I'm going to try my best not to do him the way he's always done me by casting judgment. I'll leave that up to God, but right now, Lisa—"

"Lorna. My name is Lorna."

"Right now, Lorna, I'm not interested in having a relationship with you. It's hard enough for me to maintain a relationship with my two kids and my fiancé. Having one with you would probably be impossible."

"I understand, and I'm sorry that I bothered you."

The next sound I heard was a dial tone.

"Let's try this a different way," I said to myself as I logged off the office phone and stuck my hand inside my purse, searching for my cell phone to call Val. As much as I didn't like dealing with her, for something like this she was the first one I wanted to call, because she and I were so different. Knowing her, she wouldn't be as surprised as me about it.

"Bo, you got a day off from work? I don't believe it," I said to Val's husband as I walked out of the Tech Center. "Put Val on the phone."

"Call her on her cell. She's at Dollar Tree and she's supposed to be right back."

"I'll try to catch her on her cell, but if not, let her know that I'm on my way over."

My fingers couldn't press the buttons on my cell fast enough.

"Hello," Val shouted, nearly bursting my eardrums. "Who is this?"

"Winona."

"Hello. Talk louder, I can barely hear you."

There was loud noise in the background and lots of talking. "Are you at the casino?" I shouted as I walked through the parking structure toward my car.

"No, I'm at the store."

"Save that lie for your husband. What time will you be home?" I asked.

"I'm on my way back now."

"What do you consider now, Val? An hour or two?"

"I should be leaving in the next thirty minutes so I probably won't be back for an hour."

"Oh, Val, hurry up. I have to tell you something that is going to blow your mind. It's about Dad."

"Tell me now. I'm listening. I got a few seconds before I play the next hand."

"Trust me, I can't shout this over the phone. Just hurry home."

"What is it?" Val shouted.

"Dad has other kids." I said, just as my signal faded.

When I arrived at Val's house, I didn't see her car in the driveway, but I did see Bo's, so I thought maybe Val's was in the garage. I'd given her enough time to get home. I stopped by the mall and parked in front of Neiman's, dashed inside to the shoe department, and bought the shoes ten minutes before closing. By the time I made it to Val's, an hour and a half had passed, but who was I kidding? She'd be at the casino until it closed—and casinos didn't close.

Bo answered the door with the vacuum cleaner handle in one hand and a look of disgust on his face. Their daughter, Raven, was walking down the stairs as I walked through the door. It was obvious from her high heels and short black dress that she was going to a club. This from a young lady with a set of one-year-old twins she was raising without the father because she'd decided during childbirth that she wasn't into the family thing. They assumed it was the pain of childbirth that made her tell her babies' daddy that she was tired of him and she wanted him to leave for good, but she meant it. Now, from what I could gather from Mom, Raven wasn't working and hung out at some club called Tonic in Pontiac and at St. Andrews Hall in downtown Detroit. She was into white boys now, because she thought black men had too many hang-ups and very little power. And as angry as I was at one black man in particular—well, two—I would never say something like that about all black men. She was the female version of my brother, Trent, who married a white woman and had never been attracted to black women.

"Why can't your sister do right?" Bo asked me.

I shrugged in response to Bo's question. "Raven, when do I get to see those babies again? They should be walking soon, shouldn't they?"

She laughed but didn't say two words. She was always quiet around me, probably because she felt like she didn't really know me since I'd been away from Detroit most of her life.

"I'm serious," Bo said. "Why can't that woman do what she's supposed to do? Is it fair that on my off day, I have to work while I'm home? That I have to clean behind her junky ass." He picked a blanket off the sofa and started folding it. "Have a seat."

"No, Bo, it's not fair. So have your daughter do it, since she's not working." Raven looked at me and rolled her eyes. "You're too pretty to look so mean." And she was too pretty—the spitting image of her father. She was slim but still curvy. Tall compared to other women, but not too tall for the average man. Her jet-black hair was long and straight. Most women assumed it was a weave. She had big eyes and deep dimples, a pleasant face that made you smile at first sight, until you realized she was angry at the world or maybe just black men.

Raven took her father's wallet from the coffee table and took a couple hundred dollars. Then she stuck her hand out for the keys to his SUV. He didn't even question her. She was twenty years old with a set of twins. She needed to keep her butt at home, and if she was my child, I sure wouldn't be watching her kids while she went out to party. I knew how I was at twenty when I had my first. I sure wasn't clubbing.

"I married the wrong Fairchild," Bo said. "You're never out running the street, gambling. You work every day. Your man is lucky to have such a good woman, but your sister. She's trifling and you know it."

Yes, I knew it. She was pretty trifling, which is why the two of us would never be close. We were too different—like night and day.

"I think she may be cheating, but she ain't gonna cheat no-body but herself when I leave her ass, because she won't find another fool like me. You want a drink?" I shook my head. "You don't even drink. A good, wholesome woman. It's bad when you've been married for over twenty-two years and you have to fantasize about what it would be like with some-body else." I wasn't sure if that somebody else was me, but I sure hoped not. I didn't want to think that my brother-in-law, who I'd known since I was fourteen years old, had thoughts like that—even though I did have the biggest crush on him back in the day, but what younger sister didn't have a crush on her older sister's boyfriend?

"That's what I do nowadays." He walked over to the wet bar that was built into the living room wall and took a bottle of Crown from underneath, a glass from overhead, a few ice cubes from the minifridge, and drank it straight. "I'm fed the fuck up."

I didn't know what to say, other than good-bye, because after looking at my clock and realizing how late it was getting, I was ready to leave. Porter was at the fire station and was expecting a call from me by midnight. And I was expecting a call from Dr. Bryce in the next fifteen mintues.

"Well, Bo," I said, looking down at my watch again. "Doesn't look like she's going to show." I stood. "I guess I'll talk to her tomorrow."

"You just got here. You might as well wait a little while longer. I'm about to go in the basement to throw clothes in the wash and then I'll be out your way. But do you see my point though?" He finished his first glass and another.

"You know that I see your point," I said.

"If I'm going to have a wife who lies to me, spends all my money, and holds back on the sex, I might as well not have a wife, don't you think?"

"Bo, that's something you need to talk out with your wife." Even though I agreed wholeheartedly with what he said, one thing that I didn't and wouldn't ever do is comment negatively about someone's marriage. Let them work it out. "I really do have to be getting home."

"I know you do. All right then, I'll tell your sister to call you tomorrow. If I see her tonight or tomorrow. Who knows, she may try to pull something like she did last week and stay out all night."

He escorted me to the door and opened it.

"Tell Val that it's an urgent matter."

He nodded and said, "I sure will."

I felt my phone dancing in my purse as I walked to my car. As I dug, I wondered who it might be, hoping it was Dr. Bryce. Whenever it was him and I could talk, I felt like I won a prize. It would be so much easier if I put him on a special ring tone, but I didn't want to make him a priority. The more tingly feelings I had associated with him, the further I moved away from reality—my reality, which was that I was in love with Porter, and I wasn't just saying that to convince myself. He was the man I needed to be with.

I fished around and fished around. One more ring and I'd miss the call, which I did, but he called right back.

"Where are you?" Dr. Bryce asked. "I need to see you."

"I'm just leaving my sister's house."

"Can I see you?"

He sounded anxious and rushed. I didn't like it. His demeanor was always calm but now he sounded desperate.

"I can't. Not tonight."

"You're seeing Porter tonight?" he asked. I didn't like it when he mentioned his name. It made me realize how unfair it was that he knew about Porter but Porter didn't have the slightest idea about him. Once again, it was my fault for giving him the name. "Do you ever ask yourself how is it that a man who doesn't have HIV can stay with a woman who does?"

"No, I don't ask myself that because he's already explained to me how he could. I take it you couldn't."

"I'm not saying I couldn't, but I would have concerns about sex and transmission. Are the two of you having sex?"

"No, we're not."

"Do you want to?"

"I would never want to risk giving him the disease."

Dr. Bryce said, "I'm not talking about having sex with him. I'm referring to me. Do you want to make love to me? Because I can't get the thought of making love to you out of my mind."

"You know just because we're both HIV positive doesn't mean it's safe." I was surprised to learn that fact, but it was true, according to a sex therapist who specialized in HIV-positive patients. She was a guest speaker at the Sisters Living Positively support group. She'd asked members of the group to raise their hands if they thought that if you and your partner are both HIV positive, you don't have to use condoms or other protection. We all raised our hand. *Not true,* she'd said. She explained that even though we are HIV positive, you can get more of the virus from having unprotected sex. There are different strains of HIV, and different types of HIV may be stronger than others and harder on the immune system. So it is possible to get reinfected with more or different HIV in your system.

"Who do you think you're talking to? Have you forgotten my background? I know that we'd still have to have safe sex. I'd have to use a condom, but at least you wouldn't feel guilty."

"I'd feel guilty."

"Let me rephrase my statement. You wouldn't feel guilty about giving me the disease since you know I already have it. And there are a lot of things we can do without a condom where the risk is so slight that I'd be willing to take it."

"Like what?"

"Well, of course I could kiss you. Kiss your lips—both sets."

When he said that, my vagina tingled.

"Stop talking like that," I demanded.

"Why, am I turning you on or something? You're not having sex with him, Winona, so I hope you're not naïve. You do know that he's having sex with someone. Porter is a man. No man is going to be with a woman and not have sex and not get it from somewhere. And how long have you been with him?"

"Almost a year."

"Oh, yeah. I can guarantee you he has someone. You think this guy in his late thirties is celibate and loving it?"

"He's not in his late thirties."

"Oh, I assumed he was around your age. He's older?"

"Younger. He's twenty-nine."

"Twenty-nine. Oh, he's fucking the city and the suburbs too," Dr. Bryce said, and when he did I literally had flashes of Porter doing women. Women I'd seen him look at on the sly while we were together. He'd wait until the woman passed us; then he'd turn his head, not all the way around, but to the side so he could catch her through his peripheral vision. Dr. Bryce was right. Porter was. I knew he was.

"I have to go."

"I'll let you go as long as you promise to think about me, because I'm going to be thinking about you."

The only thing I was going to be thinking about tonight was that phone call I received at work. I had a sister, and she wanted to meet me and only me. Now I wanted to meet her too.

"So, Dr. Bryce wants sex?" I asked, because it seemed as if he'd woken up from a wet dream and decided to dial my number. I felt like a booty call.

"No, Dr. Bryce wants to make love to the woman he's falling in love with."

"When is the last time you've had sex?"

"Look, I don't want to talk about that."

"Well, I do. When was it?"

"I haven't had sex since I was diagnosed. I hadn't had the desire to, but I have it now and it's strong . . . and it's all for you."

"Good night, Dr. Bryce."

"Promise you'll call me that while we're making love."

I hung up the phone. Temptation was going to make me lose everything.

27 Porter

I must have called every hospital in the city before I dialed the Barbara Ann Karmanos Cancer Institute. They wouldn't release any information to me over the phone, other than to confirm she was a patient. So I went in person with my identification and family photos, bills with my name and her address, a birth certificate, just to make sure they'd take me to my mother. Instead, I followed a nurse to an office to wait for a physician to talk to me. I just wanted to see her.

The female physician walked in, shook my hand, and sat behind the desk. She opened a medical chart and studied it for a few minutes.

"So you're Porter, Mrs. Washington's son. She's talked about you frequently."

"I want to see her."

She cleared her throat and said my name as she rubbed her hands together. The door opened and a male doctor entered and sat beside me.

"You're mother is under our hospice care."

"A hospice is for dying people. Are you telling me that my mother is dying?"

"Our hospice program provides support and care for terminally ill persons. Your mother is in her final months, and she's receiving care in a new home that she purchased with your father. I spoke to your mother about allowing us to notify you but she didn't want to bother you."

"Bother me?" I asked, my voice crackling. "Can I have her address, please? May I please have her address?"

"I can call your father and ask if we may release their telephone number and address."

"We're talking about my mother," I said emotionally. "My mother." I cleared my throat when my voice began to crackle. "Call him right now with me in the room. That is my mother."

"I will call him right now," she said as she picked up her office phone, looked at the file, and began dialing. I listened to the doctor as she spoke to my father, advising him that I was in the room with her. Then she handed me the phone.

"Dad," I said, clearing my throat. "I want to see my mother."

"I want you to see her. She wants to see you. We love you, son."

"I love y'all too."

"We're sorry, son."

"I'm sorry too."

Dad gave me their new phone number and address. They'd moved to a ranch in Novi, a suburb of Detroit. "She's asleep right now, but why don't you come early in the morning."

"I'ma be there early. How early can I come?"

"As early as you'd like. She's usually up by six."

"I'll be there."

I got there at four a.m. and camped out in my car in their driveway. It was too early in the morning to ring my parents' doorbell because I was afraid that would disturb my mother. I'd dozed off and didn't awake until after I heard a knock on the driver's side window. It was my father, standing in his robe and slippers, holding the *Detroit News*.

I let my window down.

"Come on in, son. You didn't have to sleep outside."

"Wait, Dad. Can you sit in the car for a second? I need to ask you some questions." I unlocked the car door for him. He looked around the interior of the Magnum once he sat inside. "This is nice."

"It's okay," I said. "How did this happen?"

"Your mother was never the going-to-a-doctor type of woman. I felt the lump on her breast. I told her to go in, she kept saying nothing was wrong. She started having a discharge. She was tired. Her stomach was hurting all the time. Son, by the time she finally did see someone it had spread to most of her vital organs."

"I want to see her."

"She doesn't look the same. I just need to warn you of that."

"I don't care how she looks."

"You won't recognize your mother."

"Is she really dying?"

"Yes," my father said and he broke into tears. I'd never ever seen my father like this and it frightened me. He was always the macho man. The one that nothing or no one could faze. "I wish we could trade places to make up for all the wrong I did to her." He took a handkerchief from his pocket and wiped his eyes. "Are you ready to come in? She's up."

I nodded and followed Dad into the house.

"Hi, Porter," she said in a frail voice. I'd barely walked through the door. "That's my son," she told the nurse. "Isn't he handsome? Come here," she said, patting her hand against the mattress. I walked up to her bed and kissed my mother lightly on the lips. She didn't look herself at all. Her face was thin and her skin lighter than usual. Her head was bandaged. Dad had told me she was bald. She struggled to smile. "You kissed your mother." She put her hand to her lips and closed her eyes.

"I love you, Mom. I am so sorry." My eyes started to water. "I am so sorry for everything I have ever said to you that was wrong and mean-spirited. You did the best you could at the time."

She shook her head. "Some ... times ... the best"—she cleared her throat—"isn't good enough. Isn't good enough." She took my hand. "I asked God to forgive me for all the wrong I'd done. I'm going home now."

"I'm not ready for you to go home. I need my mother."

"Your mother . . . you'll always have your mother . . . just like you'll always have your brother. Listen to me." She closed her eyes and swallowed, which let me know that she was having a hard time talking.

"Mom, that's okay, don't talk."

"Don't tell me not to talk. I want to tell you something. I want you . . . I need you to be happy and do great things in your life. Life is so short. You can either live well or wait to die. Don't wait to die. I'm not going to be here much longer. I guess God just wanted me to see you before I go." I sat on a chair with my mother's hand in mine. The tears overtook me. The nurse handed me a box of tissues and I wiped my eyes. "I'm going to say hello to Richard for you. I saw him the other day and he told me to tell you that it wasn't your fault. Do big things, baby."

"She needs to rest now," her nurse said.

"I love you, Mom," I said as I knelt down and kissed her. My senses were numb. If I could tell people one thing, I'd say, don't take life or loved ones for granted. Tomorrow is never promised.

28 Winona

Porter and I were sitting at the table, fully dressed and ready to go to the dance. He didn't feel like talking about his visit with his mother the night before, so I figured that I'd wait on him to bring it up.

"She looked so bad," he said as he bent over to tie his dress shoes. "I didn't even recognize her. She didn't look at all like herself." He shook his head. "They gave her two months to live, but I doubt if she makes it half that time."

"Don't be negative, Porter. She can still beat it."

He looked at me with a strange glare. "Do you know what a hospice is, Winona? It's for people who are dying. People they've given up on. My mother is dying and I don't handle death well. I can't handle seeing sick people either. Not when I can remember how they used to look. I couldn't handle seeing you that way."

I dropped my head. My throat had a big lump in it.

The phone started ringing and I jumped up to answer it. Anything to get away from Porter and his present mind-set was appreciated right about now. I took the handset off the wall and walked into the living room before I answered.

"I've been calling you all day," Val said through the speaker of my BlackBerry cell phone.

"I'm sorry. Things have been so crazy around my house. Porter's mother is dying. She has cancer and the whole thing was sudden and so sad."

"Oh, girl, I understand. I just was curious about what it was you wanted to tell me since you said it was about Dad. Can you tell me now?"

I walked into the bathroom and shut the door. "I don't want the kids to hear me."

"Is it that bad?"

"It's worse. Nothing you could ever imagine. At least I didn't."

"What is it?" she shouted so loud I had to move the phone away from my ear. It even frightened my black Lab, Samson, who had been lying on one of the white rugs. He slowly raised his head and cocked it to the side.

"It's okay, boy."

"Boy? Who you calling boy?" Val asked.

"I'm talking to my dog."

"Skip that dog and tell me what's going on."

"You're not going to be ready for this but I don't know how else to tell you besides just telling you. Dad has more kids. Three more kids."

She sighed. "What? Who told you this lie?"

"Oh, no, it's not a lie. I talked to one of them at work. Her name is Lori, something like that. He has two daughters and a son by some woman. I should have gotten the woman's number or more information but I wasn't in the best mood when she called."

"You don't know who that girl was. Just because she claims all this don't make it true."

"It's true. The girl knew too much about Dad and our family for it not to be."

"And you didn't get her number?"

"No," I said, angry at myself for not getting contact information. "I was like you at first. Thinking it was a lie or a mistake or something, even after she told me more and more so I would believe her. It wasn't until later that night that I realized I should have found a way to contact her."

There was a loud bang on the bathroom door.

"We're going to be late," Porter said. "I don't want to miss Norma Jean Bell's performance. She comes on at eight."

"Look, Val, I have to go, but I was thinking that maybe you and I should take Mom out to lunch just to feel her out."

"You mean to tell her? I know you, Winona. Dad doesn't call you a signifying monkey for no reason. How are you going to tell Momma that before you ask Dad if it's true?"

"Did I say tell her? I said feel her out."

"What's to feel out?"

"Look, if you don't want to go, you don't have to."

"If you paying for it, I'll go. I don't never turn down a free meal."

"Winona," Porter shouted. "Let's go."

"I'll call you tomorrow with the time. In the meantime, call mom and tell her—"

"Tell her what? You must be crazy if you think I'm going to tell her that her husband has three more kids that she don't know nothing about."

"No, tell her we're taking her out. I got to go." I hung up and quickly applied some makeup. Then I released my hair from the banana clip, allowing my freshly permed locks to fall well below my shoulder. "I'm coming Porter. I'm almost ready," I shouted because I knew he was about to bang on the bathroom door again.

"If we don't leave in the next five minutes, we're going to be late. I'm in the car."

I was almost ready. The only thing I had left to do was slip on my dress that was hanging on the bathroom door in a plastic garment bag and put on my shoes.

My phone started ringing—three quick tones, followed by one long one. I now had Dr. Bryce on a special ring tone. I wanted to answer so badly, but if I did I wouldn't make it downstairs on time. Now I only had two minutes. But if I didn't, he'd probably ring my phone off the hook. "I can't talk. I'm on my way out the door. The Roostertail," I said, before thinking. Maybe he shouldn't know where I was just in case he was the type to show up.

"I'll see you there," he said, confirming my latest fear that he had stalker traits.

"Why are you going to see me there?"

"Winona, I just need to see you. I've been thinking about you every waking moment. What are you doing with a man who is ten years younger than you and not HIV positive? What are you doing?"

"Don't worry about what I'm doing. Worry about finding

a cure for HIV. That's what you said your sole purpose in life was . . . so act like it, because people like me need you to succeed. I want to be cured."

"You will be, and you're also going to be with me."

Porter blew his car horn.

"I've got to go."

We were in the glass-enclosed Palm River Room. There was a pretty decent DJ playing old-school jams from the 70s and 80s mixed in with chart-topping R&B and rap music. But the real highlight of the evening was the wonderful performance by Norma Jean Bell, a local artist who'd been on the music scene for years.

My eyes were closed tightly, squeezed together because I was making a wish that I desperately needed to come true. I wanted my life to return to normal without Dr. Bryce in it. I wanted to be the type of person who meant what she said. I wanted to stay committed to Porter and not let any outside influences convince me that my man was cheating. I didn't want to worry about things that I had no proof of and I didn't want to be the jealous type who was always looking for proof.

My head rested comfortably against Porter's muscular chest as we slow-danced to Luther's "Love Won't Let Me Wait." Porter was singing softly in my ear. I remembered when that song came out in the late 80s, but I couldn't place what I was doing then besides living in Texas with a man I didn't love who also didn't love me.

For the most part I was happy. My support group seemed to be helping, as was the book I was reading. In fifteen days something was supposed to change. "Get out and enjoy life,"

Brenda said at the last meeting. "Do things you wouldn't normally do." Which is why I agreed to attend this dance. That was definitely something I wouldn't normally do. The romantic evening out with my fiancé now seemed worth it. I was in the arms of my knight in shining armor, a man ten years my junior who entered my life just in time to save it. I loved Porter. Not Dr. Bryce, who I barely knew, even though we seemed to click. I loved Porter. Maybe I had to keep telling myself that to convince my mind it was true. I loved Porter and nothing could ruin this night . . . or so I thought.

"Winona," a familiar male voice said. "How are you?" I opened my eyes and spotted Derwin dancing right beside us. I tried to speak but for some reason my mouth felt nailed shut. I felt like someone had abruptly snatched the needle off the record that was playing because when I looked up at Derwin, I immediately heard a screeching sound and Porter and I both came to an alarming halt.

What is he doing here? I thought.

Everything about Derwin irritated me—how light his skin was, how thin he was, the awkward and out-of-date way he wore his hair with a short tail sticking out in the back, and yet he had the nerve to pierce both ears as if somehow trying to be in touch with the younger generation. But tonight, what bothered me most was mainly his devilish grin. I came back to Detroit, my hometown, two years ago not only for a job promotion but also to reunite my son with his father, Derwin, a man my son never met or even knew existed. I'd always told him that Keith, my daughter's father, was also his. But now that they'd developed such a tight bond, I had to admit it bothered me that a couple months could erase all those years that

Derwin obviously cared less about his only child because he never tried to find him. The only solace I had was in knowing that Carlton's main reason for spending time with his dad was to see what he could get from him. If Carlton was staying around him this long, most likely he was milking him dry.

"I'm doing fine," I finally said to Derwin. "But I'm surprised to see you here. You didn't miss out on your prom like I did."

"No, I can't say that I did," Derwin said.

"You just stood me up for mine," I said underneath my breath.

"I'm sorry, I missed that," Derwin said, leaning his ear toward my mouth. "What did you say, Winona?"

I drew my head back, away from Derwin. Porter was standing beside me on the dance floor with his arms shoved in his pockets, looking annoyed. "She said you stood her up for hers. So, in other words, you messed up one. Why did you have to show up and mess up this one?" Porter took a firm hold of my hand and yanked me off the dance floor. We walked over to our table beside the window overlooking the river. "I'm waiting."

"For what?" I said. My hands cupped the small glass candleholder as I studied the light while it flickered.

"For you to fuss me out about what I said."

I looked up at him. "There wasn't anything wrong with what you said. He did mess it up," I said, but then I thought about it. The only way he'd mess up my evening is if I let him. I was tired of giving that man credit for ruining things in my life. I remembered what Brenda said: *The best way to take control of your life is to embrace your failures the same way you embrace your accomplishments. Hindsight is 20/20 but at the time of your mistakes you were blind.* "I take that back," I said to Porter. "I am having a wonderful time."

Porter winked at me, then took one of my hands and kissed the palm right before he began singing Luther Vandross' "Love Won't Let Me Wait." I'd never paid that much attention to Porter when he sang, but now that I was, I realized how good he sounded: "And I need your love so desperately and only you can set me free, when I make love to you, we'll explode in ecstasy."

"But we have to wait," I said as if he'd asked me a question, because indirectly I knew he had. He placed his finger to my lips so I wouldn't talk, so I quickly stopped and went back to enjoying the dance.

I closed my eyes. I couldn't wait either, but what other choice did I have?

We walked out of The Roostertail holding hands. Porter was walking slightly in front of me. He tugged my hand so I would slow my pace. When he turned to look at me, I noticed Dr. Bryce sitting in his 6-series BMW, black with red interior.

"What are you staring at?" Porter asked.

"I liked that car. You know me. I'm one that will always notice a good automobile design." Porter looked at the car for a moment.

"Maybe it's my imagination, but the two of you seem to be staring at each other."

I shrugged. "No, I'm just looking at the car and I'm not sure what he's looking at."

The valet opened the passenger door for me and I tried my best not to turn toward Dr. Bryce, but it was hard. Porter got in the car and stuck his key in the ignition. He turned toward me. "Are you okay? You're sitting real stiff."

"I'm fine."

He started the ignition, and just when he was about to shift the gear into drive, I squeezed his hand. "Are *you* okay?"

"I'm afraid to lose my mother. And I still miss my brother."

"Your brother is your angel and your mother will be too," I said.

"Beware of false prophets," Porter said. "Do you know the rest?"

I shook my head. "No, Porter. I'm afraid I don't."

"Could you hand me the Bible from the glove compartment?" he asked, which I did. I watched as he turned to find the verse. He read: "Beware of false prophets, which come to you in sheep's clothing, but inwardly they are ravenous wolves. Ye shall know them by their fruits. Do men gather grapes of thorns, or figs of thistles? Even so every good tree bringeth forth good fruit; but a corrupt tree bringeth forth evil fruit. A good tree cannot bring forth evil fruit, neither can a corrupt tree bring forth good fruit. Every tree that bringeth not forth good fruit is hewn down, and cast into the fire. Therefore by their fruits ye shall know them. Not every one that saith unto me, Lord, Lord, shall enter into the kingdom of heaven; but he that doeth the will of my Father which is in heaven. Many will say to me in that day, Lord, Lord, have we not prophesied in thy name? and in thy name have cast out devils? and in thy name done many wonderful works? And then will I profess unto them, I never knew you: depart from me, ye that work iniquity."

"Are you trying to call me a false prophet?" I asked,

concerned that he may have figured out I was looking at more than Dr. Bryce's car.

"No. Not you. Why would you even say that? My brother said a few things about my bishop that have made me wonder."

"Your brother?"

"Yes, my brother, Winona. He speaks to me." I nodded my head slowly as he looked over at me.

"He speaks to you?" I asked. "What does he say?" He could probably tell from my tone that I found it hard to believe.

"He talks to me the same way you and I talk, only when he talks to me, he's trying to give me advice or to warn me about something." He kept his eyes on me through every word.

I straightened my body and looked ahead. "What kind of advice, Porter?"

"Do you love me, Winona?"

"I love you very much. Now let's go home. I can barely keep my eyes open."

"I guess we better." He put the car in drive and pulled out of the space. "Will you go to California with me?" he asked.

"Porter, I need to think about it. That's a big step. I have two kids. I'd have to quit my job."

"I'm just talking about for a couple days. Keena's management company sent me two first-class tickets and they're paying for our food and hotel. It's just for this Friday and Saturday. Will you?"

I nodded. "I guess I can take off. I can go."

Winona

29

My mother entered the restaurant first. Then I walked through the carved mahogany front door of the Blue Nile. On the ride to the restaurant, Mom mentioned that my sister Val went to Zeidman's and pawned her wedding ring months ago. Bo found out through the notice in the mail that the ring had been sold, and supposedly that was the final straw. So now I understood why I received a last-minute voice mail from her saying something had come up and she couldn't join us for lunch. She must have been trying to save her marriage. Maybe Val not showing worked out for the best, because I wasn't sure if I was going to tell Mom what I'd found out or not.

I chose the Ethiopian restaurant in Ferndale because Dr. Bryce recommended it, and I loved the idea of eating with my hands. The all-you-care-to-eat menu consisted of chicken, lamb, beef, collards, cabbage, and several varieties of split peas and lentils arranged on a round, flat, spongy bread called *injera*. My mother and I used the smaller pieces of *injera* to scoop up the food.

I can't remember the last time my mother and I went anywhere together just the two of us. Not even when I was a teenager because I wasn't allowed to drive and Mom didn't like to. She was forty when she finally got her driver's license. After she did, she and Dad were driving down Hubbell near Six Mile. As they approached a yellow light, Dad said turn, and Mom did—without looking. The car jumped the curb and hit the side of a party store. I think about that a lot. How Mom would do so much of what Dad said without taking the time to think for herself. It used to anger me. If she'd just use her head or a little common sense, she would've seen that she needed to get to the light before she turned or else she'd hit a brick wall. After that incident, Mom pretty much swore off driving and had to depend on Dad or my brother to take her anywhere she needed to go. But Mom was driving now. In fact, she drove her Chrysler Pacifica to the restaurant today.

"Do you really like being married?" I asked as I picked up a piece of lamb with my hands.

"Why would you ask me that, Winona? Do you think I'd stay married for nearly fifty-five years if I didn't?"

"Well, I know all of those fifty-five years couldn't have been exactly paradise. Were they?"

"No, of course they weren't. And any woman who expects her marriage to be is in for a very rude awakening. Your father and I had to grow together. Any- and everything two people can go through in a relationship, we did."

"Cheating?" I asked with my eyes downward, focusing on the food.

"This was very nice of you to invite me for lunch, but what was the occasion?" Mother asked, completely changing the subject.

I shrugged. "I just wanted to spend some one-on-one time with my mother. When was the last time we did?" My cell phone started ringing. I opened my purse and looked at the caller display. It was Dr. Bryce, but I decided not to answer.

"Was that your friend?" Mom asked.

"Friend?"

"Yes, Sosha said you have a friend. She didn't call him your friend, but that's what I'm saying. She said he's over there nearly every night. Is that true?"

"Well, if he is, I'm grown."

She frowned. "That's not a good idea. Not in your condition."

"What's my condition, Mom?" She made me so mad that I wanted to tell her. Right then, just blurt it out and let her deal with her feelings. Hurt her with my words the way she was hurting me with hers.

"You know your condition and you shouldn't even be thinking about marriage. Does he have the same condition?"

"No, Mom, he doesn't have the same condition. Are you ready?"

"If you are," she said. "I didn't mean to upset you."

"You didn't upset me. I'm the only one who can say something to upset someone right now." And in true Mom form, she didn't ask me what I meant by my last statement. She didn't ask what I would say to upset someone or who it would upset. She treated my words as if they were meaningless. She was so oblivious to everything—even to her own life and to what her husband had been doing for all those years. Even if I told her, she'd just pretend she didn't hear it so she could go about her mundane life as usual. Dad could have twenty kids for all I cared. She wasn't finding out by me. "I'm ready."

When I walked into my house, Porter was in the kitchen talking on the phone.

"Do you have to invite that woman?" I heard him ask. "Don't expect me to acknowledge her."

He hung up the phone and turned to face me, and when he looked into my eyes, he broke down crying. I held him in my arms and didn't say a word.

"I can't believe she's gone," he said.

"I know," I said.

"Mom had such a feisty personality. I thought she'd live to be a hundred." He pulled back from me and punched at the air. "I can't believe I did that. How could I have been such a damn fool? I was the only child my mother had left and I stayed away from her. That's just one more thing I have to live with."

"Don't fault yourself for being angry. Be thankful that you had an opportunity to see your mother before she passed away, and do know that she has gone to a much better place."

He nodded. "I'm going upstairs to take a nap. Can you wake me up in a few hours?"

"I will." I watched Porter as he walked slowly up the stairs. The loss of his mother made me think of my mother and how angry I was at her less than an hour ago. I picked up the phone to call her.

"Hello," my dad said.

"Can you put Mom on the phone?"

"Who is this?"

I rolled my eyes. "Your daughter . . . Winona." I felt I had to clarify which one now more than ever.

"Didn't you just leave her?"

"Dad, will you please just put Mom on the phone?" He yelled out her name, and a few seconds later she picked up another line. "Mom, I just want to tell you that I love you very much. I'm sorry if it seemed like I had an attitude."

"It didn't seem like that to me. I had a nice time. I was telling your father about the food and how we ate with our hands. I'm going to take him there one day."

"I don't want to go out nowhere and eat with my hands," Dad said. "I can stay home and do that."

"Donald, hang up the phone."

"Why did you have to call your mother to tell her that you loved her? Don't you know that your daughter loves you?"

"I know, and I still like to hear it," Mom said.

"Porter's mother died."

"Who?" Dad asked.

"Porter."

"Donald, that's her friend."

"Friend. You mean that's that man she's living with, don't you? I don't understand how you can be living with a man—"

"I'm sorry to hear that, honey," Mom said, cutting Dad off.

"Me too," Dad said. "When is the funeral so we can send some flowers?"

"I'm not sure. He just found out, and now he's upstairs taking a nap. When I find out I'll let you know. I just called to tell you that I love you, Mom."

"You don't love me?" Dad asked as I was hanging up the line.

30 Porter

I couldn't work so I called in. And honestly, I didn't know if I was ever going to be able to go back. My mother was dead. I was having a real hard time coming to grips with that, and so was my father. I went to the house to check on him and to help arrange the funeral and put together the obituary, and just as I'd suspected there were a lot of relatives from both sides coming in and out. My aunt Monique from my dad's side and her husband, Frank, were over. So were Mom's three first cousins: Detra, Eve, and Betty.

We were all in the dining room sitting at the table with photo albums and loose pictures scattered around, reminiscing about the past, when out of nowhere Eve said, "Did she mention a will?" Aunt Monique rolled her eyes. "What? I was just asking. I mean, you know Jolene was my girl and I miss her. I was just wondering if she thought about me at all. I was just asking what the rest of us probably want to know. Oh, and did y'all own the building the restaurant was in or were you leasing?"

Monique stood up. "I know it's taking Richard everything he's got not to curse your ass out. But not me. I've been waiting for this moment ever since I saw the three of you musketeers walk through the door. Jolene was my best friend and I feel safe in saying that she didn't leave any of you shit." Monique and my mother weren't blood sisters, but they were cut from the same mold, and neither could bite their tongue. "If she left anyone anything it was to Porter and her husband. As for whether or not they owned or leased the building, why are you so damn concerned now when your ass never showed up over the last fifteen years it was open to support it? Whenever you did decide to drop by, you expected your cousin to give you the food for free." Monique got so excited that she had to take out her inhaler and breathe through it.

"Calm down, Aunty," I said, rubbing her back.

"No, I feel like I have to speak up for your mother. These are her so-called cousins but when's the last time any of y'all even talked to Jolene? But now you damn near planning on camping out just to see if your stankin' asses are going to get something. I watched her suffer. Where were any of y'all?" My aunt broke into tears. I walked with her outside and sat with her on the back porch.

My aunt took out a tissue from a small package in her purse, wiped her eyes, and blew her nose. "I'm sorry that I acted a fool in there," she said to me. "I just couldn't help myself. Those women in there aren't your mother's family.

You know who your mother's family was? The three of us. You, your father, and me. We were all she had."

I shook my head. "I feel so bad. I don't know what to do. I blamed my mom for so much and wasted a lot of time carrying around anger." I balled up both of my fists just thinking about what I'd done. "Who knows why a person does what they do? It wasn't my place to judge."

"Porter, your mother had a really hard childhood. Your grandmother had a bunch of kids by different men, all of them called Uncle somebody. Men coming in and out the house, around your young daughters, that's not something I'd do. It was hard for your mother. It's the reason, I think, she decided to get married so young, so she could get out and away from that situation."

"Was my mother sexually abused growing up?"

My aunt nodded. "It's not that your mother didn't hear what you were saying. She heard you, because she'd talk to me about it. She just didn't want to accept it. And then there was the feeling that since she had boys, they'd be safe. Never figuring her mother would bring home an uncle who liked little boys. Your mother understood your hurt and your pain because she'd been through it herself. I believe that she didn't know what to do or to say to make up for what had happened so she chose to ignore it. I spent a lot of time with your mother while she was sick"—my aunt held my hand—"and she wanted nothing more than for you to be happy. And right now, I know you're sad because your mother has passed, but do you think you can try to forgive your mother and move on with your life?"

I nodded. "I have already forgiven her. "She did the best she knew how at the time. I honestly believe that."

31 Winona

"**W**ho was that on the phone?" Porter asked as I ended the call that came through my cell phone. I was in the garage looking in my car for my Fred Hammond CD because I was in the mood for some uplifting gospel.

"Dr. Bryce," I said quickly. I figured it wouldn't be a big deal since I'd already explained to Porter that I was trying a combination of traditional and holistic medicine and Dr. Bryce was an expert in alternative medicine and herbs.

"You mention his name a lot . . . almost too much."

"Not really," I said as I swept passed him on my way into the house.

Porter grabbed my arm and pulled me back to face him. "Yes you do. And every time you're on the phone with him and I come in the room, you get off real quick. Why did you have to come out here to talk to him?"

"I came out here to find my Fred Hammond CD."

"Your Fred Hammond CD is in the house in the bedroom. You were listening to it this morning. I'm no fool, Winona."

"Fool about what?" I asked as I looked at his hand that had a tight hold on my arm.

He loosened his grip. "Go on. I can't make you love me."

"You know I love you."

"I do?" he asked as he shook his head. "Then marry me. Go to California with me and marry me." I hesitated. Why did love have to come with all these life-changing conditions? "That's what I thought. I'm going to California. Are you still going with me?"

"Going with you? This is the first I'm hearing of this."

"Winona, I told you about this. It's just for a couple days to check it all out, remember?"

"You told me about this?" I asked, trying to pretend I'd forgotten about it, because I couldn't go, didn't want to, but I couldn't tell Porter that.

"So you forget that quickly? Maybe you need to ask your doctor if memory loss is a side effect of the medication you're taking."

I shook my head. "That hurt."

He shrugged. "What you're doing does too." He walked out of the garage, leaving me behind. I understood the reason he was acting that way. It had to do with the death of his mother. He probably needed some alone time, some space.

* * *

I told myself I'd go to Dr. Bryce's quaint store that sat on the corner of Woodward near Jefferson not far from the City-County Building. But when I did, Dr. Bryce wasn't there. I wasn't sure how to classify the place. It was part health food store, part coffee shop, part bookstore, and a whole lot of aromatherapy. A woman had just walked out of the acupuncture treatment room in back and another woman came out a separate door singing praises about the deep-tissue massage she'd just received.

Dr. Bryce was upstairs in his loft, not feeling particularly well, and he didn't even call me to let me know. He opened the door in his pajamas and a thick robe.

"Are you cold?" I asked after walking into his loft and felt the heat. I looked at his thermostat, which was set to eighty-five.

"I'm freezing," Dr. Bryce said, shivering. "I need to get back in bed. You can come with me, if you like. You can take care of me, if you want to."

"It's almost ninety degrees outside. If you're cold you might be sick."

"I'm fine," he snapped, but then apologized quickly. I'm just not feeling well," he said as he rested his back against three fluffy pillows. "That's all this is. I'm not trying to take you away from him. I just—well, I guess that's a lie. I guess I am trying to take you away from him. But how can you blame me for that?"

"Do you need me to fix you anything before I go?" I asked as I stood. The room was as dark as his mood seemed to be and my energy level was dipping. I was ready to leave.

"No, I don't need anything, but I would like for you to stay a little longer and watch a movie with me. Can you keep me company for a couple hours? Just to watch a movie on HBO or one of my DVDs?"

I probably should have left, but I decided to stay.

32 Porter

I don't handle death well, and a funeral, to me, was the worst part of dying. I hated seeing my mother's lifeless body lying in the casket, arms folded across the chest. She was wearing a short wig and a colorful dress. She looked so young, like a child almost, but the sad part was that she didn't look like herself, which made it even harder for me to accept that she was dead. If I could have looked into the casket and seen my mother, instead of a face that didn't resemble her at all, maybe her death would be a little easier to accept.

We had the funeral at Perfecting, which was the church my mother attended. Hundreds came out: everyone who had ever worked for her came, including Vanity; people who had eaten at the restaurant, especially the regular customers; her relatives, more than I realized we had; even several of the men she'd dated. I didn't see her mother, but I wasn't looking for her either. Maybe she did what was best and stayed home.

I stood at the casket, holding my mother's hand. My father was beside me, broken and barely hanging on. I tried to console him, but he told me to leave him alone. "Let me deal with this, son. You just can't imagine how hard this is." Oh, I could imagine. What he was going through couldn't have been half as bad as what I was going through. I turned to walk back to my seat, and that's when I spotted her. She'd just walked to the front of the church with a cane in one hand and a man's hand in the other—a man who looked to be half her age if that. My grandmother was completely gray but her face wasn't wrinkled. She'd be a pretty woman if she didn't wear her bitterness all over her face. She refused to look at me, but I knew she saw me. A lot of years had passed, but she had to feel my presence as strongly as I did hers. After the house fire and the insurance denied the claim, my grandmother moved back to Pine Bluff, where she was raised. She never called, at least not that I knew of. Never came to visit. Just up and disappeared. If I did speak to my grandmother, she wouldn't want to hear what I had to say.

My father had a houseful of relatives on both sides. I was talking to them, especially those who came all the way from California, but at the same time I was keeping an eye on my grandmother.

One of my cousins was telling me about the cost of living in California, how expensive housing was. Winona and I looked at each other; her look seemed to be one of reservation. "It's nothing to pay sixteen hundred on a one-bedroom out there . . . a small one-bedroom," my cousin Til said. "And be prepared for the traffic. No, I can't even say be prepared because nothing can prepare you for that. Two hours to get most places because of all the cars. But I wouldn't trade it for the world."

I saw my grandmother walk up the stairs alone and I waited a few minutes and went up behind her.

"I'll be right back," I told Winona.

I walked in three of the bedrooms before I realized she'd gone to the bathroom off the hallway. I heard the toilet flush and I stood outside to wait.

"Hello, Florence," I said, startling her. "Do you know who I am?"

"Richard or Porter," she said.

That angered me. "Richard?" I asked. "You can't remember that Richard died in your house. Are you senile or something?"

"No, I'm not senile. I just said that to piss you off. What you want with me? I don't have time for your foolishness."

"You may not have time," I said, leading her into one of the bedrooms and shutting the door. "But you about to make time right here and right now. You knew what was going on. Didn't you?" I said, my voice rising.

"I don't know what you're talking about," she said as she held on to the footboard. "Going on when?"

"In your damn house. How could you let a man touch your grandbabies? What kind of person are you that you would let a man abuse your own blood? I didn't need that shit in my life. Do you know how much I've had to deal with because of it? At times, even questioning my own sexuality—not because I liked what happened to me, but just because the shit happened. How could you do it? You did that."

"You talking crazy, boy," she said, shaking her head like

she'd lost her mind. "I don't know what you're talking about. Ain't nothing happen to you in my house."

"You right about that. Your perverted boyfriend took me out and raped me in his car. How could you do that?"

"Porter, open the door," my father said, banging on it.

"I want an answer or I swear to God I don't know what I might do to you."

"I didn't know nothing," she said as she sat on the bed. "Nothing at all."

I looked over at her old run-down body. Barely enough energy left to breathe.

"Well, since you didn't know, let me tell you. Uncle Ray. That's what you called him, but we knew he wasn't our damn uncle, didn't want you, couldn't stand having sex with you because he liked little boys. You claim you didn't know but you did. I know that you did because desperate women like you always do."

I walked to the door to unlock it. My father and Winona were standing outside.

"Are you all right?" Winona asked as she held on to me.

"That's her," I said to Winona as I took Winona's hand and guided her over to my grandmother. "That's the woman who let her boyfriend abuse her own blood. That's the woman who ruined my life. There's not enough forgiveness in the world for you."

Winona stood shaking her head as she looked down at Florence.

"Come on, Porter, let's go," Winona said as she took my hand and guided me out of the room.

33 Winona

I felt guilty. Porter was going to be in California for a couple days starting tomorrow and all I could think about was Dr. Bryce and how much time I'd have to spend with him. I didn't see him as much as I talked to him on the phone, and that was mainly at work during my lunch hour. We shared one kiss. What was it about him that I liked so much? I'm sure it was the promise he made of a cure. Porter could accept my condition, but Dr. Bryce might be able to cure me of it, and that's what I needed.

"Are you feeling better today? You sound better," I asked him as I sat outside on a park bench in the courtyard of the Tech Center and talked to him on my cell phone. The first fifteen minutes of my lunch break, I ate a tuna sandwich on rye and read my book. In ten days, something was going to happen. I could feel it. Did I think my entire life would change in a little over a week? No. But I did think that I'd be on the road to something new and exciting.

"I'm fine. It was just a twenty-four-hour virus. I think really, it was my body shutting down and demanding that I rest. Sometimes I work so hard I forget to go to sleep."

"That's one thing I never forget to do. I love getting my eight hours."

"So are we still getting together this Saturday?" Dr. Bryce asked.

"If you'd like," I said. "Was there anything in particular that you wanted to do?"

He laughed. "Anything in particular? Never ask a man that question. No, sweetheart, I'll leave that up to you."

"Can I read you something from my book?"

"If you'd like."

"It is God himself who has made us what we are and given us new lives from Christ Jesus, and long ages ago he planned that we should spend these lives in helping others."

"You're reading the Bible?"

"No, I'm reading *The Purpose Driven Life*."

"But that was taken from the Bible. I believe that's from Ephesians."

"It is. Second chapter, tenth verse. That came from Day Twenty-nine, even though I'm on Day Thirty, but I wanted to read that to you because what you're doing is helping others. I mean I know it's helping yourself as well, but you're giving hope to a whole lot of people and then you're doing your best to get out and spread the word that you might have a cure."

"There's no might. I do. Why are you reading that book?"

I looked over at the Tech Center. "Because there has to be more to life than this. What is my purpose? Why did God put me here?"

"My purpose is to find a cure for HIV/AIDS."

"How did you know that was your purpose?"

"Long before I was diagnosed HIV positive, when I was treating patients, I wanted to do more than prescribe medication. I saw the hopelessness in many of my patients' eyes and I understood it, but I didn't want to. I wanted to give them something to look forward to. You're lucky, Winona. You haven't experienced sickness, and have very few side effects. But some people are struggling living with the disease."

"I'm struggling mentally. I'm thinking about quitting my support group."

"Why? It seems like a pretty nice group with a positive agenda," he said.

"We meet once, sometimes twice a month, and every time I'm there I'm wondering who's going to walk through the door that knows me. I don't like that feeling."

"So what if someone you know walks through the door? People spend way too much time worrying about what other people think of them. I don't care what anyone thinks of me. Judge me by my works. Not by how much money I have. Not by how good I look. Not by my body. But what I contribute. But then again, I have a different way of looking at things. Have you decided where we're going on Saturday?"

"No, I'll let you know then."

"Spontaneous. I like that."

34 Porter

California

They put me up in a two-story, one-bedroom penthouse in an exclusive hotel by the name of Casa Del Mar. I flew in late the night before and by the time the limousine dropped me off it was a little past one, but I was still on Detroit time, which made it four in the morning.

I put in a wake-up call request for eleven in the morning so I would have enough time to get ready for my one o'clock lunch meeting. Then I collapsed on the bed on top of the bedspread. Danzo called me thirty minutes before my wake-up call.

"Do you know where Chez Jay is?" he asked.

"This is my first time in California. I'm afraid I don't."

"It's very close to where you're staying."

"I'll find it." All I had to do was ask the concierge.

After the call ended, I lay on the bed with my eyes open until the wake-up call came through. Then I dragged myself out of bed and into the shower. I was getting ready to meet a star, but I didn't understand why I wasn't really that excited. I guess I had other things on my mind. Like my mother. I was still grieving, still kicking myself for being so stubborn and staying away from her like I did. I was starting to put my life into context. Yes, it went on, but now life to me had a different meaning. I started shaving and thinking about how I was in Detroit yesterday, and now I'm in Santa Monica, California. Was that how I wanted my life to be? Going from city to city touring with Keena, performing with her band as a drummer when my interest now was the saxophone. When I gave my word to something, it was bond, but I hadn't given my word to this yet.

I waited at the restaurant for an hour, before this huge entourage arrived. I guess it was fashionable in Hollywood to be late. Damn, I could have sworn a rapper was entering the restaurant, but it was Keena, with her long auburn weave. She wore her dark sunglasses the entire time. And even though she spoke only a few times, I could tell that she wanted to say more. She constantly stared in my direction.

We ordered a tableful of appetizers and plenty of drinks. I met the bass player and the piano player. They seemed to be cool guys, but it was something in my spirit that told me I didn't belong there. Danzo did most of the talking. The rest of us ate and pretended to listen.

"Bottom line, Porter," Keena said. "Are you going to

move your ass to California and drum for me or not? Yes or no."

I sighed. "Since I had to wait for an hour, I had a little time to look through the *LA Times* real estate section. If I move here, I won't be coming alone."

"You won't?"

"No, I'm engaged."

"Oh, I didn't know that," she said with a slight attitude.

"It's just not conducive for a family. We can't live in an apartment. And even the apartments out here are high as hell. Not to mention, if I drum for you, it's not a year-round gig. I've got to look at the big picture."

You're obviously interested or you wouldn't have flown all the way out here," Keena said. "You want more money. Right?"

"Money is definitely a big factor. But also, I'm starting to get away from drumming and moving toward the saxophone. Eventually, I'm going to want to go solo and I need to know how performing in your band will benefit me."

"First of all, I don't need a saxophone player. If I did, I'd get someone like Boney James to lay down a track with me. I need a drummer. I've never had luck with my drummers and that's all I need. Now this saxophone shit, put all that aside and look at the big picture."

"What is the big picture?"

"I'm not local-level Detroit, baby. I'm international." I could have burst her bubble if I wanted to, but I'm sure it wouldn't have been too easy because it was so obvious that she was full of herself. Yes, she was all that at one time, but she's nothing now.

"Well, how about this. How about tomorrow afternoon we get together again, but maybe this time at the studio so we can both showcase our talents?"

"That might work."

"What's wrong, Porter?" Winona asked. I guess she could hear the disappointment in my voice.

"I'm not feeling this." I was flipping through the television stations out of boredom and disgust.

"Not feeling what?"

"This whole scene. I'm not feeling it."

"But you haven't even been there for a whole day."

"I know but I'm still not feeling it. It's expensive to live out here and I'd never ask you to leave your job and move out here with Sosha if I didn't think I could support you. And then I want custody of Portia too. I won't be able to afford a family out here."

"But what about your music? You're just going to give that up?"

"No, I'm not going to give that up. But my music isn't the drums anymore. My music is the saxophone."

"Then come on home. We'll figure it out. If you don't want to drum anymore, that's your answer right there."

"The only reason I accepted this stupid trip was for us to get away for a weekend, but then you decided not to even come so I really could have stayed at home."

"Make sure this is the right decision because once you turn her down there may not be an opportunity to come back."

I turned off the television. "I don't want to come back . . . not here."

35 Winona

I met Dr. Bryce at Xochimilco's, a restaurant in Detroit's Mexicantown. I hadn't had any Mexican food since I'd moved home. Back in Texas, not a week went by that I didn't stop at either Taco Bueno for something quick or Pancho's whenever I wanted to take the kids to an inexpensive buffet. What I really had a taste for were some beef and chicken fajitas and a margarita.

As I waited inside the restaurant, I looked at all of the METRO TIMES READERS' POLL plaques hanging on the wall right above the picture of Virgin Mary. Best Mexican Restaurant for 1988, '90, '91, '94, '96, '97, '98, '99, and 2001. I looked around the restaurant and it dawned on me why the two-story building was so familiar. The last time I ate here I was in high school and Derwin and I had just finished making out in the car in some creepy downtown alley. Afterward, he'd smoked a joint and got the munchies. So we went here at close to two in the morning because it was the only restaurant still open. I sat and watched him devour a large basket of loaded nachos without offering me one. Yet I was the fool to still deal with him. I shook my head at the thought and headed for the door. I didn't feel like dealing with the reminders. But as I approached the door, Dr. Bryce was walking through it.

"Good choice," he said. "I've always wanted to try this place out. Sorry I'm late. It was a hectic day at Tree of Life." We followed a young Mexican girl to a table in the middle of the restaurant and took our seats. I didn't even need to look at the menu so instead I studied Dr. Bryce while he did. "You already know what you want?"

I nodded. "Fajitas."

He smiled. "I think I want to try something different. I'm going to get the Platillo Mexicano."

I opened my menu and read the description of his entrée. "That's a lot of food."

"I can handle it."

"Have you had enough time to look over the menu?" the waitress asked.

"Sí," Dr. Bryce said.

"Ooh. Buenas tardes, señor y señorita. De que tiene gusto de comer?"

"I'm sorry, *sí* is about all I know. I had one semester of Spanish in high school and that was a long, long time ago."

The waitress laughed. "I said good afternoon and I asked what would you like to order?"

"We want to start with an appetizer." Dr. Bryce looked

over at me for agreement. I nodded. "Can you recommend one?" he asked the waitress.

"The *botanas* and the super nachos are very popular," the waitress said.

"What's a *botana*?" he asked.

"The *botana* is a bed of corn chips topped with refried beans, cheese, avocado, tomatoes, and jalapeños. It's an appetizer, but if you add beef or chicken it can easily be a meal."

"Would you like that?" he asked me.

I nodded. "As an appetizer I would."

"One more question," Dr. Bryce said to the waitress. "Well, two. How do you pronounce the restaurant's name?"

"So-she-MIL-co," she said.

"So-she-MIL-co," he said. "And what does that mean?"

"It's named after the famous floating gardens that's just south of Mexico City."

After a few more of Dr. Bryce's questions were answered, we placed our appetizer and entrée orders as well as our drink request. The margaritas came out first, followed by the *botana*, which *was* big enough for a meal, so I didn't eat too much because I wanted to save room for my fajitas, which came out sizzling.

"Have you ever been to Greektown?" I asked him. He shook his head. "That would be another nice place to go. I like it when they bring out the flaming cheese and say *Opa!* real loud. Pegasus would be a good restaurant to go to."

"You seem to really enjoy eating out," he said with a smile.

"Unfortunately, I don't do much cooking. But most of these places I'm mentioning I haven't been to since high school."

"What high school did you go to again?"

"I'm not sure I ever told you that I'm a technician."

"You went to Cass? No, you didn't tell me because I would have remembered that. But I don't think you and I were there at the same time. You're thirty-eight, right?" I nodded. "I'm five years older than you." He snapped his fingers. "I just missed you."

"Were you premed then?" He nodded. "I guess you always knew your purpose."

"Let's talk about this purpose thing, because I can tell that it's constantly on your mind. You have no idea at all what you would like to do?"

"There are plenty of things that I'd like to do. I'd like to get on *Oprah* during her favorite things or wildest dreams broadcast. But as far as what I want to do with my life, I have no idea."

"What about marriage? Is that something that you want to do? Are you really going to marry him?"

"Mmm. I don't want to talk about that."

"What do you want to talk about?"

I shrugged.

"Can I tell you what I want to talk about?"

"If you'd like."

"Us."

"Us? What about us?"

"There's a reason that we talk on the phone nearly every day. There's a reason that we've made time to see each other. At least for me there's a reason. Maybe there isn't one for you. Is there?" He seemed to study my face for the answer.

It took me a moment before I responded because a million and one things zipped through my mind. Was today going to be the day that I whacked my hair off? Not all of it. Nothing like Angela Bassett's character did in *Waiting to Exhale*. It took me too many years to grow my hair out this long. It tickled me when I turn and catch women, black and white, looking into my head as if in search of tracks. I think to play it safe I was going to get a trim and take maybe an inch away.

"I'm comfortable when I'm with you," I said. Then I started thinking about my pedicure. I loved the spa pedicure. The whole experience was pure pampering. And I'd been getting pedicures ever since I was twenty-two. Back when I didn't have any money and knew that twenty-five dollars would have been better spent on a tank of gas or lunch money for the week, I still went ahead and treated myself, which helped me to strive harder.

"Are you still with me?" Dr. Bryce asked as he waved his hand over my head.

"I'm still here. I really enjoy our phone conversations. It's nice to talk to someone who can relate to what I'm going through. *And* you're not too bad to look at either. For a light-skinned man, which has never been my preference after one dumped me at the altar."

"Well a dark-skinned woman has always been mine," he said as the waitress brought our entrées to the table.

"Wow, that's a lot of food," I said as my eyes expanded. My cell phone rang. I took it out of my purse and looked at the caller ID. It was Porter, but I decided not to answer, even though I wanted to talk to him. I wasn't sure what lie to tell when he asked me where I was.

"Do you need to answer that?" he asked. I shook my head. "So after we eat, will I still have the pleasure of your company?"

I looked at my watch. "I have a hair appointment and a manicure and pedicure. Today is my beauty day."

He set his elbow on the table and rested his chin on his hand while he stared at me. "You don't need a beauty day. You're naturally beautiful." I didn't comment. I wasn't much for compliments because I thought people who gave them were full of it for the most part. Even though Dr. Bryce didn't seem to be like that. "When are we going to see each other again?"

"I don't know. As long as we can continue to talk—"

"I want to do more than talk," he said, interrupting.

"Right now, all we can do is talk. Is it wrong of me to want you to be my friend?" I tried my best not to look at him because he had a way of looking at me that made me melt. Much different from the sympathetic looks Porter sometimes gave me. Dr. Bryce gave me a look that said he liked what he saw.

"Is it wrong of me to want you to be more than that?"

I didn't answer.

"Oh, by the way, the next time you see your friend, give her this." He pulled out several folded sheets of paper and handed them to me. I glanced at the first page and read the heading, ELEMENTS OF A HOLISTIC SUPPORT PROGRAM. "There's a holistic approach for everything, including the treatment of uterine fibroids," Dr. Bryce said.

Some of the suggestions for holistic treatment were to make dietary changes by eating a low-fat, high-fiber diet, which should help decrease estrogen levels. Avoid dairy, red meat, refined sugar, fried foods, saturated and hydrogenated oils, and trans-fatty acids, which are found in margarine and hydrogenated oils. Increase the amount of whole foods, and fresh fruits and vegetables. Eat organic. Eat cold-water fish regularly, such as salmon, herring, mackerel, anchovies, and tuna.

After lunch he walked me to my car and stood blocking my door. "I wish you were mine."

I frowned. "How can you? We barely know each other. And besides that, over time things change."

"I want you to stop all of that negativity. I listen to you and more negative words and ideas come out your mouth than positive. I know you think you have a lot to be bitter about, but you have a lot to be thankful for too."

"Stop with the speech. I know what I have to be thankful for. But I also have a lot on my mind as well. I have a fiancé who just lost his mother. He's in California trying to work on his dreams. I have a best friend who desperately wants to be carrying a baby in her stomach instead of a massive fibroid. And I have a half sister—actually, I have two half sisters and a half brother that I just found out about and I don't know whether or not to tell my mother about them, ask my father, or just keep it to myself. And that's just what's been going on in my life over the last month. Let's not even look back over the years. Yes, I'm bitter." My eyes started to water. "But I am working on it."

He stepped away from my car door. "Just as long as you continue to work on it." He opened the door for me after I released the lock with my remote.

"I will." I sat inside my car and we played tug-of-war with my door. Dr. Bryce won. He leaned inside to kiss me on the cheek but moved his lips over toward mine and I let him, but then I pushed him away when I realized how wrong that was.

"I just want you to think about me. In every way. Not just as the man who might cure you, but as the man who can love you too."

* * *

"What do you mean you are no longer doing hair, Gina?" I asked as I was driving to her house. She'd called me to ask if I'd received her messages. She was canceling my hair appointment.

"What do you mean what do I mean? I mean what I said. I'm not doing hair. I'm tired of standing on my feet all day. I'm tired of doing perms and color and wraps and all that. I want to concentrate on having a baby."

"Gina, you can do hair and have a baby."

"It's not a matter of what I can do. It's a matter of what I want to do. I'll do your hair today. But that's it."

When one door closes, usually another will open. I didn't want her doing something she really didn't want to do, and I didn't want to be selfish. After all, Detroit was dubbed the hair capital. If I couldn't find a new stylist in Detroit, then may the Lord help me. "That's okay, Gina. I'll try to find a stylist. Any suggestions?"

"There's Alonzo Palmer. He works out of Alta Moda Salon. There's Mr. Little. He works out of Better Fashion on Seven Mile."

"Are these those guys from Hair Wars? I'm not trying to have a spiderweb on my head."

"Those were fantasy hairstyles, Winona."

"Still, I'd rather go to a woman."

"A woman. Let me think. Okay, you can go to Jackie. She owns Salon Jacqueline in Southfield on Northwestern Highway."

"Where on Northwestern Highway, Gina?"

"It's in a strip mall. I think it's in the strip mall next to Fishbones. I can't remember. She's good. If you can get an appointment on such a short notice. You know Saturday is the busiest day for hair."

"I know this, so for the life of me I don't understand how you could cancel on me at the last minute."

"It's not last minute," Gina said, raising her voice. "I can't help that you don't check your voice mail."

I called Salon Jacqueline but I couldn't get an appointment with her or any of the other stylists who worked there on such short notice. I ended up going to what looked like a little salon on Livernois called NuLook, but looks can be quite deceiving because when I entered it was much larger than I thought. The sign on the glass door said WALK-INS WELCOME, so I did—hesitantly. But I figured, how could they really mess my hair up if I wasn't getting a perm, color, and for now, not even a trim? Just a simple body wrap.

When I walked into the salon, I was reminded of why I stopped going to them—wall-to-wall people, half of whom were there for the same stylist and most of whom had the same appointment time. I couldn't get with the concept of double- and triple-booking. I could remember the Saturdays I spent what felt like a day at work just waiting for my name to be called to go to the shampoo bowl. I swore I'd never do that again, and here I was. Walk-ins welcome. I needed to walk my ass right on out.

All eyes were on me as I sat down, took out my miniature *Purpose Driven Life*, and finished reading Day Thirty-two: Using What God Gave You.

I felt a light tap on my shoulder so I pried myself away from page 253 to turn to the lady on my right.

"Have you been coming here long? Do you use their products?" The woman had a scarf tied around her head.

"This is my first time."

"Oh." She dragged out her words. "I thought you were one of the success stories from their hair-growth program."

That's when I started looking around at the before and after pictures on the walls. I even had to stand up and study each of the photos one by one. In less than six months, most of the women displayed on the Wall of Mane had gone from barely an inch to over a foot of hair. How was that possible? They claimed it was from their hair-growth serum that they kept well protected in a glass case. I was impressed by the packaging, but not so impressed by the clinical atmosphere of the shop. I took my seat but nearly fell out of it when a woman holding a chart called me to Dr. Taylor's office for a consultation before my shampoo. *What the hell?* I thought. At Hair Wars they were calling themselves hair entertainers, but now they're physicians?

The woman led me to a large office, where I was motioned by a tall, dark-skinned man with a press-and-curl.

"Have a seat," the man said as he walked around his desk and stood beside the chair I'd sat in. His hands started fishing in my hair. "Didn't you used to come to me a long time ago?"

I shook my head. He wasn't about to put me on his Wall of Mane. My hair had grown halfway down my back not due to any of the products sold at his salon but because of the way I cared for it: kept the direct heat away, trimmed it regularly, washed it once or twice a week, and took hair vitamins. I could write a book for black women on hair care. Gina knew how to style, but I knew how to care for hair, especially for my hair. I was the one who had to tell Gina when to wash out my touch-ups. I didn't like my hair getting bone-straight. Just get the kink out. I had to tell Gina not to trim my hair every four weeks.

Every eight to ten weeks was fine; let it get a little length before you whack away what has grown. I was constantly bringing new conditioners and treatments to Gina's house to try on my hair. So, I said, "No, I've never been here before in my life."

"Can you say you have?" He looked at the lifeless expression on my face and said. "Just kidding." He walked to his desk and sat down. "I'm going to prescribe a wash, deep-penetrating scalp treatment, and conditioner/blow-dry and curl. The cost will be eighty-five dollars and includes a trial pack of our products."

"Eighty-five who for a what? First of all, I won't let anybody blow-dry my hair. And curl as in with an iron?" He nodded. "Hell, no. Have you ever heard of a body wrap or a spiral set?"

"We only press and curl or blow-dry and curl."

I stood up. "Then I'm in the wrong place." I walked out of the salon and into my car, dialing Gina frantically. When she answered, I said, "Listen, I know you have given up hair, but you have to do mine today. I couldn't get an appointment at Salon Jacqueline. I tried lucking up by walking in to one and that was a disaster. So please, Gina, I'm begging you, just this one time, and after that I should be fine because I did make an appointment with Jackie for next week."

Gina took a big sigh. "Only because you're my best friend. Come on."

Gina was digging her long acrylic nails into my head while she vigorously massaged my head. It felt so good that I'd dozed off with my book resting in my lap.

"My purpose is to be a wife and a mother," Gina said after she rinsed out the shampoo and poured a sweet-smelling herbal conditioner on my hair and brushed it through. "That's what I want more than anything." I sat up after she put a plastic cap on my head. "I hate my stomach." She said as she sucked it in and held it with her hand. "I can't wear the kinds of clothes that I want. I get tired of people looking at it."

"That's your imagination. No one's probably paying your stomach any mind."

"No, Winona, they are. I've tried wearing girdles, sucking it in, of course diets and exercising, but that fibroid isn't going anywhere until I get it cut out, sucked out, or whatever the hell they do. I don't want to get cut up."

"Try eating salmon. My doctor friend said there are plenty of holistic options for treating fibroids. He even gave me some information to give you that should help reduce your fibroids."

"Your doctor friend?" Gina asked. "Are you sure he's just a friend?"

"Positive." I reached in my purse, pulled out the papers, and handed them to Gina. "Here. Read them over when you get a chance. There are plenty of options for you. Don't be depressed."

"Next time somebody asks me if I'm pregnant, I'm going to say yes. Save us both the embarrassment."

"Go on, girl. Claim it, because you will be soon enough."

36 Porter

It's funny how just when I thought I had it all figured out something happened to make me realize I was wrong. It was as if none of what I thought I knew about the things in my life—especially my place of worship, the place that I had selected as my church home—was as it appeared. Or at least that's how I started to feel this morning as I sat in the third row at Faith in the Word church. I drove to church with the bishop's sermon from the Sunday before blasting through the speakers because I was hoping I'd catch the spirit and clear my mind of all its negativity. But it was hard because I knew Winona was still in bed sleeping when she of all people needed to be praying. I realized she had a late night, since she picked me up from the airport at one in the morning. But I was the one in the air for all of those hours, so if anyone should have been tired it was me.

Deaconess Myra Lane walked to the podium with her head hanging low. Was she going to do the announcements before the praise team came out? If so, that would be a first.

As she began speaking, the recorded music of "Jesus Loves Me" cut off. The only words I heard her say were "missing" and "in your prayers." Then I heard gasps. So I asked the woman sitting next to me what happened.

"Deaconess said Bishop is missing. This Sunday's service will be canceled but we should all stay and pray for his safe return."

I stood and walked out of the church because I heard a little voice say *Leave now*, and that's exactly what I did.

I didn't tell Winona about the bishop, but she found out through the evening news and became upset with me for not mentioning it. The news had a lot more on the story. The bishop's wife reported him missing Saturday morning. The last time she'd seen him was Friday afternoon. He'd left their home around two in the afternoon for a business meeting, because in addition to his role as bishop at Faith in the Word, one of the largest churches in the city of Detroit, he also owned several apartment buildings throughout the city.

"Would you wait?" I asked Winona as we sat beside each other on the sofa.

"Wait for what?" Winona asked. I figured she was preoccupied with her own thoughts after I noticed her pupils moving rapidly.

"What are you thinking about, baby?"

"Would I wait for what?" she repeated.

"To call the police if I didn't come home one night."

"The police? Yes, I'd wait to call them. A moving truck, no. I'd call them right away."

"A moving truck? Why a moving truck?"

"Because if you ever stay out all night, I'd assume it was because you were up to no good with some woman. And if you were, you gotta go. Gotta go, gotta go. I don't forgive infidelity and you need to know that in advance."

I shook my head. "Don't ever forget that a woman did me dirty. Men aren't the only ones who cheat. So you think the bishop is with another woman, as much as he preaches on infidelity?"

"Another woman . . . another man . . . someone other than his wife. I don't put anything past any man, even a so-called man of God. They can be the worst ones."

And there it was right there. Winona had said something—something that I didn't understand how she could know or even suspect since she'd never been around the bishop that long. *How could she say another man?* The thought had crossed my mind. It was nothing he'd done or said to me personally. I just noticed the men who were in his close circle and the way they interacted with each other. I sensed that they might be gay. It wasn't something that I could explain. And even though most of them were married, what did that really mean? "Why do you say another man?"

"I can't say. I know I shouldn't assume but I think he's gay. And I think his disappearance is foul play."

37 Winona

I had driven by the Tree of Life on the day Dr. Bryce was conducting his first of a series of healthy-living seminars for people living with HIV and AIDS. I didn't go in. There were too many camera crews out front. Too many reporters sticking microphones in the face of every person who walked by.

When I entered Tree of Life, on a day when there wasn't all the commotion, I spotted the back of Dr. Bryce's head and his long dreads. He was standing on a ladder, pulling down a box of herbs for a customer.

Dr. Bryce stepped down from the ladder and handed the box to one of the employees. As he dusted off his hands, he looked over at me and smiled.

He walked toward me. "Pleasant surprise."

He wasn't going to think it was pleasant when I got finished telling him what I had to say.

"Can we talk in private?" I asked as I looked around the store and its many customers.

"I don't like the way you said that. What's up?" he asked as he stood in front of me with a stern look. "You coming to give me a Dear John?"

"Can we just talk for a minute?"

"Where? In my office?" he asked.

"It's a nice day out. Let's just take a walk around Hart Plaza. It'll be good exercise." Hart Plaza was a central gathering spot in downtown Detroit that sat next to Cobo Hall. It was a few blocks away. Once we got there, we sat for a short while and listened to jazz at the outdoor stadium. While I was sitting there, I was trying to put together my thoughts on how I was going to say what I needed to, but my mind was drawing a blank.

"I'm ready to go. The music is okay, but I want to know what you want to talk about," he said in my ear.

I shook my head and stood. He reached out his hand for mine, but I didn't take his. I couldn't hold his hand in public. I walked through the crowded stadium seating, excusing myself along the way. He followed me as I walked through Hart Plaza to the riverfront area.

"I'm in love with Porter. I'm blessed to have a man who loves me in spite of it all. I'd be a fool to throw that away. It took me a minute to realize all of this, but now that I have, I feel like a completely new person. I figured out a lot about myself and what I want to do. I love my job with Chrysler, but it's not my passion. I'm HIV positive and there's not a damn thing I can do to change that. Maybe one day they'll find a cure, but for now I'm thankful that I'm undetectable and I haven't been sick."

"You don't want to see me anymore. If that's what you wanted to tell me, just tell me. I don't have time for a long speech."

"No, I don't."

"It was nice while it lasted."

He didn't have time to waste. I remembered him telling me that the first day I'd met him. *Maybe saying good-bye was a waste of his time,* I thought as I watched him walk away from me.

When I pulled into my driveway, I noticed a couple in Andrea's yard planting flowers. They had a black Lab like mine, only theirs was a puppy that was so cute it made me want to get another one. Andrea had mentioned to me in passing that she was moving to Illinois. I guess it was relatively easy for a flight attendant to relocate. She'd said that she was keeping her home and using it as rental property. I'd asked about her husband. The last she'd heard he received probation and was ordered to do community service and attend anger-management classes.

The first thing I did when I went in the house was turn on the television. I expected to hear a new development on the disappearance of Bishop Coles after nearly a week with no mention. I'd been watching the news every day but it hadn't come up again. But today, as soon as I flipped to channel two,

I saw a reporter standing in front of a dilapidated house on the east side of Detroit with a flatbed in the background raising a silver Bentley onto it.

"Mike, back to you," the female reporter said.

"The cause of death has not been released. An autopsy is expected to be performed early this week."

"Carlton and Sosha," I yelled as I walked up the stairs. "Are either of you watching the news?" I went to Sosha's room first. She had the phone receiver superglued to her right ear while she sat on the bed. "Get off the phone and do your homework."

She walked over to her desk with the cordless, picked up a stack of papers, and handed me two tests, both with A-plus scores along with what looked like completed homework for three subjects. Why was I tripping, as smart as she was? Grades were the least of my worries. How quickly she was developing was my true concern. I think she may have had overactive hormones because her breasts seemed even larger today.

"Well, you need to take an oxygen break. Who are you talking to anyway? It better not be a boy."

"It's Stephanie, Mom."

"It's always Stephanie. Don't you all run out of things to say?"

I walked out of her room and over to Carlton's. He was sitting at his computer desk logged on to the pgatour.com Web site.

"Dreaming, huh?" I asked.

"Yeah, Mom, dreaming . . . dreaming you'd believe in me," he said sarcastically.

"I believe in you and you know it."

"No I don't."

"Well, I do. I'm trying to find out what happened to Bishop Coles from Porter's church. It was on the news. I think he was found dead."

"I need to talk to Porter about a few things," Carlton said.

"Can you check the Internet for me?" I asked as I stood over him.

"What's his first name and the name of the church?" Carlton asked as he switched from the PGA Web site to the search engine.

"The name of the church is Faith in the Word. I think the bishop's first name is Freddy."

Carlton started typing. "His name is Franklin Coles and it says he was found dead in a hotel off Woodward."

"What? What else does it say?"

Carlton started reading the *Detroit News* article. " 'The slightly decomposed body of forty-six-year-old Bishop Franklin Coles was discovered at the King Garden Inn on Woodward in Highland Park at 5:45 a.m Saturday. The motel's surveillance camera showed the bishop entering the inn a few days prior with a young black male who police have identified as twenty-four-year-old Lonnel Hicks of Detroit, an ex-con who served three years at Carson City Correctional Facility for grand larceny. The man is currently being held in custody in connection with the murder. The room, which displayed a DO NOT DISTURB sign on the doorknob, was opened after complaints of a strong odor. When the hotel manager entered the room, he discovered Bishop Coles' naked body bound to a chair. The victim was gagged and blindfolded.' That's it. Do you want to e-mail a comment?"

"No. Print that for me."

"Naked body bound to a chair," Carlton repeated. "He was a bishop at Porter's church." Carlton turned up his nose as he handed me the article. "What kind of church is that?"

"Exactly." I took the article and went into my bedroom to use the phone.

"Tell Porter I'm coming by the station tomorrow," Carlton said as I walked out of his bedroom."

"Hello," Porter said.

"Did you hear about the bishop on the news?"

"Yeah, I know. I guess you were right since the motive doesn't appear to be robbery. His wallet was still on the nightstand with five hundred dollars and all his major credit cards."

"Oh, is that what the news said? I had to go online for the story. Still, it could have been robbery because they did take his Bentley."

"Life is so strange. It seems real weird to me now. Just like California. I thought for sure that was going to work out, but when I got out there, I just wasn't feeling it."

"Something's going to happen real soon, Porter."

"I sure hope so."

"Oh, by the way, Carlton's coming by to see you. I have no idea what it's about. Probably graduation."

"Carlton wants to talk to me? I thought he put me down for Deep Pockets?" he said, referring to Carlton's father, Derwin.

Porter

38

Carlton came by the station the next afternoon. "Can we leave the station?" he asked. "I'd feel better in a more private setting. What I have to tell you may just blow your mind."

I drove around the neighborhoods of east side Detroit with the radio volume kept low. I was waiting for him to start talking. I had only an hour before I'd need to head back to the station.

"What is it, Carlton? What's on your mind?" I asked as I stopped at a red light.

He turned to face me. "My mother is going to be mad at me for this. I have a baby and I'm not going to college in the fall. I'm going to try to go pro."

"What?" I asked. I didn't move when the light turned

green and the Cadillac behind me blew its horn. "A baby, Carlton? You have some girl pregnant?" I asked as I pulled off and turned down a side street, parking in front of an abandoned house.

"No, we already have the baby." He shook his head. "Mom's going to find all this out soon enough, but I wanted to see if you could drop a few subtle hints."

"What kind of hints could I drop that would be subtle, Carlton?"

"I don't know. I'm confused right now. I'm scared and confused. The very thing Mom never wanted me to do, I've done. She's so proud of me, and we've been getting along really good lately. That probably has more to do with you than me, but still, whatever it is, I don't want to ruin it. What should I do? How should I tell her?"

"There's nothing like having a relationship with your mother. Don't ever take that for granted. I'd give anything to have my mother back, if just long enough to tell her that I love her."

"I'm not going to take it for granted. I love my mom."

"I know, Carlton. But you're going to have to understand. Your mother is dealing with a lot."

"My mother has it made. She has a good job. She has you. She's at the best place in her life right now. I'm almost grown. I'll be eighteen in a couple months."

"Eighteen is hardly grown."

"It's grown enough. She has to realize that if I fall, it's up to me to get back up."

I should have taken some time to think before I said,

"Your mother is HIV positive, Carlton. She's dealing with a lot."

"My mother's what? You gave my mother AIDS."

"No, Carlton. First of all she doesn't have AIDS. She's HIV positive. I didn't give her the disease. Sosha's dad did."

He twitched his nose. "I never liked that punk. He was a punk, wasn't he? I could tell he was one. I never liked him. I knew that midget wasn't my dad," he said right before he fell into a long silence. "Does that mean my mother's dying?"

"She's very healthy. Even though she has the disease, it's being controlled by medication. I just don't want to see her undergo a lot of stress. She's stressed out enough as it is. How and when are you going to tell her?"

Carlton took a deep breath. "I'm really not sure yet. That's why I want you to help me. Throw out some hints. Get her ready. She needs to know and she needs to know soon. It's been rough trying to hide all of this. And tomorrow's graduation." I looked over at him. He had a blank expression on his face as he stared straight ahead.

"My mother is HIV-positive. Now I understand." He sighed and shook his head. "That explains a lot."

"**D**o you want me to get out and get them?" Sosha asked as we pulled in front of my parents' home. Finally the day had come, Carlton's high school graduation from the University of Detroit. I was extremely excited because he was graduating with honors and had been offered athletic and academic scholarships to numerous universities. He had planned to announce which university he'd be attending over dinner. I was praying for the University of Michigan in Ann Arbor so he would still be fairly close to me. Carlton was in my life six years before Sosha was born. Whenever I wanted to throw in the towel and give up, I'd remember that I was someone's mother and I owed my life, if not to myself, to him.

"Let's just sit here for a minute in peace." I glanced over at the house that I'd resented for years, and not just the house, but myself for not being able to let go of my painful past. I knew there were children in the world who had it way worse than I. Children who grew up in poor areas with not enough food to eat or who were getting beat or, in Porter's case, sexually abused.

"Mother, please," Sosha said, trying to sound grown. "I want to see my grandparents."

Sosha had her arms folded and attitude written all over her face.

"They'll be out soon enough. I'm sure they see a stretch limo in their driveway, but just in case they don't, I'll go ahead and call them." I pulled out my cellular and started to dial, but then I noticed my family piling out of the front door. My sister Val first, followed by her husband, Bo, and my other sister Colleen, then my parents. *Good thing we rented a stretch.* I turned off my cell phone and threw it in my clutch purse.

I looked over at Porter, who was half asleep, and studied his perfect profile: his smooth chocolate skin, his long eyelashes, his pointy nose and heart-shaped lips. I took my elbow and nudged him. He had been up most of the night fighting an apartment blaze that he didn't want to talk too much about, and his lack of sleep was causing him to doze in and out now.

"Damn, I'm up," he said.

I stared out the window at my family steadily approaching. After being at odds for years, Father and I had finally made up, but now I had his infidelity to try to deal with.

The driver stepped out of the limousine to open the car door for my family.

Val got into the limo first. She was wearing clothes that

were inappropriate for the occasion, my son's graduation. Her dress was too short and showed off her large thighs while hugging her big hips. She had on a pair of three-inch glass-heeled sandals and a gold herringbone ankle bracelet. Her hair was swept off her face in a beehive hairstyle that added a couple inches to her height. Her husband, Bo, had a toothpick stuck in his mouth. He was in his mid-forties but he looked good with his dark reddish-brown complexion and his black wavy hair. He was wearing an expensive suit and a pair of equally expensive alligator shoes, and he could afford it with all the overtime he racked up working on the Ford assembly line.

My sister Colleen got into the limousine next. She was still plain and outdated. She had an Afro that needed shaping, and her man was the same way, even though he wasn't with her today. Mom had already told me that my brother, Trent, and his wife were meeting us at the restaurant. They couldn't attend the graduation because of a prior engagement that they couldn't get out of, which was one more thing upsetting me. He did more things with his white wife and her friends and family than with his own.

"Mmm," Val said as she looked at Porter. "You ain't tell me you went out and found you a man that looks almost as good as mine."

"Almost?" I questioned. "Yours looks good, but I think mine looks better."

"And I guess that's why you're not getting paid to think," Val said.

"I think you've got me confused with yourself, because actually I do get paid to think, and quite a bit for that matter."

"Say, man," Bo said. "Why they talking about us like we not even here?"

Porter shook his head.

I was surprised to see Val and Bo joking around again after the wedding ring mishap, where Val lost her ring to the pawn sale.

Val grabbed Porter's hand and shook it slowly. "Nice to meet you, Porter."

When my father got in the limo, he looked around it like it was a big waste, or maybe I felt that way because I knew he was cheap.

"How much this cost?" Dad asked as the limousine backed out of the driveway.

"Sometimes it's not about cost. It's about occasion," I said.

"It's always about cost in my book. Because occasions are always coming up, and if you keep thinking about occasions and not cost, your ass will be broke."

I rolled my eyes. "Okay, whatever you say."

"Carlton," my mother said in her soft sweet voice. "We are so proud of you. Your gift is at the house. We didn't want to bring it because we knew we were going out to dinner afterward."

"We're going to Red Lobster, right?" Carlton asked.

"No, we're not going to Red Lobster. We're going to Benihana."

"Benny who?" Carlton asked.

"Benihana. It's a Japanese restaurant and the chef cooks the food right at your table."

"What does Japanese food taste like?" Carlton said. "Why do we have to go there? Why can't we just go to Red Lobster? You know that's my favorite."

"It's for the occasion," Dad said. "You got to spend more money."

"It's my day, and I want to go to Red Lobster."

"We're going to Benihana," I said. "Aren't you tired of Red Lobster?"

"Okay, Mom, if that's what you want." Carlton was quiet the rest of the drive.

In fact, the entire family barely uttered a word all through the graduation ceremony, the ride to the restaurant, and even during our twenty-plus-minute wait time for a table. We stood in the bar area staring around at the fish tanks and the people who seemed to be enjoying themselves. Porter ordered a rum and Coke because he said he needed something to take the edge off. That was his first time meeting my family and he hadn't seen them in action yet. Val and Bo ordered drinks too. I just had water.

"You okay?" Porter asked as he stood over me.

I shook my head. "No, not really."

When our name was finally called, we followed the greeter down a long hallway into the sitting area. Although the restaurant was crowded, Derwin's face was the first one I noticed. "What's he doing here?" I said before realizing it. "What is he doing here?" I asked Carlton. I knew if Derwin was here it was because of Carlton, who had suddenly allowed Derwin to become his father overnight.

"I invited him."

"And his snooty mother?" I asked.

"Mom, she's my grandmother."

"Your who? Please don't get me started."

We had two tables side by side that each sat seven. Porter, Sosha, and I sat at the table with my parents, Val, and Bo. Carlton, Colleen, and her man sat with Derwin and his mother. A few minutes later, Trent and his wife, Felda, walked in and sat with Carlton.

While the chefs were preparing the meals and doing tricks with their knives and the shells from the seafood, our table was silent. Carlton's table was lively with conversation and laughter. My eyes were fixed on Derwin with anger.

As I ate my hibachi shrimp, I started thinking about how your family can really mess you up—fuck you up is what I need to say because that's how strongly I feel about the subject. Part of my problem was the men from my past. The other was my family and how I never fit in. If they had been different, I would have been different. Self-respect and feelings of security are learned behaviors when you're a child. But how can you feel good about yourself when your father is constantly pointing out what you haven't done right instead of what you have? How could I have felt good about myself when I was ten years old and brought home a report card that had all As and one B, and he zoomed in on the B and practically made me give a thesis about why I got a B instead of an A. Or when I was thirteen and went to the hairdresser for the first time and I had to sit at the dinner table and listen to my father tell my mother that they wasted their money because my hair didn't look any better than it did before I got it done. I probably wouldn't have allowed men to use me if I'd known what respect was.

Throughout dinner, my family and I made some forced small talk. Carlton seemed to be enjoying himself, but I couldn't wait to go home with Porter. I was looking forward to curling up in bed so I could wake up in the morning and start a new day.

Carlton stood up when a young lady holding an infant walked in. He took the newborn from the young girl's arms and walked the baby over to me.

"Mom," Carlton said. "This is my girlfriend, Carnisha."

"And what is that you're holding?"

"Your grandchild."

I nearly fell out of my chair.

"My *what*?" I screamed. "This isn't happening. I'm having a nightmare. Please tell me I am. Somebody wake me."

"It's okay," Derwin said. "They're good kids and everything is going to work out for them."

"Which leads me to another major announcement," Carlton said.

"That wasn't it?" Val asked.

I was sitting with my mouth partially open, still in a state of shock as I looked over at the young girl who appeared so innocent.

"No, I have an announcement to make about the university I've decided to attend," Carlton said as he stood between the two tables. "Everyone is not going to agree with or understand my decision, but I'm young and at this stage in my life I feel like I can take a few risks, which is why I've decided not to go to college."

"What the hell do you mean not go to college?" I asked.

Derwin's mother held her napkin up to her chest and rolled her eyes as she looked at me in disgust.

"Mom, hear me out," Carlton said.

"The only thing I'm willing to hear is your decision on the

college you are going to, not some bullshit about not going to college." I snatched my napkin from my lap, stood, and threw it over my dish. "And I still haven't processed in my mind yet that you have a child. My worst fear in life was that you would get some girl pregnant and you did. I have half a mind to slap you all the way out this restaurant."

"Winona, calm down. We're in a public place," Val said. "I mean, even I'm not that ghetto."

"I don't care where we are. This is the place he chose to tell me that he wasn't going to college. What, you're going to get a job at Kroger bagging groceries so you can support your new family?"

"No, Mom. I'm turning pro and that's how I'm going to support my family."

"Pro what?" I asked raising my voice even louder. "Pro golf? So you think you're that good?"

"No, I don't think I'm that good. I know I'm that good."

"Who told you that? Him?" I jabbed a finger at Derwin. "You never stop, do you?"

When Derwin stepped out of his seat, so did Porter.

"What are you talking about, Winona?" Derwin asked.

"Ease up," Porter said as he placed a wedge between Derwin and me with his hand. We were now the center of attention in the restaurant.

"What do you mean by I never stop."

"Is everything okay?" one waiter asked.

"Everything's fine," a few of us barked back.

A man in a suit rushed toward me.

"I'm sorry, but is there a problem or something that we can help you and your guests with?"

"There's a problem, but nobody is going to be able to help me or my guests with it."

"Is it possible for your party to pay and perhaps move the conversation to a private area so you won't disturb our other guests?"

"It's very possible," Porter said as I snatched my clutch from the table and stormed out of the seating area. Derwin and Porter were following close behind me.

We walked out of the restaurant and into the parking lot where the limousine was waiting. "He has a future in golf, Winona," said Derwin. "Maybe you can't see it but I do remember telling you that I have an uncle who's a professional golfer. He plays on the senior tour now and golf is his life, his profession. He's played with Carlton. He said at his level right now, he's easily one of the ten best golfers in the world among the pros—at his level right now, and he's only eighteen. I'm not up to anything. I'm not trying to hurt you or my son. I'm footing the bill and it's not going to be cheap. I'm paying for his pro, his caddie, his apartment in Florida, anything he needs. He's going to be on the PGA tour card. You watch."

"I hate you," I said to Derwin. "You ruined my life. That one decision of yours to leave me standing at the altar cost me more than you will ever know. And now you're trying to ruin my son's life too, but I'm not going to let you. Just because he has a child doesn't mean his life has to be ruined too."

"You might as well leave, man," Porter said as he walked over to us.

"I'm not trying to hurt her or my son. Some people are gifted. Carlton is one of those people. I understand it all sounds like a long shot, but sometimes you have to take those in order to come out ahead."

"Man, just leave. She's not hearing you," Porter said as he held my head against his chest. "Carlton will be eighteen and he can make his own decisions."

"This is a good thing and I wish she could see it that way. My uncle knows what needs to be done. He's connected. It's going to happen. By this time next year, Carlton's going to be a millionaire. And as far as the child goes, things like that happen. It's not the preferred way, but the baby is here now. Carnisha comes from a good family."

"You've met her family? You knew about all this before I did, about his decision not to go to college, about the baby? You've been an invisible man for eighteen years and you are given more courtesy than I am about what's going on in his life now? I hope you get hit by a car on your way home and you die the same way Keith did," I said. And I didn't feel bad about it either.

He walked to his car, where his mother was waiting with her arms folded.

"I'm not riding back in that limo," I said. "I don't care if we walk. I'm not riding back with those people."

40 Porter

"I found your mother's will," Dad said, "and I'd like for you to come over so I could go over it with you." He'd called me late, close to eleven. Winona and I were already in the bed. She still had a headache from the night before.

"You tell me when and I'll be there," I said.

"I'm in Chicago right now on business. I should be home in a couple days and you can come over then. I'll call you."

A will. Just as soon as he said it I tossed it out of my mind. Not like I wasn't grateful to my mother for thinking of me, but whatever it was that she left behind for me, be it the restaurant or a little money, wouldn't bring her back.

Winona's head was resting against my bare chest. I was still replaying what happened at the restaurant the night before. Damn, how she must have felt, and what was Carlton thinking to spring all of that on her in a public place and in front of Derwin of all people?

The phone was ringing but this time I let it go straight to voice mail. Then I turned the ringer off so it wouldn't disturb Winona's head or our conversation.

"Was that your father?" she asked.

"Yes, mom left me in her will. He wants me to come over and discuss it when he gets back in town."

"That's good. I know you miss your mother, but I'm sure when she put you in her will she was thinking about your future. Right now you're afraid to go to California because of the high cost of living, but who knows, you may not have to worry about that."

I frowned. "Mom left me something in her will. Not a whole lot because she didn't have a whole lot. Anyway, I don't want to talk about it. How are you feeling tonight?"

"I was just thinking about my family and how fucked up we all are. And restaurants in this city should ban us from entering because it seems like every time we go, something happens. Do you think it's too late for me?"

"Too late for what?" I asked.

"To be happy. Thirty-eight years old, halfway through my life and I find you, but I still haven't found my purpose."

"You will. And no, it's not too late for you."

"Don't you want a young woman?"

"Okay, yeah I do."

"You do? Really?" she asked as she raised her head and looked down at me. "I knew it."

"It's amazing how I can tell you exactly who I want, which

is you, and you can't hear that, but the minute I lie and tell you what I don't want, you hear all that."

"I know," she said resting her head on my chest again. "I'm so strong until you put a man into the equation, and then all of my insecurities start to surface. Sometimes I think I should be alone for the rest of my life, especially with my disease."

"Let's just make a pact that we're not going to let anything bother us. That we can overcome anything."

"I'm a grandmother, Porter, and I'm not even forty. I can't overcome that. I'm still trying to get used to the fact that I'm a mother with two kids, and now one of my kids has a kid." She looked up at me. "I don't want to wear you down. I can understand if you don't want to be with me anymore."

"You're not wearing me down. I have a very high endurance level. And why wouldn't I want to be with you anymore? Joy is going to be restored in your life. I guarantee it, and I'm waiting for the day that I can see you at peace with who you are. That's the one missing link with you."

I heard the door slam and heavy feet run up the stairs.

"Mom, can I talk to you?" Carlton said after knocking on our locked bedroom door. He didn't come home the night before.

"I don't want to talk to him," Winona whispered to me.

"Talk to your son."

She shook her head. "I'll talk to him tomorrow. It's almost midnight."

"Mom, this is very important. I need to talk to you."

"Go on and talk to him," I said, raising her up by her arms.

"I'll be in your room in a minute," Winona yelled. She got

out of bed and slipped on a pair of sweats and a T-shirt over her bra and panties. "I won't be long."

She was walking toward the door with her head down.

"Hey," I said as I sat on the edge of the bed. "Regardless of how you may feel about the situation, you have to deal with the here and the now. The baby is here now and there's no taking that back. Don't go in there trying to tear him down because I know that's not what you feel in your heart. We all make mistakes, but maybe he doesn't feel that what he's doing is a mistake. And you need to consider that."

41 Winona

I walked out of our bedroom thinking about Porter's words. Maybe this was what Carlton wanted for his life: to be a father, to give up his golf scholarship and his academic scholarship to try to become the next Tiger Woods. As I thought back on it, it didn't really surprise me that he got a girl pregnant, the way he'd run after girls ever since I could remember. He was into them way before the age most young men would have been.

When I entered Carlton's bedroom, he was standing at the mirror as if rehearsing a speech. I sat on the edge of his bed and waited for him to say something first, because if I opened my mouth he surely wouldn't like what was likely to come out of it.

"My decision not to go to college wasn't an easy one, Mom. I knew that you wanted me to go, and I want you to know that I do think more about making you happy than I do my father because you raised me and I know he wasn't around. I wasn't trying to disrespect you, and I guess I shouldn't have picked the restaurant as a place to tell you all of this stuff—"

"But what about the baby, Carlton? How could you go and get some girl pregnant?"

"She's not just some girl. Carnisha is going to be my wife."

I flapped my hand in the air. "You're not even eighteen years old—what do you know about a wife? And how old is she—sixteen or seventeen?"

"She's nineteen. And she just finished her freshman year at Wayne State."

"Nineteen? When did you get involved with a nineteen-year-old college girl?"

"Like that's so much older than me. It's one year Mom, not ten," he said, slyly poking back at me by using Porter's and my age difference.

"Listen to me, Mom. I would never disrespect you by putting what my father wants before you." He paused and swallowed. "I know that you're not feeling well.... I know, Mom, and I know that if I can make it pro and earn millions, then I can make sure you have the best doctors like Magic did and maybe you can get better the same way he did. I don't care what anyone says, money buys a lot and it can buy your health back."

"Like Magic? What do you mean by that? Who did you hear this from and what exactly is it that you think you know?"

"Mom, I know," he said as he looked at me sympathetically. "I know, and what I'm about to do on the pro circuit is going to help you and our family . . . believe me."

"What do you know, Carlton?"

"I know that you're HIV positive."

"Oh, my God, what?" I said as I stood with my trembling hands covering my mouth. "Who told you that?"

"Mom, what's wrong? Why are you shaking? Are you okay?"

"Who told you that?"

Carlton didn't say a word.

Porter rushed into the bedroom. "What's wrong?"

"He knows. He knows I'm HIV positive," I said as I put my head against Porter's chest and peered over at Sosha, who had walked into the room. A look of fright covered my face. "Your grandfather told you, didn't he?" I asked. "He's the only one that would. And that's why I can't stand him."

"Mom, can't you see this is why I want to do this? I don't want you to die—"

"She's not going to die," Porter said, jumping in. "You don't know about the disease like I do. People with HIV live a long time. And your mother has the disease but she's very healthy. So don't stand here saying she's going to die."

"I never said she was going to die. I said I don't want her to die."

"Whatever you said, don't even say die. We're all going to die sooner or later."

"I did not want them to know," I said, feeling myself lose control.

"Mom, it's okay. Mom, I love you," said Carlton.

Sosha looked at me like she was scared.

"Sosha loves you too, Mom."

"She's scared of me. She doesn't want a mother who's HIV positive. She already told me when I picked her up from school, because a classmate has a mother who is." I wiped the tears from my eyes.

"She loves you, Mommy."

"That's the straw," I said as my anger inside intensified. "How dare he do this shit to me again!" I screamed. The next thing I knew I was tearing my car out of the driveway.

The lights were on in the den. I was cursing as I slammed my car door, marched to their front door, and started ringing the doorbell furiously. I looked at my watch. It was a few minutes before ten so they should've still been up. I knew Dad, the one I needed to talk to, would be sitting in the den watching television.

Mom opened the door and slid the latch off the hook with a look of concern. I pushed my angry presence inside.

"Winona, what's wrong with you? Why are you coming over here looking and acting the way you do?" She looked down at my mismatched shoes.

"Don't you know what's wrong, Mom? For once in your life, take your head out your ass and open your eyes. Your husband hates me."

"Baby, why do you say that? What did he do?"

"What did he do?" I repeated right before I let out a devilish laugh. "Well, for one, he told Carlton that I'm HIV positive and that wasn't his place. It wasn't his place to tell Carlton about Derwin either and he did that too."

"That's not true. Your father wouldn't do that."

The door was open and Porter walked in.

"Tell her, Porter," I said.

"Winona," Porter whispered.

"He told Carlton, Mom. He did," I said.

"Why?" she shook her head. "I don't believe he would do that."

"He did it," I said with anger. "Where is he?"

"Donald," Mom yelled as she held on to the banister. "Donald, please come down here. This is very important."

A few minutes later my father walked down the stairs, standing at the landing, looking down at the three of us as we stood in the large foyer.

"What?" he asked.

I looked up at my father and lost control of my emotions. I was crying so hard I could barely speak. "You told my son that I was sick, and I'll never forgive you for that."

"Winona," Porter whispered as he grabbed my wrist.

"Wait a minute, Porter. I'm not finished with this man who calls himself a father, but he's not just my father. He's not just Val and Colleen's father. He's Lorna's father too. Should Mom know about your illegitimate children or does she already know?"

"Shut up," my father said. "Don't say another word. I didn't tell Carlton nothing about you being sick, so if he found out, he found out on his own."

"Mom," I said, turning to face her. "I'm not trying to hurt you."

"You shut up," my father said as he stepped toward me. Porter had to block his way.

"No, I'm not going to shut up. I've done that for too long. This man"—I pointed at my father—"who came home every night for years and plopped in front of that television, has three other kids. He's disappointed that his children didn't turn out to be perfect when he himself is far from that." I looked over at Mom's expressionless face. "Did you hear what I said?"

"Yes, I heard you."

"Don't you have anything to say? He has three illegitimate children."

"I already knew," she said.

"You already knew? If you already knew, why didn't your children already know?"

"Winona, sweetie, I'm going to lie down," Mom said.

"See what you did?" Dad asked. "You upset your mother. That's why I don't bother with you kids. Each and every one of you are selfish, but especially you. Get out of my house."

Porter and I walked out of their house and stood in the walkway embracing. I tried to do what Dr. Bryce said by telling myself that this too shall pass, but these were my parents and that was my mother I'd hurt. I felt selfish. I felt childish. I felt things that words couldn't express. I wanted to fight back my tears because Dr. Bryce said tears weren't good. Crying was stressful. *When you feel like crying, laugh instead,* he'd said. I tried that but it didn't work.

I left my car at my parents' home, because I didn't feel like driving and I rode with Porter back home. As Porter was turning into our driveway, he said, "Baby, your father didn't tell Carlton. I did."

"You did?" I said, trying to understand what he'd just said. "You did?" I repeated, not willing to accept what I'd just heard. I shook my head. "Please tell me you didn't. Please tell me that you didn't, because if you did it's over between us."

He pulled the keys out of the ignition. "It's not over. I love you. Yes, I was the one who told. I found out Carlton wasn't going to college next year and I knew it would upset you. I told him so he would keep your health in mind when he made his final decision."

"You did," I said, shaking with anger. He put his hand on my thigh. "Don't touch me. You had no right, no right to tell my child anything." I flung the passenger door open, stood outside the car, snatched off my engagement ring, and threw it into the bushes. "This isn't going to work, so I need you to get all of your things out the house and I never want to see you again."

"No," he said, grabbing hold of my arms.

"Yes," I said, trying to yank free.

"No," he said, shoving me around. "You can't do me like this. Yes, I told Carlton. I'm sorry. Maybe I shouldn't have, but you're not going to throw our relationship away because of that, are you?"

I nodded, "Yes, Porter, I am. I honestly thought we could make it. I finally came to the conclusion that it was going to be tough, but we'd see it through. And you had to go and deceive me."

"Deceive you? How?"

"How do you think?" I asked, shaking my head. "It doesn't matter. I loved you and this is what you do to me." It was over. My heart was breaking. Something inside didn't feel right. I knew deep down we could repair our relationship if we really tried. I felt like we were ending it prematurely, but what Porter had done couldn't be excused.

"I'm going," he said as he walked up the stairs to the bedroom. I followed behind him to harass him with my words. I was angry and he was going to get an earful this evening. He started taking the clothes from the closet and the dresser drawer.

I tossed several pairs of his socks and underwear into his suitcase.

He pulled his large suitcase from the bed and started

walking down the stairs. I walked down the stairs after him. We stood in the foyer facing each other. He had the suitcase in one hand and my wrist in the other. "No matter what you do or say to me, I'm never going to stop loving you," he said. There were tears in my eyes, but I didn't respond. I looked down at his hand until I loosened my grip. I walked up the stairs and slammed my bedroom door.

I peeped out my bedroom window and watched Porter as he walked out of the house. I pushed my window open.

"Wait a minute," I said. He stopped, turned, and looked up at me. "I'm coming down."

I ran down the stairs as fast as I could and out the front door.

"Can we start all over again?" I asked.

"Depends on what you mean by that," he said.

"This is Day Thirty-eight. I'm two days away from Day Forty and I don't want to find my purpose and not have you be a part of my life. I love you, Porter. I don't like what you did, but I know you didn't do it to try to hurt me, and I don't want to throw our relationship away because of it."

He dropped the bag from his hand and held me. We stood in a tight embrace.

"You're the only thing good that has ever happened to me. I'm not going to throw this away, so don't you."

Porter

42

I pulled up to my father's house with Winona. He'd called me the day before and we set up a time to meet. He asked me if I was into investments, and for a second I thought maybe he was saying that because Mom had left me a large sum or the restaurant, which he probably figured I could sell. Doubt all that.

"Are you ready?" Winona asked.

I nodded and took a deep sigh. "I don't like the way this feels, like I'm here for money or something. I love my mother. I don't want her to think that I could stay away from her all that time and then flock around her house when I find out she put me in her will."

"Porter, you were only away from her for a few months. She can forgive you for that the same way you forgave her for the times she was away from you. Parents include their children in their wills to help better their lives, and that's what this is going to do."

I nodded in agreement. We got out of the car, walked to the front door, and rang the doorbell.

"Good to see you again, Winona," my father said as he opened the door. "Are you my daughter-in-law yet?"

"Not yet," I said as I walked in. "But soon."

Winona and I sat in silence on the microfiber sofa in the living room. My father milled around for a few minutes, offering us food or drinks, which we declined. After a few minutes, he sat across from us with a file folder.

"Porter, unannounced to me, your mother took out an insurance policy when you were young. We'd divorced and I guess it was something she wanted to provide you in case she did pass. When I was clearing out her things, I found it." He cleared his throat. "It's quite substantial."

Winona and I looked over at each other.

"It's two million dollars."

"What?" I asked in shock. Winona covered her mouth. "Two million dollars?"

"Yes, two million dollars."

"She also left you the restaurant. And this DVD that your mother made for you."

"She left me the restaurant? What about you?"

"I signed that restaurant over to her years ago. I just provided advice from time to time, but you know I was off into my other ventures."

"What about the DVD?" I asked, more excited about that than anything. "Is Mom on it?"

"Yes." My dad looked at both of us. "I'm happy for you. What are you going to do?"

"Well . . ." I took a moment to think about it. "Winona's going to quit." My mind was racing.

"I am?"

I nodded. "And we're going to use some of the money to renovate the restaurant and turn it into a jazz supper club. Mom was never thrilled about the whole firehouse theme, so we're going to change that, and the name, and give Seldom Blues a run for their money. Are you up to being a restaurateur?"

"Yes, but Porter, what about California?"

"California is a nice place to visit, but I wouldn't want to live there. Besides that, I'm moving away from drumming and toward making a name as a saxophonist. I have a demo and I'm going to do something with it."

Winona had the biggest smile on her face. "I have so many ideas for the restaurant and how to make it a success."

"Keep me posted. Send me e-mails and pictures," my dad said.

"Where are you going to be, Dad?" I asked.

"In Jamaica, mon," he said.

"What about your own business?"

"I sold two of the hair magazines. The only one I have left is *Millennium Hair* and the Web site, and I was hoping"—he stared at both of us—"that maybe you could manage it for me. Mail me my checks."

"Dad, with the magazine"—Winona put her hand on my thigh—"I know somebody who can run it. She's an experienced stylist and she's retired, but this will be right up her alley."

"Gina doesn't want to do that. I thought you said she was concentrating on getting pregnant?" I asked.

"She is, but just the other day she told me that she needs something to keep her mind occupied so she won't be so focused on getting pregnant."

I shrugged. "Have fun in Jamaica. You're going to live there or just visit for a while."

"I'm moving there. Me and your mother's ashes."

On the ride home, all I could think about was the DVD. The first thing I was going to do when I walked through the door was go into the bedroom and put it in the DVD player.

Winona left me alone. It was something that I wanted to watch alone.

When I pressed PLAY, Mom came on the screen, sitting in her garden. "Porter, unfortunately when you watch this I will no longer be alive. I don't know—you know I'm a movie buff and this is something I saw in the movie *My Life*. So a few days after I found out that I had cancer, late-stage cancer, I had your father buy a camcorder, and he's going to be following me around, recording me. I hope that before I die, I'll be able to see you. And I hope that you will forgive me for what happened to you when you were a child. That was my fault."

"It was my fault too," I heard my dad say.

"This is my tape, so just let it be my fault, Richard."

"Okay, but it was my fault too."

"Okay, it was our fault, since that will make your dad feel better. But I'm going to make it up to you. I want you to enjoy your life and make the most of it. Don't let anybody tell you what you cannot do. I'm going to provide you with everything you need to succeed. And then the rest, baby, is going to be up to you. I understood what you were saying happened to you and your brother as a child. It's the same thing that happened to me. I guess I was naïve in my thinking that because I had boys I wouldn't have to worry about that. Please forgive me for leaving you and your brother in that environment. At the time, I was thinking solely of myself. Whatever you decide to do with your life, do so unselfishly and do so by keeping God's intention for your life in mind. Find a good church home and worship. Marry Winona. Have babies—that's if she wants any more. Take care of Portia. Build a legacy . . . something you can leave behind."

The tape played for several more hours. She showed pictures that I'd never seen before of Richard and me when we were infants, pictures of us at Mackinac Island and Belle Isle. When I was finished playing the DVD, I called Winona into the bedroom.

"Are you ready?"

"Yes."

"You know what you have to do tomorrow at work, right?"

"Yes."

"We're closing that chapter and starting a new one."

"Yes, closing that one and starting a new one. I'm more than ready for that."

"And then we're going to plan our wedding, right?"

"Yep, I even have the date—September tenth. That gives us a few months to plan."

"I love you, Winona."

"I love me too—I mean I love you too."

43 Winona

I want to thank you for all you have done for me here at DaimlerChrysler Corporation. It's been a pleasure designing for the company. Fortunately, I have decided to embark on a new career that is not auto-related. It is with both excitement and sadness that I have decided to tender my resignation.

My eyes began to water as I typed my resignation. I rushed from my desk to the ladies room and immediately rinsed my face with warm water. Even though I knew that I was doing the right thing, I was nervous. I walked back to my workstation, unlocked my computer, and continued typing my letter.

My last date of employment will be July 29, 2005. This decision has nothing to do with the exceptional opportunity you have provided me here. You and the company have been more than fair with me, and I genuinely appreciate all your support.

I wish DaimlerChrysler continued success, and I want to thank you for allowing me to be a part of your team. Please feel free to contact me at any time if I can be of further assistance in helping with a smooth transition.

Sincerely,

Winona Fairchild

After staring at my letter on the computer screen for nearly thirty minutes, I sent three copies to my HP DeskJet printer, and with two copies in hand I walked over to Angel Templeton's office. If there was one person who I felt I owed an explanation, it was Angel, my boss and mentor, another African-American who had risen far within the ranks of the corporation and was very active in DCAAN, which helped bring diversity to the managerial and technical workforce. Angel believed in me from the very beginning, and she made sure that my work was noticed. She'd been off all week attending a trade show in New Orleans. The other person was Jennifer Theater, my old college roommate, but as usual she was overseas on business.

Angel made a hand gesture to invite me into her office after noticing me standing patiently outside her door.

"I wanted to give you this." I walked up to Angel's desk

and placed it on top of a small stack of papers and turned to walk away.

"Resignation!" she shouted. "Not so fast. Close my door and come here, Miss Fairchild. You know I'm not going to let you leave us."

I closed my eyes and prayed for the strength to say what I needed to help her understand my decision. I turned and walked toward her, my eyes watering with each step as I tried not to focus them in Angel's direction.

"I can explain," I said softly.

"Have a seat and explain," Angel said as she directed me to her chair with her hand. "Who thinks they're getting you?"

I sat in front of her speechless for a moment, but then I told myself to just tell her the way it is.

"I'm not leaving the company to go to another one. I'm not leaving it to pursue my career. I'm leaving it to pursue a new life. I never shared this with anyone here and I'd appreciate it if you'd keep what I'm about to say between the two of us."

She nodded. "I'm HIV positive."

That's really all that I felt like saying, and I hoped that the rest would be understood, but I knew I had to continue because the look on Angel's face was one of shock. I could tell she didn't know what to say.

"I love my job, but I feel within my heart that there's something more for me to do out there. I used to want to be around long enough to see my first grandchild born, but that's already happened." I shrugged. "Now I just want to be around. I want to live to be a hundred. My fiancé and I are going to be entrepreneurs and I'm so excited about what's in store."

"And you should be." She stood and walked around her desk with her arms extended. I stood and hugged her. "Well, Winona, I don't know what to say. Of course, I wish you the very best. The very, *very* best."

"Thank you, Angel. Your presence in the company has meant a lot to me. Seeing is believing, and every time I saw you I believed that I could go really far with this company. It's just that my life has taken on another course."

"You can always come back. I wish you all the success, but know that you always have a place here."

I gave her one tight squeeze and told her again how much I appreciated her. Then I walked back to my desk just as my phone started ringing.

"Winona Fairchild, design team."

There was silence. I was getting ready to hang up when a woman's voice said, "Hello, Winona, this is Lorna again."

"Lorna? My sister Lorna? I'm so glad you called back. I was so mad at myself for not getting your number."

"Really?" she asked. "I was almost afraid to call back. You seemed like you really didn't want to be bothered."

"No, it's not that. I was just having a bad day, but I'm glad you did."

"I really want to meet you, Winona. I'm not sure why after all these years it's been placed so heavy on my heart now. Do you think we can?"

"The next couple months are going to be really busy for me because I'm getting married, and then we're opening a new business."

"I understand," she said as her voice dropped.

"But we can see each other."

"Could we?" she asked.

"Yes, we can see each other one day next week. And while I have you on the phone, can I get your contact information?"

"Sure," she said, reading off her address and phone numbers.

"You live in Coppell, Texas. Nice area."

"Yeah, I guess," she said. "But everything that glitters is definitely not gold."

"But we're not looking for everything, right? We're just looking for the one thing that is," I said.

"I can't wait to meet you, Winona. I should be in Detroit in September."

"I can't wait to meet you either, Lorna."

"You got my name right."

" 'Bout time, huh? I'll see you soon, sweetie."

It was hard for me to stay focused at work, and when I finally left at my stopping time, which was the first time I'd done that in months, I felt like I had found my purpose. Like all these loose threads that had been hanging from me had finally been sewed together. I'd figured it out. I'd been an auto designer, but I would leave that to design a whole new life. And I was so excited about what lay ahead.

At home, I took out my book and turned to Day Forty: Living with Purpose. "Many are the plans in a man's heart, but it is the Lord's purpose that prevails." The first line sent chills through me.

"Living on purpose is the only way to really live. Everything else is just existing." How long I had just existed. Now I really knew that I had found a reason to wake up.

Porter walked downstairs and joined me in the den.

"We're supposed to be reading this together, remember?"

"I remembered, but I didn't think you did."

"It's never too late to start."

"I'm not starting from Day One. Are you kidding me?" I asked as I looked over at him like he'd lost his mind.

"Start from the beginning of the last chapter."

"Oh, I can do that. Are you ready?" He nodded. "Living on purpose is the only way to really live. Everything else is just existing."

I continued to read the book, and for the first time in the forty days—give or take one or two—that I'd been reading the book, I felt like Porter was listening. Now I understood how life could be beautiful yet different for each one of us.

it's like that

cheryl robinson

A CONVERSATION WITH CHERYL ROBINSON

Q. *It's Like That* is a follow-up to your first novel, *If It Ain't One Thing*. How difficult was it for you to write a sequel and how long did it take you to complete it?

A. Writing a sequel was very difficult for me to complete. It took me over a year and I changed the theme of the book several times in the process. I believe it's always hard to revisit the same characters. For me, I'd received so much feedback from book club members and readers about the characters that in some cases it influenced me. For instance, I had no intention of bringing back Vanity, but decided to have her make an appearance after a good friend insisted I consider writing her back in.

Q. Tell us about your decision to have a character who was living with HIV. Do you have any personal experience with the disease?

A. I had a friend who died of AIDS seventeen years ago. He was a high school classmate of mine who contracted the disease from a married man while serving in the army. I'd seen him at the earliest stage when you couldn't tell all the way to the last stages shortly before his death when he lost his eyesight and had to walk with a cane. For those who may have read the self-published version of *If It Ain't One Thing* entitled *Memories of Yesterday* at the end of the novel Winona learned she was misdiagnosed. In one version of *It's Like That* I had written the misdiagnosis in but decided to remove it because there are so many people living with HIV who haven't been misdiagnosed. I thought my character would be much more authentic and interesting to read if she was living with a serious illness. I'm sure there are many people who will read my book who will be able to relate to what Winona is going through. Perhaps they're not personally living with HIV, but maybe a family member, close friend, or coworker is.

Q. Some readers may think that the book took a negative look at church and church leaders. What is your feeling about this issue?

A. At the time that I wrote the church subplot into the book, there were some things going on in Texas involving a couple prominent church leaders who were always in the news and I was so disgusted that I let my writing take over. It was a way to vent.

Q. How much of *It's Like That* is based on your own experience?

A. I could relate most to what Gina was going through with her fibroid tumors. I have them and so do many of my friends. Fibroid tumors are very common in women, especially African-American women. I'm in the process of searching for a gynecologist to remove them and researching what I think will be the best procedure for me.

Q. Why is *The Purpose Driven Life* such a big theme throughout your book?

A. At work there were so many people with the book that one day I decided to pick up my own copy. I bought the book and the journal and proceeded to start my journey. When I started reading it, I knew that a book like that was exactly what Winona needed to help change her perspective on life and the theme fit in very nicely with my characters' lives.

Q. What do you hope readers will take away from *It's Like That*?

A. The older you get the more interesting life becomes. To me, life is a series of choices. The better you make your decisions the better your life will be. I want readers to be entertained while reading *It's Like That* and uplifted. I don't want to write a depressing book, but that's not to say that some of the things that may occur in my books won't be sad or depressing. It's all on how you handle the challenges that arise in your life.

Q. Are you working on another project? Any plans for a trilogy?

A. I'm writing a book that centers around one of the characters who was briefly introduced in *It's Like That* and ties in with Tower, a character from my self-published novel *When I Get Free* that I am still praying gets picked up. And yes, there is another installment to Porter and Winona's story that I'm working on as well.

QUESTIONS FOR DISCUSSION

1. What did you think about the novel? If you read *If It Ain't One Thing*, do you feel this was a good follow-up? Please explain your answer.

2. Who were your favorite and least favorite characters in the novel? Please explain your answer.

3. Winona is living with HIV. What do you think the quality of life can be for a person living with this disease? Do you think there will be a cure found soon? How do you feel about holistic medicine as an alternative?

4. Although Porter and Winona are in a monogamous relationship, Winona expresses to herself that it would be unrealistic for Porter to remain faithful to her. If she had found out about his indiscretions do you feel she would have forgiven him? How do you feel about the two times he cheated on Winona?

5. *The Purpose Driven Life* was a major theme throughout the book. Winona's big push was to change her life within forty days. What about your life would you like to change

and how do you feel about the concept of change in a relatively short period of time?

6. Winona met Dr. Bryce, someone who was also HIV positive and could relate to what she was going through. What did you think of their relationship? Do you feel they were better suited for each other than Winona and Porter?

7. Porter was a Christian who attended a church that was led by a bishop who was leading a double life. Over the years, there has been a lot of scandal in the church. Do you have any personal experiences to share?

8. Porter stopped communicating with his parents due to some issues in his past that he had a hard time letting go of. By the time he tried to reach out to his mother again, he discovered that she was terminally ill. Do you think his reason for alienating himself from his parents was justified?

9. Winona learns that her father had two families and that she has two half sisters and a half brother. She is torn on whether or not to tell her mother and when she finally decides to, it is only out of revenge. Do you think Winona should have told her mother? How do you feel about the fact that her parents hid the truth that their children had siblings?

10. Winona discovers that Carlton has a child and won't be going to college. She also learns that Porter was the one

who told Carlton that she was HIV positive. How did you feel about both of these things?

11. What was your feeling as the book ended? Obviously they are about to embark on a whole new life and their life has changed. Do you think a jazz supper club is a good move for Porter? What about Winona giving up her good job for the unknown?